AF076232

PLËRoMA

✝HE ΠEC✝AR ✝RILOGY
BOOK 1

Pleroma
Book One of the Nectar Trilogy

Published by:

 ShastaCor Press
www.shastacorpress.com

All rights reserved. No part of this book may be reproduced or transmitted in any form or by any means, electronic or mechanical, including photocopying, recording or by any information storage and retrieval system without written permission from the author.

Copyright © 2010 Steve Thomason

ISBN: 0-9840670-7-8
13-Digit: 978-0-9840670-7-7

Cover Artwork: Spot Studios, Inc.

Printed in the United States of America

*To Jamin, Micki, Ethan, and Leah
my very own Pevensies*

PLEROMA

CHAPTER 1

The air bit his skin. Every pump of the pedals pushed him harder against the cold and reminded him of the danger that waited at home. Normally this was a leisurely ride where Lane took in the sights and sounds of his suburban neighborhood and the cool autumn air washed over his face like a refreshing splash of water. Not today.

He had to get home before his father did. Josh was there, all alone. *If Dad gets there before I do...* Lane squeezed the thought from his mind and dug harder into the pedals to gain speed. *Don't think about it, just get there. I can't believe I let this happen!*

The bike skidded around the corner. He kept it together and pressed on for the last stretch of his ride.

The Murphys' house, the O'Briens' house, the Hogans'. Home. *Please don't be there, please don't be there.*

Lane's heart jumped to his throat. Dad's car was already parked next to the house. He was too late.

With one fluid motion he slid the bike sideways, laid it down, and jumped over it and onto the front porch. The doorknob was stuck. On the third twist it gave way. He slammed his body against the door and stumbled into the tiny entryway.

Fear pierced his body. His worst nightmare played out in front of him. Two figures stood in the living room; neither reacting to his abrupt entrance. Lane's father stood hard, eyes full of rage and riveted on the small figure standing in front of him. Josh stood dwarfed and paralyzed.

Dad cocked his right hand back to deliver a blow to the boy's face. Lane lurched forward and pulled Josh back.

"Run, Josh! Get up to your room and lock the door. Now!"

Lane pushed Josh toward the stairs behind him. *Crack!* He turned and met the hand that was meant for Josh. It crashed against his left cheekbone and threw him to the floor.

"What do think you're doin', you stupid brat?" The words spewed from the man's mouth. "You think you're so smart. Don't get in the way when I'm trying to discipline my kid."

The staggering man scanned the room behind him. He grabbed an empty beer bottle from the coffee table.

Lane shook his head and popped back to his feet. He stood strong and squared off to counter the attack. He was tall for a sixteen-year-old, but his dad's three-inch advantage was magnified by the drunken rage.

For an instant they locked eyes, and time froze. Spidery red veins intensified Dad's gray blue eyes. In spite of the rage, there was a softness there. A hesitation. In the small space of a heartbeat, the man's face morphed until he looked like the father Lane once knew—the kind man from when Lane's mother was still alive. It was the faint image of a time when things were different. He hoped.

Lane reached out his hand to touch Dad's shoulder.

His touch broke the spell. As quickly as it came, the soft moment was gone. The spark of hope was snuffed out by fear, and the image of that other man was replaced by the rage of a drunken beast.

"Dad, no!"

The bottle swung through Lane's left peripheral vision and grazed his temple, spinning him backwards. He twisted and stumbled toward the stairs, slamming against the wall.

Through the flashes of light in his vision Lane could see that his father was coming after him. He had to get upstairs now! Lane scrambled with his hands and feet up the short first flight. He was on his feet by the landing, took the hard right turn, and leapt up the last flight in two big steps. A hard left down the short hallway and he was at his bedroom door.

Josh. His father's footsteps were halfway up the stairs

and Josh's room was halfway back down the hall. Did he have time?

Lane doubled back down the hall and twisted on Josh's door handle. Locked. Good. Dad was at the top of the stairs now, and just a step away. Lane spun back around, ran down the hall in one big stride, flung open the door, and threw himself into his room, slamming his body against the door.

Click! It was locked. He was safe.

Usually this was it. The locked door somehow stopped his father's rage and sent him back downstairs to the couch, where he would drink himself to sleep. Today was different for some reason. Instead of going away, he started pounding on the door and screaming. Pounding and pounding. Was he kicking it? *He's gone crazy.*

Lane didn't know what to do. His dad had never been this angry before. What would happen if he actually broke the door down? Lane rubbed his arm where the "accident" had happened three years ago and shuddered at the thought.

I have to hide.

The closet was so crammed with books and clothes that there was no way he could fit in there. Under the bed! Lane flopped down on his hands and knees and threw back the comforter to see if there was any space. It was dark and dusty, but there seemed to be just enough room between the boxes to squeeze in. He backed himself under the bed so he could watch the door.

There he was, a big, teenage, high-school junior hiding under his bed like a scared little kid. He didn't care what he looked like. A drunken, raging man was breaking down his door. He was scared out of his mind.

Lane buried his face in his arm and beat the ground with his other hand. *Oh God. Help me! Somebody help me!*

The door burst open. The bed shook. The floor rumbled. *He's in the room. He's on my bed!*

The shaking and rumbling got louder and louder. Not only the bed shook, but the floor heaved as well. The wooden floorboards rattled and bounced out of their places, shooting puffs of dust up from the cracks. The whole floor billowed like water.

He was sinking.

What's happening?

His fear shifted. Dad's ominous threat was shoved to the side. A shot of adrenaline focused his attention on the fact that he was definitely sinking down into the floor. Was this an earthquake?

The weight of his body pushed the floor down and pulled all the boxes and toys in on top of him. He reached up to grab the bottom of the bed. *Snap!* The floor broke away underneath him. Falling...and floating?

It was silent. Everything was light. Blue light. Then white. Was that a cloud? Was he in the air?

The floating sensation only lasted a second, and then reality rushed in around him. Lane was falling through the sky. Tumbling and falling. Cloud, sky, ground. Cloud, sky, ground. The ground grew larger. A big patch of yellow expanded beneath him. Cloud, sky, yellow...*thud*...black.

His eyes cracked open, and he was conscious enough to feel pain shoot through his body. He was on his back, on the ground. There was blue sky. Where was he? His eyes closed. Black again.

Chapter 2

Earlier that day...

The alarm beeped. 6:30am. Lane didn't move. The book he had been reading the night before lay open across his chest.

The alarm beeped again. Reluctant eyelids slowly opened to reveal the familiar greeting of all his closest friends. They surrounded his bed and looked down at him from their hedge of protection. Every morning they were there when he woke up, and every night they tucked him into bed. Safe, secure, predictable. He loved his books.

A heavy hand silenced the alarm. His head flopped back on the pillow, and his body melted into the sheets.

Just five more minutes, that's all I need.

Then, as though electricity shot through his mattress, Lane sat straight up, flinging the book to the foot of the bed.

"It's today!" he shouted.

He swung his legs over the edge of the bed and planted his feet on the floor. Paper scraps and doodles flew everywhere. He went to the door to tear it open, then stopped short. Excitement succumbed to caution, and he opened the door slightly.

Through the small crack he could see that the door at the end of the hallway was open. That was a good sign. He crossed to the window that faced the garage in the backyard. Breath held tightly, he looked out. Dad's car was gone.

The air rushed from his lungs in a great flow of relief, and Lane's excitement returned. Once again he sprang to his door and this time flung it open.

"Josh! It's time to get up! Come on, man."

He banged on the door.

"Josh, get up!"

He checked the knob. Locked. That was good.

"Come on, Josh. You know I can't get in there to pull you out of bed. We can't be late today!"

"Uh-huh," came a muffled response from inside the room.

A few moments later a very small, seven-year-old boy stood in the doorway. Heavy eyelids barely revealed his large blue eyes.

"Come on, little J." Lane tussled his fingers through Josh's hair. "We've got to get this rat's nest under control and get ready for school."

The one bathroom in the house was very small. Two grown people could not stand in front of the sink and look into the mirror at the same time. Fortunately for Josh, he was not a grown person.

Lane stood in front of the sink and looked into the mirror. The few hairs that sprouted on his chin stared back at him. It was a good day to shave.

Josh stood to the side, step stool beside him on the floor, and tried to wait his turn. Inch by inch, as if Lane didn't notice, Josh scooted his stool closer to the front of the sink. Impatience won out, and a wild-haired head popped up into the bottom of the mirror, launching the two boys into their morning dance around the sink.

By the time Josh made it to the top step he was fully awake, and his bright eyes fixed on his big brother. Then the questions began. Usually he would ask things like, "Lane, why is the sky blue?" "What makes a lightbulb glow?" "What really lives under my bed?"

Lane didn't mind answering the questions. They kept his mind sharp.

Today the questions took a more personal nature.

"Lane?"

"Yeah, little J."

"Why are you so excited about today? Are you getting a new baseball mitt? I didn't think you liked baseball."

"A baseball mitt? What are you talking about?" The toothbrush hung out of Lane's mouth. He rinsed and spit, sloshing Josh's words in his brain.

It hit him. "Oh, mitt!" Lane laughed and patted Josh on the shoulder. "Not baseball mitt, Josh. *M-I-T*. It stands for Massachusetts Institute of Technology. I'm excited about today because after school I am going to be taking a test that will tell me whether or not they will let me apply to a special early admittance program next year at MIT."

"What's so special about that?"

"MIT is just about the best school you can go to if you want to study all the really cool stuff about science and technology. You know, if you want to be the first person to invent time travel or something like that."

"Cool! Do I get to come to school with you?"

"Well," Lane placed his toothbrush back in the holder. "MIT is a long way from here." He screwed the cap back on the toothpaste tube and weighed his next words. "I would have to move away from home if I went to MIT."

Josh's eyes dimmed.

The morning routine continued without another word. Hair combed. Breakfast eaten. Clothes on. All with a tense silence that hung thick around them.

Lane walked into his room to find Josh standing in front of his small desk. He was looking at a solitary photograph that stood in its frame, tucked securely between the Chronicles of Narnia boxed set and the tattered Lord of the Rings books. Four very happy people beamed back at him through faded ink. A man and a woman, dressed in formal attire, held each other close. The woman held a toddler in her arms. On the man's shoulders sat a ten-year-old boy with a big, wild head of hair and a huge, laughing smile.

"Lane, tell me again. What was she like?"

Lane couldn't speak. He looked around the room at all the books that lined the walls. His fascination with the world and his love of learning were because of her. Tears blurred the photo.

Things were different when that picture was taken. Back then they were a family. They laughed together. They went places. They played and talked and read stories. That photograph was the last memory Lane had of his mother. It was taken the night of the accident. She was gone...and so was his dad. Sure, Dad was there physically, but ever since that day, as far as Lane was concerned, neither his mom nor his dad ever returned. The man who lived with them now was scary, angry, and dangerous. What was Lane supposed to do? His stomach turned. He had to go to MIT, for her, but he couldn't leave Josh behind with Dad.

"Oh, Josh." A single tear fell on the desk. "I wish you could have known her. She loved you very much. I remember when they brought you home from the hospital. Her face lit up so bright. She said she had brought me the best present I could ever imagine—a little brother."

He pulled Josh close to him.

"You don't remember this, but she would take us both up on her lap and read stories. I never got tired of it. 'Read another one, Mommy' I would always say. Even though you were just a baby, you didn't seem to get tired of it either. I think it was the sound of her voice. It was so smooth and rich. I loved that voice. Man, what I would give to hear it just one more time."

They both stared at the photo in silence.

"Whoa, Josh, what are we doing? We're going to be late!"

Quickly they ran down the stairs, out the back door, and to their bikes. Side by side they rode down the driveway to the street and stopped at the sidewalk. Lane needed to go right to get to school, and Josh needed to go left.

"OK, little J, don't forget. I'm going to be later than usual today, so, when you get home, go to your room. I'll make sure I'm here before Dad gets home, so don't worry." Lane gave Josh a reassuring smile and one last tussle of his unmanageable hair.

"Don't worry, Lane. I'll be all right."

They rode off in separate directions.

PLEROMA

Chapter 3

Lane loved the ride to school, especially on fall mornings. The last hint of summer's green was fading from the trees that lined the street. Soon they would burst into a blaze of oranges, reds, and yellows.

He methodically pedaled his bike and allowed the crisp air to wash over his face. The cares and tension of home fell away and skidded on the road in his wake. This was one of the few times during his day when he felt free.

At the end of the street, a park formed a large square that was full of tall oak trees. The trees stood too far apart to call it a forest, but there was enough cover to form a leafy archway over the path. It ran diagonally through the park and led directly to his school on the other side.

He rode up to the large brick building. Its massive stone staircase opened wide from the front door. Lane dismounted and hoisted the bike over his shoulder. He was allowed to store his bike inside because several episodes of vandalism had rendered his last one unusable. This one had been a special gift from some of his favorite teachers, and they didn't want anything to happen to it.

"Hey, geek boy. How's it goin' with the ladies? Have you figured out what those are yet?" heckled one of the boys who perched like crows on the staircase.

Lane kept his eyes forward and moved past the heckling flock, fighting back images of violent retribution falling on their heads. Idiots.

With the gauntlet of mindlessness behind him, Lane focused

on what was otherwise his favorite place and procedure. First, he dropped off his bike in the storage closet. Once he had secured it, he slung his backpack over his shoulder and headed off to Ms. Mitchell's homeroom class. Moving, invisible, past several sets of indifferent eyes, he found his seat and welcomed the next moment: a greeting from the girl in front of him. Heather Jyles.

She spun around and flashed her wide smile full of perfect teeth. Her dark eyes twinkled. He always loved the way her short, dark curls bounced when she spun around to look at him like that. Every time she smiled at him something in his belly jumped. What was that look in her eye? Was it one of affection, admiration, or pity? Lane decided it had to be pity. It couldn't possibly be the others. It might be admiration. After all, he was at the top of his class academically, and Heather was one of his leading competitors. It would only be natural for her to admire her notable rival. But she was too pretty and too popular to have affection for him. On good days he thought it was admiration. On particularly bad days he was convinced it was nothing more than pity coming from a truly kind person.

"Well? Are you excited?" Heather asked. She crossed both arms on the front of his desk. Her eyes sparkled with enthusiasm.

"What?"

"The test, you dork. Are you excited?" Heather teased. "This has got to be one of the coolest things I've ever seen. How many kids get to take this test?"

"Yeah, I'm excited, I guess."

"Right. You don't fool me, I know you're busting at the seams."

The bell rang and the rest of the students slipped into their seats. Before she turned around, Heather leaned over to Lane and whispered, "I know you're going to do great. You're my hero, you know." She paused and looked at him with her dark eyes. They flashed, and then she turned away to face the teacher.

He was stunned. Hero? If he hadn't known better, that last look might have been more than admiration. Impossible.

PLEROMA

The homeroom class proceeded as normal, and the bell rang, dismissing everyone to begin their day. Heather turned around and looked at Lane.

"Good luck today. We're cheering for you."

His eyes followed her as she disappeared into the hallway.

"Heather Jyles, huh?" Ms. Mitchell said. She walked up to Lane's desk.

"What?" He shook himself from a dumbfounded stare.

"I saw how she looked at you, Lane. I was a young girl like her once, you know." Ms. Mitchell smiled and looked at him with motherly admiration.

"Heather? Me? Come on, Ms. M." He vigorously shook his head. "First of all, you know I don't have time for that sort of thing. And, secondly, she is way out of my league." He shrugged it off.

"Well, don't underestimate yourself, young man," she scolded him. "Which reminds me...don't forget to be right here after school. Three thirty sharp. They allowed us to use this room. It should make you feel nice and comfortable."

"That's great," Lane replied.

"I'm so proud of you. I just know you're going to do great. Now, you better get moving, or you'll be late and you'll have to take the test from detention hall."

The rest of the day went smoothly. It started out in Mr. Lancaster's AP Physics class.

"Yes, Derek." Mr. Lancaster hadn't had a chance to begin class when a hand shot up in the back of the room.

"Mr. Lancaster," Derek said, "I watched a show last night that talked about parallel dimensions. Do you think there really are alternate realities?"

Mr. Lancaster's eyes brightened beneath his bushy white eyebrows. He squinted his left eye, which bunched up the skin at the corner like folds of leather. When his head tilted to the side everyone in the class shot excited glances at each other.

They got him. Everyone knew Mr. Lancaster was a sucker for science fiction and discussing the bizarre aspects of physics. All the students leaned forward to enjoy the ride.

All but Lane. He slumped back in his chair and raised his hand.

"I don't mean to be rude, sir, but is this really what we were supposed to discuss today?"

Audible groans echoed around the room as Mr. Lancaster's spell was broken.

"Look, everybody," Lane said, "it might be cool to talk about having to slingshot around the sun to go back in time or finding your alternate personality in another dimension when you are watching science fiction, but I thought this class was about science reality. Don't get me wrong, I love a good story, but I'm here to learn something that is actually going to get me somewhere in life. Can we get back on the subject please?"

Mr. Lancaster smiled. His pure white hair and slightly hunched back did not conceal the impish mischief that lay behind his eyes. He sat back in his chair, put his arms behind his head, and stared at Lane.

"Mr. Reality, huh Lane?" he said. "It's all about the tangible, the concrete, and the here and now for you, isn't it?"

"Pretty much, sir. I used to be into all that fantasy stuff..."

His mind wandered back to the times his mom would sit with him on his bed and read classics like *The Lion, the Witch and the Wardrobe* and *A Wrinkle in Time* to him late into the night. The two of them would dream together about all the magical places that might be lurking around any corner and about how cool it would be to find one of them. Now that was all gone...

"...but I don't have time for that kid's stuff anymore. The world is in too much danger, and we need to use science to do something real about it."

Mr. Lancaster lifted his eyebrows and redirected his attention to the topic at hand. "OK, you are the whiz kid after all."

After physics it was calculus, then AP Lit, AP History, a brief stretch of the right brain with an art class, and finally German.

Three fifteen, and the final bell rang. The moment had come. Lane stopped off at his locker to gather his things and then made the trek down the main hallway to Ms. Mitchell's room. As he walked through the doorway, things seemed different somehow. The room that was usually bristling with the energy of his homeroom classmates was now strangely still. It was almost suffocating.

"Hey, Lane, are you ready?" Ms. Mitchell greeted him.

"Yeah, I guess. But could we open the window or something? It seems really hot in here." Lane rolled up his sleeves and opened his collar a little more.

"Sure." Ms. Mitchell slid open the archaic window.

"Now, find a comfortable spot, and when you're ready, I'll give you the packet."

Lane scanned the room and decided that the most comfortable spot was the seat that had been his since his freshman year. He sat down and looked up at his teacher.

"I'm ready."

She placed the thick stack of paper in front of him.

"You'll have one hour from the time I say 'go.'"

The clock on the wall said it was 3:30. He'd be done by 4:30. That would give him plenty of time to take the exam and be home before his father came home from work.

"Perfect." He looked up at his admiring teacher with a confident smile.

Ms. Mitchell situated herself behind her desk and then looked up at Lane.

"I just want you to know how proud I am that you are even able to take this exam. Now, just relax." She picked up the timer and pressed the button.

"Begin."

He cracked open the test packet and opened to page one. The first question actually made sense to him. That was a good sign. He progressed through the questions, carefully taking them one at a time, not wanting to look ahead.

The time went by quickly. Fifteen minutes passed, then thirty. The pages turned, and the wheels in his mind spun wild and fast. The questions energized him, and he reveled in the stimulus they provided for his mind. He loved it. He hadn't felt this good in a long time. It was 4:15 and he was on the final question. Perfect.

His enthusiasm came to a screeching halt. His breath caught in his throat. In big, bold letters at the bottom of the page he read the words "YOU MAY NOW TAKE A 10 MINUTE BREAK BEFORE PROCEEDING TO PART 2 OF THE EXAM."

What? Part two? Lane looked up at the clock then darted his eyes to his teacher.

"Ms. Mitchell, it says there is a part two on this test." His voice cracked as the words squeezed from his tightened throat.

"Yes? Is that a problem?"

"Well, I...just...wasn't expecting that." He looked up at the clock again. His foot bounced on the floor, racing with his accelerating heartbeat.

"Lane, I'm sorry. I thought you knew it was a two-part test. You have one hour to complete part one and one hour to complete part two."

He studied the clock and tried to make the calculations in his head. His mind was so scrambled now he felt like he couldn't even tell time. *It's four thirty now. If it takes an hour, that will put me at five thirty. I'll have to get my bike and ride home. I'll barely make it home by six. What day is it? Thursday? Does he get home early or late today? Oh man, I can't remember.*

He fidgeted in his seat. "Ms. Mitchell, is there any way I can take part two tomorrow?"

Her face showed deep concern as she began to piece together what was bothering him.

"Oh Lane, I'm so sorry. The rules clearly state that once you open the packet the test must be completed in the allotted time, or else you will forfeit the opportunity."

He rolled his head back and raked his hands through his hair several times, massaging his brain to come up with an alternate solution. The timer beeped and his ten-minute break was over.

"Lane, it's time to start part two."

Perhaps some kind of miraculous intervention would happen. Maybe the fire alarm would go off. Maybe Mr. Lancaster would barge into the room and finally ask Ms. Mitchell to marry him and carry her away. Maybe aliens would suck him out through the window.

No help came. He dropped his head in defeat.

The page weighed a hundred pounds. The words of the first question were thick and meaningless. A heavy head pressed into his hand, and he wondered how he was going to make it through part two.

Pull it together, man. Just breathe deeply and focus. You can do this.

The next hour took an eternity. It was amazing how different he could feel from one part of the test to the next. In part one he felt brilliant and energized. Now his mind felt splintered, and all his knowledge dribbled out his ears. Loud clicks from the minute hand marked his trudge through each thick question.

Five twenty-seven. It had taken him the full hour to slog through the boggy test. He wasn't sure if he had understood the questions, let alone answered them correctly. Hopes of MIT melted away as he placed the packet on Ms. Mitchell's desk. He would be stuck here with no hope of getting out...and away from him.

It's all his fault, again. Anger surged inside him. Teeth clenched, he stared a hole through the desk.

"Lane, what's wrong?"

Ms. Mitchell's question jolted him back to the moment. He looked up at her and then at the clock. The anger was quickly displaced by fear.

"Josh!" He bolted for the door. "I've gotta fly, Ms. M. I'll see you tomorrow."

He slid out of the room onto the green and black vinyl floor of the hallway and scrambled to make the turn. A frantic stop at the storage closet produced his bike, and soon both were out the front door, down the big stone staircase, and onto the path that led through the park.

He had to make it home in time. Couldn't he pedal any faster? His legs started to burn, but he had to keep pedaling.

PLEROMA

Chapter 4

Later that day...

The sound of voices was the first thing he heard. Whispers, really. Muddy words swirled around in Lane's mind like milky clouds. As the sounds became clearer, so did the pain that shot through his head. Where was he? The darkness around him was not the heavy kind of darkness that he would expect to feel when stuffed underneath a bed. It was a bright darkness. Even through closed eyes, white heat burned in his vision. Sunlight? He didn't dare open his eyes.

"Jethro!" The muddy whispers formed words. "Jethro! Come here." The voice was a whisper trying to be a shout. "Jethro!"

Sounds like snapping twigs or peanut shells underfoot moved away from him and disappeared. More sounds emerged. A light breeze blowing through leaves, the occasional buzz of a flying bug, and a rhythmic beating of some sort. The beating was not a deep boom, like a drum beat, but more high-pitched and short—like the sound of a bean bag falling on the ground. It was distant and very faint, but it continued, consistent and rhythmic.

Under ordinary circumstances these would be the calming sounds of a lazy summer afternoon in the park, but Lane was anything but calmed. The pain in his head grew stronger, and every muscle in his body was tensed and hard.

Did he dare open his eyes? Where could he possibly be? Waves of possibilities whirled in his mind. A tingling sensation coursed through his body. First in the ankles, then shooting up his back, it exploded like the feeling of ginger-ale bubbles at the base of his head. Was this fear or excitement...or both?

Just as he was about to open one eye, footsteps approached. Two distinct sets of footsteps swished through the sound of branches brushing, bending, and snapping back into place.

"Jethro, do you see what I mean? Just look at the size of him!" It was the voice he had heard before.

"Hmmmm," a deep growl rumbled from the second set of footsteps. "You are definitely right about his size, Gustov. I will grant you that," the grumbler said, "but how can you know if he is the one?"

"Jethro! Slap yourself! Look at him. What other explanation can there possibly be?"

"Gustov, keep your voice down. You do not want to attract attention to this thing. No matter what he is, we have to figure out what to do with him."

Footsteps paced back and forth from one side of Lane's head to the other, snapping twigs, pausing, then moving again.

"We cannot very well have him stand up. The guards will spot him for sure. If they see him then all kinds of trouble will rain down on us."

"That is true," Gustov agreed.

The three of them were silent for a while.

"I am telling you, Gustov, nothing good will come of this. We should just walk away from this right now and let the guards deal with him."

"The guards? How could you possibly think about letting the guards learn of him? That is just the opposite of what we should do. No, we have to come up with a plan. You wait here and keep an eye on him. I will be right back."

One set of footsteps faded into the distance. Lane could hear the heavy breathing of the voice he now knew as Jethro. Did Jethro just growl?

"Oh, this is just lovely," grumbled Jethro. "There I was, just minding my own business, working on my row like a good little worker, and then you have to show up and send Gustov into a fit. *Pleroma*...that is a bunch of rattlescat if you ask me."

Pleroma? What's he talking about?

Lane felt a sharp poke in his right shoulder. Another jab

poked into his ribs.

"You are probably dead," Jethro growled.

A twig cracked, and then something came extremely close to his head. Warm, moist air tickled his ear. It was very difficult to lay still when his personal space was being violated by...whatever it was that was violating him.

What is Jethro? Why is there a Jethro? I'm supposed to be under the bed in my room.

A sharp, pinpoint pain shot into the top of Lane's head.

"Ow!" the exclamation jumped from Lane's mouth and sprung his body to a sitting position. His eyes popped open. Lane's sudden movement sent the mysterious Jethro sprawling backwards into the shadows.

Trying to match the sounds with what he saw was disorienting. It took a few seconds for the two senses to come in sync. Lane was definitely outside. The clear blue sky sprawled above him, and the sun shone brightly overhead. It was midday. Yellow and green dominated the color palette. He sat in the middle of a field of plants that stood straight and tall. They reached a little higher than the top of his head when he was sitting up. A cluster of buds crested the top of each tall green stalk and revealed a small stripe of yellow down their sides where they were starting to break open.

The plants completely surrounded him and obstructed his view. Several stalks fanned around him on the ground, apparently crushed by the impact of his fall. If he wanted to see any more of his surroundings he was going to have to stand up.

Just as he pulled in his legs to hoist himself to a standing position, a voice shot out from the plants in a constrained, whispered shout.

"NO! Do not stand!"

Lane froze. It was the voice of Jethro. Lane stared into the wall of stalks. His stomach churned as he anticipated what was about to emerge from the plants. He was sure it was going to be grotesque and frightening. He just hoped it would not hurt him. Lane braced himself.

Jethro stepped out from the wall of plants and into the sunlight. A laugh escaped from Lane's mouth before he could catch it. What stood before him was anything but an intimidating or grotesque creature. Jethro was a pint-sized, middle-aged man wearing a simple, beige tunic that hung loosely from his torso, brown pants, and some dirty leather boots.

The top of his head came to just below the tops of the plants. His body was well proportioned, except for the fact that his head seemed a little too large for the rest of his parts. His arms were thick and strong, culminating in wide and calloused hands. A thick, bushy mustache tucked under his bulbous nose and blended in with an equally thick beard that hung down to mid-chest.

The most unusual feature on this strange little figure was a lack of feature. Jethro had no ears. Dark eyes blinked in the sunlight, revealing strange, goatlike, horizontal pupils that constricted vertically in the brilliance. Other than these two things, his features were very humanlike.

"Did you just laugh at me?" Jethro scrunched up his nose and scowled.

Lane didn't respond. After all, what do you say when one minute you are under your bed and the next minute you open your eyes and you find yourself staring at a Munchkin?

"I'm sorry?" Lane hunched his shoulders and opened his hands, palms up.

They stared at each other for a few uneasy moments, and then Lane resumed his attempt to stand up.

"No!" Jethro ran full speed toward him.

Jethro's impact knocked Lane backwards onto his rear. The momentum of the charge caused Jethro to tumble on top of Lane. They both lay on top of some newly crushed plants.

Jethro looked at the plants he had crushed and lamented, "Oh no, more flowers destroyed. We are going to pay for that. What is worse is we are going to have to explain it as well."

Jethro looked up at Lane and squinted in the bright sunlight. "Pleroma, huh? I think you are nothing but bad luck. Humph!"

Before Lane had a chance to respond, a rustling sound approached them from the other side of the clearing they had formed. Another small man appeared from within the plants. Overall, this man was very similar to Jethro. He had no ears, and his pupils were goatlike. His face, however, was round and jovial. He had cherry cheeks that smashed up into his smiling eyes. Thick salt-and-pepper sideburns covered the sides of his face and grew down his jawline, took a sharp turn below the corners of his mouth, and converged to form a thick mustache. This left his chin exposed and clean-shaven. He was not fat, but his body was round. Combined with his rosy cheeks and the gleam in his eye, it gave him an aura of Yuletide.

"Oh, Great Father, he is awake!" Lane recognized the voice as that of Gustov. "This is wonderful."

"Wonderful?!" Jethro protested, "Look at all these crushed flowers. How are we going to explain this, Gustov? I am telling you, this thing will be the death of us. We need to run away, now!"

"Oh, stop it, Jethro," Gustov waved him off. "Just look at him. If this is not the one, then I do not know what else it could be."

"Trouble," Jethro muttered under his breath. "That is what it is."

"Well," Gustov said, "we will just let the council figure that out."

Lane sat, speechless, and stared at his two new companions. Perhaps he was dreaming? But it all seemed so real. He could feel the stalks of the plants under him and the breeze blowing against his skin. The warmth of the sun beat on his head. Sweat beaded on his forehead, and a drop ran down the side of his face. The sounds, the textures, the colors, they were all so vivid. It couldn't be a dream. What was it?

Gustov walked closer to Lane and planted himself in front of him. At full height, the round halfling's eyes were even with Lane's when he was sitting down. Horizontal pupils scanned Lane up and down. They stopped and looked deep into Lane's eyes as if searching for something. He felt awkward, but somehow knew he shouldn't look away. Gustov's stare penetrated deeply and lasted for several minutes.

A smile spread across the round face, and Gustov's eyes disappeared under the upward thrust of rosy cheeks.

"Ah, yes, Jethro, he is the one. I can feel it."

He stood back, tapped his index finger against his lips, and searched the ground for answers.

"What to do, what to do."

Gustov looked up at Lane. "Well, Jethro is right about one thing. We cannot have you standing up and getting noticed by the guards. We will have to wait until nightfall before we can bring you into the village."

Gustov slapped his hands together with a great flourish. "It is settled, then. Jethro, you stay here with him, and you," he pointed at Lane, "blessed Pleroma, you stay down, and wait until I return."

The small, round form vanished into the plants. Jethro ran after him, leaving Lane alone. Muffled whispers volleyed back and forth, and then silence. A few moments later a very dejected Jethro reappeared. He took one look at Lane, huffed, then plopped on the ground.

"That is it then. We wait." Jethro turned away from Lane and stared into the wall of vegetation in silence.

Lane thought it was just as well that his reluctant companion did not want to speak. The silence would give him time to think through his situation. What was happening? There wasn't enough information to form a hypothesis. He would have to wait.

His head was really throbbing now. The pain and the weight of these strange events pulled him to the ground. Everything grew misty, then black. He fell asleep.

PLEROMA

Chapter 5

No more sunlight. Night had fallen while he slept, and the plants that encircled his field of vision were rimmed with bright moonlight. Sleep did not extinguish the throbbing in his head. In fact it seemed to be more intense.

A strange sensation crept over Lane. Someone was watching. At first he was afraid to look, but then he remembered his previous encounter. He turned his head and saw two sets of eyes gleaming in the moonlight, intensely fixed on him. It was Jethro and Gustov.

"Ah! You are awake!" Gustov boomed in a loud, robust voice. "Get up, Pleroma. We must walk."

The volume that bellowed from this small body was remarkable.

"You want me to stand up?" Lane asked. "What about the guards? Aren't we supposed to whisper and stay low?"

Gustov laughed.

"Good, you learn quickly. Yes, when the sun shines we must be very cautious of the guards. They watch our every move. But, when the sun goes to bed and our Three Sisters rise to guide the night sky, the guards become worthless. The nectar has done its work, and they will sleep soundly all night."

Gustov extended his hands to the night sky.

"In the day we are prisoners, at night we walk free."

The two small men walked away from Lane and into the wall of plants.

Gustov called back over his shoulder, "Come, Pleroma! Stand and walk."

He stood up. For the first time since his arrival in...wherever this was, Lane was able to see past the small patch of plants that had been his cell. The darkness cast a deep purple shadow over everything. He stood in the middle of a large field of plants that rose to his waist. Far on the other side of the field there was a long ridge of darkness. He couldn't tell if this was a line of trees or the silhouette of distant mountains. Straight ahead, another wall of darkness tore a jagged edge against the dark gray sky. It seemed to be a cluster of trees.

Two blurry dots moved toward the dark outcropping. He assumed these dots were his guides, so he followed. By the time they reached the edge of the mass, he caught up with them.

At this point it was obvious that they stood at the edge of some woods. The tree trunks were rim-lit with silky white light. The majority of the trees were of a broad, leafy type with strong, exposed trunks. Scattered amongst them stood the furry outlines of pine branches. The ground was covered with loose leaves and dirt and relatively free of undergrowth.

Gustov and Jethro did not miss a beat, but continued to press on into the woods. Lane stopped at the edge and looked back. The source of the strong rim-lighting was apparent. Spread evenly in the sky hung three moons. Each of them was nearly full. Their brightness illuminated the landscape in rich, monochromatic tones. Wide fields spread away from him over rolling hills as far as the eye could see. The fields were punctuated by dark patches of forest.

"Ah, our Sisters," Gustov said. "You are not the first man to be distracted by their beauty. When the three of them dance together it is especially captivating."

Gustov paused to bask in the moonlight.

"It also makes it very easy to see in the darkness," Gustov said, "even in the deeper woods. So, we must not waste their mercy. We need to go!"

Gustov turned and headed quickly back into the woods where Jethro impatiently waited. Lane had no choice but to follow his guides into the dark woods.

As much as the three "Sisters" illuminated the woods, it was still very dark and difficult to navigate the forest floor. He tripped and stumbled along, skinning his hands as he caught himself against the rough trunks. Eventually the ground began to rise steeply. Soon he needed to use his hands and feet to climb. The two guides were barely visible, but it was clear that they did not struggle as they climbed. Twiggy shrubs served as handles as he pulled his way up the slope. Breathing became more difficult, and his head pounded.

Finally, they came to the top of the ridge. It flattened out into a moonlit clearing about ten feet wide. The other side was edged by another wall of forest. Rocky, flat ground spread out to their right. It was a path.

Gustov and Jethro continued along the path without hesitation or instruction. He followed, thankful for a level surface that was free of trees. The two halflings walked briskly, but Lane's long strides quickly overtook them. He slowed his pace and settled into a leisurely gait in order to let them lead.

The subdued cadence of his walk, combined with the milky white moonlight and the warm summer air allowed his body to slip into autopilot and his mind to kick into overdrive.

Where was he? Who were these two strange little men walking in front of him?

One thing was certain. He had not fallen into another world. That was not possible.

I'm dreaming. That's the most logical explanation. But, I've had lots of dreams before, and none of them have been like this. This is too lucid. Everything seems so real. The bigger question is why I would be asleep right now.

His father had been in a bad place that day. Worse than usual. Why had he been so angry? *Let's see, what happened? I hid under the bed. He kicked in the door. The bed started to shake, and then everything fell in on me...*

"A coma!" Lane shouted.

His outburst stopped Gustov and Jethro short.

"A coma, Pleroma? What is a coma, and why are you shouting?" Gustov asked.

"A coma...you know...the sleeplike state of someone who

has suffered a head injury." Lane said.

Gustov stared blankly.

He stepped away from Gustov and looked up at the night sky.

"Hello!"

He ran a few feet further down the path, cupped his hands, and shouted louder.

"Hello, can you hear me? I know where I am now. You can wake me up! I get it!"

"Pleroma," Gustov said, "are you calling to the Sisters? Do you have the ability to communicate with them?"

"No, I'm not calling to the Sisters. And, oh yeah, by the way," he continued with a new sense of confidence, "stop calling me Pleroma. My name is Lane."

"Lane?"

"I told you he was not the Pleroma," Jethro said.

"Be quiet, Jethro." Gustov caught up with Lane on the path. "What does Lane mean?"

"I don't know. It's just my name. You know...Lane. That's it."

Gustov scratched his head and studied the ground.

"I suppose," Gustov said, mostly to himself, "the term Pleroma is more of a label than a name. Why can the Pleroma not have a proper name?"

He looked up with a satisfied smile. "Lane it is, then. It is a pleasure to meet you. Now, what is this coma that you say, and why are you calling to the sky?"

"Oh, right," Lane answered, "I guess that might look a little strange to you."

"A little," Jethro said. He rolled his eyes.

Lane ignored the jab and continued. "As we have been walking along this path I've been racking my brain, trying to make sense out of what's happening to me. At first I thought I was dreaming, but everything is too real for that. Then, as my head kept pounding, I remembered how my dad broke into my room. He must have slammed down on my bed and broken it. The bed fell on my head and crushed my skull."

Gustov and Jethro froze in confusion.

"You see, I'm not really here. Well, I'm here, but here isn't really here."

The confusion deepened in their faces.

He backtracked and tried again. "What I mean is that I'm actually lying in a hospital bed right now."

"What is a hospital?" Gustov asked.

"A hospital? Well, it's a place where you take sick or injured people so that they can get better. You know, with doctors and nurses."

"A place of medicine?" Gustov asked.

"Yes, that's it." Lane replied, "A place of medicine. When the bed fell on my head I must have been knocked unconscious. They rushed me to the hospital, and I am lying on a bed. The doctors are trying to use medicine to bring me out of my coma. I probably have tubes and wires sticking out of me all over the place."

His hands flailed as he pantomimed his bedridden and intubated state. Gustov and Jethro recoiled in disgust at the picture he painted.

He toned it down and continued.

"So, I've been trying to figure out what you are and what this place is. After all, how cheesy is it that I wake up in a land full of half-sized people? I mean that one is so old. That got worn out with *The Wizard of Oz*. Obviously, there aren't half-sized people with no ears and weird eyes in real life. This is too much like all those stories my mom used to read to me when I was a kid."

He slapped his hands together.

"That's when it hit me! You guys exist inside my head. You, this place, this is something that my subconscious mind has created in order for me to cope with my coma. Everything I see is an image from my memory and imagination."

There was a long, silent pause as the two halflings studied his face.

"So," Jethro snorted, "we are not real. We only exist in your mind. That is rich."

Jethro looked at Gustov with exasperation.

"Gustov, do you need to hear any more of this? Do you still believe he is the one? He does not even think we are real."

Gustov looked puzzled and hurt. His eyes shifted back and forth, scanning the ground for answers to this new wrinkle in his ideas.

He looked at Lane, "Plero—I mean, Lane. Do really think we are not real?"

Gustov's sincerity was moving. And unexpected. The two munchkins were supposed to vanish or change in some way now that they were exposed by the light of truth.

"Well…I mean…when I said you aren't real…I meant that you don't exist in the real world."

Hurt deepened in Gustov's eyes.

"No, no, I mean…that…you are very real to me…"

The furrowed brow smoothed out and Gustov's shoulders relaxed. The smile once again spread across his rotund face.

"You see, Jethro," Gustov looked back with a smug superiority, "he is not crazy. He knows this is real."

Lane deemed it best to hold his perceptions to himself. If he was going to figure out what is really going on, perhaps he should interact with this world as if it were real.

The fact that he was inside of his own mind helped to subdue his mounting anxiety. Now the task at hand was to decipher what his mind was telling him and figure out how to wake up from his coma.

"Gustov, I'm sorry if I worried you," Lane said. "I think I'm a little confused. Could you tell me where I am?"

Gustov looked at Lane and then turned his head a little to the side. "You really do not know what is going on, do you?"

"No, I really don't." Lane answered, "All I know is that one minute I was hiding under my bed, and the next minute I was falling through the sky and landed in your field."

"Hmmm… This is interesting," Gustov said. "Let us walk and I will explain everything."

Chapter 6

The three moonlit figures continued their walk along the path.

"First of all," Gustov said, "you understand that we are in Deltonia, correct?"

"No," Lane replied, "I don't have a clue where I am or what is going on."

"My, my," Gustov shook his head, "this will be complicated. Where do I begin?"

They walked a little while as Gustov gathered his thoughts. He gestured with his hands like he was drawing on a chalkboard as his lips mouthed silent words.

"All right, Lane," Gustov cleared his throat. "Let us begin with a geography lesson. We are the Deltonians, and we live in the fertile plains where the Great River flows into the sea. To the south of us, where the lesser branch of the river meets the sea, lives our cousin tribe, the Erles. They are very much like us, but, if you ask me, their women are far plainer than ours. It is a pity really."

"Now that," Jethro chortled, "is something I can definitely agree with."

"Yes, yes," Gustov waved off the remark. "Be that as it may, both the Erles and the Deltonians have lived in the fertile plains for as long as time can remember and we are mostly farmers and artisans.

To the north, where the mountains meet the sea, up where the ground is rocky, live the Gamordines. They are a hardy tribe that mostly mines the earth for metal and precious stones. They can be fierce in battle, but if one ever becomes your friend, they will be so to the death.

"Further south, beyond the Erles, the trees grow taller and the vegetation gets thicker. Down there, where the dense forest meets the sea and you cannot go any further, that is where the Bedites live. They are a wild bunch."

"Vile, if you ask me," Jethro said,

"Well, no one is asking you, are they?" Gustov retorted. "Stop interrupting."

Jethro spat on the ground and grunted.

"Vile, indeed," Gustov said. "Where was I? Yes, the Bedites. They grow not a lick of food on their own. They hunt their meat and gather the fruit that grows all year in the forest. They sing strange songs and beat their drums long into the night. The air is thick and moist there and is usually swarming with bugs. We never go to Beda, if at all possible."

Gustov paused and took in a deep breath. His shoulders slumped with the weight of his thoughts.

"Then there are the Altanians…"

Gustov stopped and looked at Lane. "Are you sure you do not know any of this?"

"Trust me," Lane insisted, "I still have no idea what you're talking about."

Gustov continued his educational walk down the path. The glowing Sisters were high in the night sky, and it was easy to see the well-worn path that lined the top of the ridge. It turned to the left and began a gradual decline.

"To the west, across the desert where the river disappears into the ground, up in the mountains, live the Altanians." Gustov clenched his jaw and became visibly agitated. "The very sound of their name on my lips makes my stomach sour. They are the reason we walk by the light of the Sisters instead of during the day like free people. They are the reason my hands are hard and calloused and my back is stiff. They came down from the mountains with the Bellator and conquered us all."

"The Bellator?" Lane interrupted.

"The Monster, you mean." A gruff bark came from Jethro.

"Yes," Gustov agreed, "he is their monster. Many years ago their goddess, Amo, gave him to them so that they could come down from the mountains and dominate us. We live in fear of him.

"I was young when the Invasion happened. There was no warning. One morning my father looked up to the western horizon and saw their war horde marching in with...him..." venom hissed in his voice, "...towering over them all. They came right into our village, and he massacred our leaders, and the soldiers corralled the rest of us into the barns. We all stood huddled in our animals' homes while we watched our homes burn to the ground."

Gustov's voice trailed off as his eyes traveled into that misty, painful memory.

They walked for a while in silence. The gravel crunched under their feet and the night creatures wailed, calling back and forth in the distance, echoing Gustov's pain.

"It was not always like this, you know." Gustov looked up at Lane to see if he was still listening.

"A generation ago, the five tribes lived in harmony with one another. Yes, it is true that over the centuries we have warred back and forth for dominance. In our ignorance much needless blood was shed. But, over time, our tribal leaders realized that life was much more tolerable when the tribes worked together and traded for the things we need, rather than raiding and pillaging for them like barbarians. So, a nice agreement was made. We and the Erles have the best farmland, so we focused on the production of grain and vegetables. The Gamordines offered their ore and stones. The Bedites contributed exotic fruit and lumber. And, finally, the Altanians brought furs and various fruits and elements that can only be found in the mountains. The trade routes were wide and easy to travel between the four coastal tribes, and the interaction was rich and beautiful. The Altanians had the most difficult piece of the arrangement, that is to be sure. Their trade route crossed the wasted plain between the two mountain ranges. It took them many days and cost much in supplies to come down to the coast. I'm sure they felt cheated, like the odd one in the bunch."

Gustov stopped as a silent debate began in his mind. He let out a soft sigh.

"I suppose, if one cares to look at it from a particular point of view, it is possible to see why they did what they did. Had we been in their situation..."

"No!" Jethro interjected, "Do not even say it. We would have never done what they have done. They betrayed us all. They broke the treaty and reverted to the old ways. They are nothing more than savages."

No rebuttal from Gustov this time. Both men stewed.

The muscles in Gustov's temples pulsed under his reddening skin. Just as it looked like he was about to explode in anger, his expression abruptly changed.

"Look at me, getting all worked up again."

The twinkle came back into his eyes. Gustov stretched out his hands to Lane.

"But now we have you. The Pleroma has come. The time of balance is about to break through. We will no longer have to rely on the light of the Sisters for freedom, but will be able to dance freely in the light of the Great Father of Lights once again."

He grabbed Lane's hands and danced around him in a circle. He bounced up and down as they twirled. As his body went up, his jowls went down, and then, as his body came back down, his jowls caught up and bounced up around his face. The sight of this half-sized, middle-aged man bouncing and jiggling around him was enough to make Lane break out in a big smile and laugh out loud. Lane even found himself skipping in step with his little dance partner.

"I am not saying that you two do not make a lovely dance team," Jethro's voice invaded their revelry, "but we are almost to the Hall. The night is nearly gone, and we have much to do before the morning work begins."

Gustov was chastened back into a focused walk.

"Right you are, Jethro," Gustov said, "there will be enough time for dancing. Come, Lane, we must get to the Hall. Everyone will be waiting for us there. It has all been arranged."

PLEROMA

Gustov still held Lane's right hand from their dance. He pulled it and led him through a small clearing on the right side of the path. They traveled silently a short way down a smaller path that was lined by trees. Just ahead, the darkness took on a different tone. A massive wall stretched up into the treetops and merged with the darkness of the sky.

A dark spot at the base of the wall marked the end of the path. Jethro reached it first. It was a door. A sliver of light sliced up its edge and then fanned across the path, sending Jethro's long shadow out to meet Lane's feet. Gustov and Lane quickly reached the door, and soon they stood blinking in the firelight of the Great Hall.

Chapter 7

Sweet. That was Lane's first thought when he stepped into the room.

First it was the smell. He could almost taste it. A sweet, meaty aroma welcomed him in and quickened his hunger, reminding him that he had not eaten all day.

Then it was the music. Pan flutes, fiddles, and dulcimers lifted airy notes high up into the rafters of the hall. They ebbed and flowed in time with the rhythmic movement of the small figures on the floor below.

Most of all, it was the faces. There was a sweetness to these people. The room was full of what, at first glance, looked like a large gathering of dancing children. They were not children, however, but small people like Gustov and Jethro. Both men and women formed tiny circles that moved back and forth and in and out like the opening and closing of flower petals. Graceful movements floated them across the floor in time with the music. Everyone smiled and laughed, and it seemed like a great celebration.

As soon as the three travelers stepped fully into the room, the music stopped. All eyes riveted on Lane. It was a very awkward moment. Usually no one noticed when he stepped into a room, let alone every eye there.

He was alarmed at first, but then the smiles captured him. The eyes that stared at him were not judgmental or condemning, but welcoming and full of anticipation. A strange and foreign sensation came over him. He felt welcome here. Even though these were strangers, he felt like he belonged here. He liked it.

PLEROMA

"Friends," Gustov said, "thank you all for coming tonight. I know we will pay with weariness tomorrow as we till the soil again. But I believe it will be worth it. Tonight, I present to you… the Pleroma!"

He stepped aside and raised his hands toward Lane.

The crowd erupted in cheers. Lane flushed and could not control the smile that spread wide across his face. All of those little people cheered for him. He didn't know why, but at that moment he didn't care. He had never been cheered for anything.

Gustov motioned for Lane to follow and then led him across the room, through a maze of people. The tops of most of their heads came only to his waist. Those close to him stopped and stared up with awe, arching their backs in order to see his face.

The hall was round and large. Two massive fireplaces sat directly across from each other. A circular chandelier full of candles hung from the center of the ceiling. Torch sconces lined the perimeter. Wild shadows shifted back and forth from the firelight and joined the dance.

They walked directly across the room to a platform on which sat a table, a chair, and an elaborate candelabra. Gustov climbed onto the platform and pulled the chair out from behind the table.

"You must be hungry. Would you like something to eat?"

The invitation doubled the hunger pains in his belly. Lane shook his head vigorously.

"I'm starved!"

Gustov stood at the edge of the platform and again addressed the crowd.

"Now, my friends, let the feast begin!"

The crowd noise swelled again with renewed cheers, and the people scattered to different places in the room. Tables and chairs were pulled to the middle. People disappeared through doors on either side of the fireplaces and quickly returned carrying platters full of bread and vegetables. In a few moments the dance floor was transformed into a banquet hall.

"Please, sit." Gustov motioned to the empty chair.

Something seemed strange about it. It was as tall as Gustov, who struggled to scoot it back. The table was also very large. As Lane neared the furniture he realized that the table and chair were his size. The other tables and chairs in the room were all correctly proportioned for these small people.

"Gustov," Lane asked, "where did you get this table? I mean, why do you have one this big?"

Gustov smiled. "I told you. We have been waiting for you, Pleroma. Please, take your seat."

Lane approached slowly. He sat down and scooted in to the table. Two young boys presented platters full of food. They hoisted them up to eye level and slid them onto the table. It was an awkward maneuver, but they did it with smiles and an authentic desire to serve.

The platters were filled with sweet meat, bread, vegetables, and a large goblet full of a frothy brew. The sight of this food pushed all thoughts and questions aside, and his appetite took control.

There was no silverware. Everyone else in the room simply plunged their bare hands into the food. A childish grin spread across Lane's face, and he plopped both hands in and shoveled the delicious food into his mouth. He couldn't remember a meal that tasted so good and was so satisfying.

Everyone settled into a rhythmic hum of eating and low chatter while two musicians mingled sweet sounds with the already sweet aroma of the food.

The scene was enchanting. Especially the women. They were not attractive or alluring. They were comforting. Kindness glowed in their eyes. It awakened something inside him that Lane hadn't felt in a long time.

Gustov's voice broke the moment.

"My friends, did you not enjoy the feast?"

The crowd cheered in unison and pounded on the tables in delight.

"Yes, as well you should. It has been a long time since we have had reason to invoke the sacred feast. I have been observing you all during the meal, and it warms my heart to see smiles again and to hear laughter. I have never lost hope, but I must confess that I have grown weary. Our lives have been stripped of joy and purpose."

The sparkling faces that had just warmed Lane's spirit were dimmed by gray, pasty masks.

"Every day we awaken to the light of our Father and the whips of our masters. I do not know why the Father has allowed this painful era in our history to occur. His light has been harsh on our backs and piercing to our eyes as we labor under the Altanians' cruel oppression. We are forced to seek refuge in the light of the dancing Sisters, where all color is faded into shadow. Our backs are bent, our hands are calloused, and our spirits have come near to death."

Gustov paused, and a hush fell over the room.

"But now, the season of our darkness is coming to an end. The great prophecy has been fulfilled. The Father's light is once again shining warmly on us, for, as predicted, another has fallen from the sky."

Gustov pointed his stubby, calloused finger directly at Lane.

"The Pleroma has come!"

In unison, the people rose to their feet, dropping the gray masks and replacing them with a cheer that rattled the sconces on the wall.

"Pleroma, Pleroma, Pleroma!"

Lane pushed himself back from the table. The sudden focus of attention left him breathless.

A flurry of activity swirled in front of him. The same boys who had set his place came and removed the dishes. Two men carried the table off to the side of the platform. From different places in the Hall a handful of figures moved toward Gustov and stood with him in front of Lane.

Six people gathered, three men and three women. Each face bore the lines of wisdom and age.

At first they stood side by side in front of Lane and stared at him, intense and searching.

What were they looking for?

The chanting of the crowd flowed softly like rushing water.

The group divided. Three of them moved to the left and three to the right. Each group circled around to the side of the platform, climbed the stairs, and then converged behind Lane. Before finding their position, each person removed a torch from a row of sconces that hung on the wall. Each torch was unique and beautiful, made of twisting golden filigree. One had cascading leaves that wove together around the handle, others bore the heads of animals, and still others oscillated with intricate scrollwork.

Six bodies, pulsing in their own torchlight, encircled Lane.

"Please rise, Pleroma." Gustov's tone was formal and deep.

Twelve eyes stared intently into the torch flames.

They waited.

Lane turned in his seat and studied the strange row of characters. The woman at the end shifted her weight and shot a glance at the man next to her. He returned the glance and cleared his throat. Neither looked directly at Lane. The silence thickened.

Gustov finally broke his gaze and looked directly at Lane with a pleading eye.

In a strained whisper he said, "Lane, stand up!"

"Oh!" Lane flushed with embarrassment, "Right. That's me. Pleroma. Got it. Sorry about that."

He sheepishly stood in the center, now completely encircled by the halflings. The liquid chanting continued to wash over him.

The circle moved. First they walked in three clockwise circles around him, then three circles in the opposite direction. After the circling finished, they stopped and, in unison, softly spoke low and unintelligible words.

When their words stopped, the crowd stopped chanting.

Silence hung in the Hall, accented only by the popping and crackling of the wood in the fireplace.

Five from the circle formed a line behind Lane while Gustov stood in front of him and faced the people. He raised his voice, half-singing and half-proclaiming.

PLEROMA

"Many years ago the goddess Amo deceived the Great Father and, through treachery and dark magic, brought forth the Bellator from murky regions beyond. She gave this creature to her favored children, the Altanians, and commanded them to descend from the mountains and conquer the coastal tribes. Since that terrible day of the Invasion, since the moment we first saw the fierce and piercing eyes of the Bellator, a shadow of fear and oppression has fallen across our beloved fields."

Some of the people turned their heads and spat on the ground as though expelling a bitter taste.

"The balance of peace between the tribes has been unnaturally spoiled and now, where once harmony reigned, only treachery and pain remain. Soil that was once rich with grain and fruit is now littered with the vile yellow flower that the Altanians crave. We work with no reward, and the fruit of our labor is taken from us as quickly as we harvest.

"Our wise men searched the signs to make sense of this upheaval, and they discovered a prophecy. It was told that when the time was right, and the Three Sisters danced together, another would come from the sky and restore balance. The Pleroma would come and deliver us from this oppression."

This last phrase caught Lane. Deliver?

Gustov continued, "In generations past, a yearly Festival was created to celebrate the union and harmony of the five tribes. This Festival was the high point of our year and our time to bring glory to the Father and all of the deities that watch over our tribes. Since the Invasion, Amo has worked her treachery and has stolen the Festival from the Father. She now controls its power. The Altanians have perverted it into a blood sport and cruelly mock us. Each year they taunt us with the idea of liberty and promise that any tribe that can offer a champion to defeat the Bellator in a battle to the death will win their freedom. Every year a valiant warrior from each tribe dedicates his life to the hope of freedom, and every year he is cruelly defeated by the monster in a bloody and disgusting mockery of the sacred event."

A knot formed in Lane's stomach.

Gustov continued, "But now, my dear friends, the prophecy is fulfilled. The Father has begun to overturn Amo's dark magic and has brought forth another to match the size and strength of the Bellator."

Blood drained from Lane's face. Objects in the room swam around him.

"The Pleroma stands before us. The Father has given us the warrior we have longed for. The Pleroma will fight for us at the Festival this year and will be victorious! Freedom is within sight, dear people!"

Excitement electrified the room as the people anticipated the finale of Gustov's speech. The more the energy increased, the weaker Lane's knees became.

"And finally, the elders have conferred. It has been decided. Our greatest leader in the art of battle will work with and train our Pleroma."

Gustov pointed at a gruff man standing at the side of the hall.

"Jethro, you have been chosen. You will train the Pleroma and be his guide between now and the Festival."

Caught up in the revelry of the feast, Lane had forgotten about his grumpy traveling companion. Now, through his spinning and blurred vision, he saw the shocked expression on Jethro's face.

In a final and grandiose gesture Gustov pointed at Lane, "Pleroma, you will fight the Bellator and defeat him. With his death you will deliver us!"

Death?

Gustov thrust his torch high into the air. The room shook as the blast of cheers erupted like a swelling river on a weakened dam.

The noise invaded Lane's mind. Everything in the room blurred into swirling color. Gustov's beaming face. Jethro's open astonishment.

His knees buckled.

All was black.

Chapter 8

Pain woke him up. Lane lay on his back, but the throbbing in his head kept him from sitting up. Maybe, if he lay very still, the pounding would subside.

Something was different. The air was stuffy, and a large presence pressed in just above his face. He was definitely not in the Great Hall any more. Did he dare open his eyes?

A gurgling sound came from somewhere near him.

Gurgling? Heavy breathing? Snoring. Someone was sleeping near him.

A loud *pop* scared him and he sat up in reflex reaction. *Wham*! The impact shot a new pain from the top left of his head down to meet the old pain on the back right side of his head.

Now his eyes were open.

The ceiling?

He sat on the side of a bed inside a small, cavelike room full of miniature furniture. A fireplace revealed the source of the popping sound.

Beside the bed, a chair contained a small, sleeping man. At the sound of Lane's thud against the ceiling, the halfling stood to full attention, rudely awakened.

"Jethro!?" Lane said in part surprise, part disgust, and part disappointment.

The gruff little man puffed and gurgled. He placed both hands on the lower part of his back and arched his head up and backwards until a loud *pop*! cracked from his spine.

"Ah! That is much better," he said.

He walked over to the fire. "I see the glory boy has awoken. I am sorry, did my snoring wake you, oh great one?"

Jethro threw a log onto the fire.

"You had quite a fall up there last night. Gave everybody a big scare. It seems the great Pleroma cannot handle his nectar. I must admit, it was quite entertaining to see all those pompous windbags scurry around like a bunch of scared *numa* when you hit the floor. *Plop*! There you were. Whoo-whee, they did not know what to do. Ha! You should have seen the look on Gustov's face when you hit the ground. He just stood there with his little eyes darting back and forth like he does when he knows he is wrong and he is trying to make up some lame excuse for how it is all 'part of the plan.'"

Jethro stoked the fire with angry thrusts.

"Serves him right for choosing me. They had no right to announce that in front of everyone. Now I am stuck. If I want to retain the small shred of respect I have left I must follow through, or...or... Oh, rattlescat!"

Jethro finally looked up at Lane. He shoved one of the chairs aside and marched over to the bed. Lane's hunched position let Jethro meet him at eye level.

"Now you listen to me!" He pointed his stubby finger in Lane's face. "I do not know what you are, or where you came from, but one thing I do know is that you are not the Pleroma. If you ask me, you seem more like a scared kid than a mighty warrior. Just look at you. Yes, you are tall, but look at your arms and your legs. You are gangly and lean. The Bellator will tear you limb from limb."

The knot returned to Lane's stomach as he remembered Gustov's proclamations.

"I do not know why they cannot see that," Jethro said. "Yes, I am the most qualified to train our warriors, but let us be reasonable. He will crush you. He will take your head in one hand and your feet in the other and then tie you up in a pretty little bow and snap you in half over his knee. *Crack*!"

With a downward thrust of his hands and an upward swing of his knee Jethro enthusiastically acted out this violent deed.

His knee was still raised when he noticed the expression on Lane's face.

"Oh, sorry," Jethro calmed his voice. "I am sure it will not be *that* bad... really. There is always the outside possibility that... that...the Bellator...well...he...might go blind, or lame...before the Festival...perhaps."

His voice trailed off and he stared back into the fire.

"No," Lane said, "you're right. You're absolutely right. I'm not the Pleroma. I don't even know what a Pleroma is. And I'm definitely not a warrior. The only fights I've been in, I've been on the receiving end when the jerks at school want to have some cheap entertainment. I'm a science geek, for crying out loud. I can't fight a warrior!"

Jethro's expression changed. He softened. For a long, uncomfortable time, he stood and stared at Lane.

"What?" Lane said, "What are you looking at? Don't you want to dance around and be happy that you were right? You obviously have some kind of authority issues going on here. Now you can rub their noses in it. Go ahead, I'm used to it."

Jethro did not respond. Instead, he slowly turned and plopped down on the chair that he had been sleeping in. His face shifted in the firelight, and the flames consumed his thoughts.

Lane sat on the edge of the bed. Jethro's silence allowed him time to scan his own thoughts.

What does this all mean? I've got a bunch of munchkins who think I'm a god or something. I've got Grumpy over here who knows I'm not a god and thinks I'm going to get pulverized by the Bellator.

The Bellator. What is that all about? They say he's a creature. A big, gnarly, man-eating creature. Oh that's good. My teachers told me I shouldn't read that scary monster stuff, but noooo, I wouldn't listen. I bet he's got one big eye in the middle of his forehead and bulging muscles popping out everywhere and claws that could slice me in half with one swipe.

The Bellator. Why would my mind set me up to fight against a vicious killing machine?

Lane's thoughts expanded and stretched out to mingle

with the flames that danced inside the hearth. The two figures sat, bathed in the firelight, and churned over their situation in silence.

"That's it! The Bellator is my coma." Lane looked at Jethro. "Are you really a good trainer?"

"What?"

"Are you really a good trainer?" Lane repeated with sincerity.

"I trained the best warriors we have ever had. Of course, they have all been killed by the Bellator, but you have to give me some leeway there."

"Then, do you think you could train me to fight the Bellator?"

"Ho, ho, that is rich," Jethro wagged his head.

"No, seriously. I mean it. I want to fight him. I need to fight him. I don't know if I'm the…Pleroma…or not. Truthfully, I don't really care. But I know that I'm supposed to face the Bellator. It may be my only hope."

Jethro studied Lane, scanning him intensely, as though he was looking for something. Lane returned the stare with equal intensity.

Neither of them knew whether or not Lane was the Pleroma, nor did they know whether Lane would survive the battle. But in that instant they connected. A mentor and an apprentice locked eyes for the first time.

Jethro would train and Lane would fight.

Chapter 9

"Now what?" Lane asked.

"Now, we wait."

Jethro moved to the small kitchen area and sliced into a large square of cheese.

"The Father is about to climb above the edge, and I will have to leave soon."

He handed a slice of heavy, dark bread and a wedge of cheese to Lane and pulled up a chair to join him.

"If I am going to train you, then we must get one thing perfectly clear right now. You must obey my instructions. What I say is the law."

Crumbs flew from his bread as he emphasized the point.

"Got it, you're the boss."

"Good. Now, rule number one." Jethro pointed to the small window next to the door. "As long as there is light in that window, you must never step outside. Never. Do you understand?"

"Never?"

"Never. It is too dangerous. If the guards saw you, who knows what they would do? They would most certainly make trouble for us. It is best if you remain a secret for now."

A splash of pale light washed away the darkness in the window. It quickly intensified.

"I have to go now. The fields are waiting. If I am late, I will pay with my flesh."

Jethro moved to the door, turned, and repeated, "Remember, stay inside."

"Right. Inside," Lane said.

Jethro closed the door behind him, and Lane slumped back onto the small bed.

Great. I'm a prisoner. This should be a fun-filled day.

Outside, footsteps scuffled back and forth. Low voices murmured and sounds of splashing water and clinking metal echoed through the window.

Soon the sounds faded away and all was silent. The whispers of nature filled the void. Birds sang. A light breeze tickled leaves in distant trees.

The sunlight grew more intense and thrust a shaft of golden light through the window. Its heat burned away the morning chill from the room.

After a while a new sound emerged. Giggles? Tiny footsteps. *That sounds like children.*

Lane crawled over to the window, careful to keep his head out of view. When he got to the wall he slowly raised his head until his eyes came above the sill and he could see out.

It was children. Like little puppies they ran and played together, clustered in the center of a large circle of small, dome-shaped huts. Rough, hairy skins covered the rounded buildings, each like half of a coconut shell sitting flat side down. In the middle of the circle, next to the children, a woman sat on a stone bench.

Four smaller, stone, circular objects surrounded this center point. From Lane's vantage point it was difficult to tell what these objects were. The children ran around them, hid behind them, and sat on their edge.

The woman stood and called them all to one of the stone circles. They all gathered around it and hopped up onto the edge. One of the children leaned forward and reached into it. She pulled back a handful of water and splashed it on her face. Soon they were all splashing water on their hands and faces. One especially small boy got a devilish grin and splashed the girl next to him. She splashed back, and all the children began sloshing water everywhere.

The woman clapped her hands and called them all back to

order. She motioned toward another stone bench that had a clay jar sitting on it. The jar had a rope tied to its handle. The tallest girl ran over to the jar and lowered it down behind the bench. She pulled up a dripping-wet jar. The bench was a well.

The children swarmed her and held out their cupped hands. One by one she poured water into their hands and they drank.

Once they had all finished, the woman clapped her hands again and walked toward the edge of the circle of huts. The children formed a line behind her, smallest in front and tallest in the back. The mother quail then led her chicks out of the circle.

It was silent again. A small, lizardlike creature scurried across the dirt of the village circle. Lane turned away from the window and slid to the floor with his back against the wall.

A small square of sunlight inched its way across the floor and slid with painful slowness up the side of the bed. Lane joined it there and lay down. The boredom and exhaustion got the best of him, and soon he was fast asleep.

Wood grated over stone. The sound woke him. Pale light faded quickly in the window.

Jethro slowly entered the room, leaning heavily on the wooden door. His hands and feet were caked with mud, and tiny red scratches streaked his forearms.

"What happened to you?" Lane said.

Jethro held an index finger to his mouth and motioned for Lane to be quiet. He closed the door and pressed his tired body against it. Exhaustion pulled on his shoulders.

Lane tried again, this time in a hushed whisper, "So, what happened?"

Shouts and clangs rang through the window before Jethro could respond. He leaned his head back against the door and closed his eyes. Was he holding his breath?

Lane slid off the bed and crawled over to the window to assume his lookout position. From the far side of the village five men entered the circle. The fading twilight painted them in eerie blue tones. They were halflings like the others, but they were slightly different. More slender. Perhaps a little taller. They wore armor: helmets, breastplates, and swords. One had a long spear.

They laughed as they entered the circle. It was a familiar laugh. Not the sound of good-natured fun. It was the cackle of a pack of hyenas looking for prey. The hair on the back of Lane's neck stood on end.

They stopped at the center stone ring. One of the soldiers covered his eyes with one hand and pointed his finger with the other. He weaved a little, unable to maintain his balance. Another soldier grabbed him by the shoulders and spun him around. He spun in erratic circles while the others howled and egged him on.

When the spinning stopped, his finger pointed at a hut across the circle. The pack moved in. One of them fell on the door and pounded.

"Get out here, now!"

Nothing happened.

He beat on the door with the butt of his sword.

"You do not want this to be worse than it has to be, do you?" He looked over at his comrades with a broad and leering smile.

"Have it your way."

He motioned and two guards tore open the door.

A shrill voice screamed inside the hut.

Jethro's body tensed at the sound. The hair on Lane's neck bristled now, and his heart beat faster. It pounded in his throat.

The two guards dragged a screaming woman out of the hut. A man ran after her but was knocked to the ground with the flat side of a sword. He lay motionless in the dirt.

Lane jumped up and moved to the door. Jethro leaned harder against it and blocked his exit.

"Jethro, what are you doing? I have to get out there."

"No. You cannot." The words scratched out of Jethro's mouth. "They cannot know you are here." Just then the woman screamed again, and Jethro clenched his eyes shut.

Lane looked out through the window. The guards dragged the screaming woman into the shadows on the other side of the circle and faded away.

It was dark now.

The circle sat silent.

Jethro's chin fell into his chest, and his shoulders hung heavy. He slid down the door and sat on the floor, arms and hands hanging limp beside him.

"I don't understand. What just happened out there?" Lane asked.

"The Switching Hour." Jethro let out a long, deep sigh, his voice heavy with defeat.

"Every night it is the same. We drag ourselves in from the fields while the guards go back to their quarters and start drinking the nectar. Just as the Father's light slips away, they choose one of our villages.

"Some nights they choose a man. The poor creature gets beaten as they play cruel games with him. Other nights they'll choose a woman. She is dragged off, screaming. Like tonight."

Jethro looked at Lane. "Did you see who they took? No, of course not, you would not know who she was. Whoever it was, she will return in the morning, but she will never be the same. The women never talk about what happens to them."

He smeared the back of his hand across his moist cheek. A swatch of mud streaked under his eye and looked like a bruise.

"The worst is when they choose a child."

Jethro stared into the now cold and empty hearth.

"They never return."

"That's horrible," Lane said.

They sat in the empty silence, fearing the worst for the poor woman.

Slowly, sounds of life emerged in the village circle. Several hollow cracks rang out, as if a pile of wood had been dropped on the dirt, the sticks knocking against each other.

"That would be Ban," Jethro said. "It is his turn to make the fire tonight. It always amazes me how quickly we recover after the Switching Hour. I suppose we have no choice."

Lane rose to his feet but was abruptly blocked by the low ceiling.

"Ow!"

Jethro let out a mocking chuckle and the dark spell was broken.

He hoisted his heavy body off the ground and carefully balanced himself, feet spread wide and leaning forward. He paused, and then arched his back quickly and came to a standing position. A deep, hollow *pop* echoed from his lower back.

"Ah, much better!" He smoothed the front of his dirty smock, took a deep breath, and looked at Lane with a strange, skeptical glare. "Are you ready to begin?"

Without waiting for an answer, Jethro quickly slipped out the door. A cool burst of evening air blew in and refreshed Lane.

It was time.

Lane crouched low in order to clear the door. As he unfolded his body, his head lifted above the top of all the huts in the circle. This giant business was going to take some getting used to.

A small man coaxed a fire into existence. Its flickering light revealed the stone objects that Lane had observed earlier during the day. From his elevated vantage point it was clear to see that there were five stone circles in the center of the village. The middle circle was the largest and held the fire, which grew in brilliance. Four stone circles of equal size surrounded the fire pit. One of them was the well where the children had been, and the other three appeared to be pools of water.

The children were the first to notice Lane. They swarmed him and danced around his feet like a litter of puppies in the pet shop. Each of them wanted to be the first one noticed.

"Well now," Lane said. "What do we have here?"

The girl who had held the pitcher of water for the others earlier in the day was the first to speak. She stood as tall as her tiny body could stretch and spoke with a clear, confident voice.

"My name is Tora."

"It is very nice to meet you, Tora." Lane leaned over and extended his hand to her. She stared at his hand and scrunched her nose, then looked up at him with eyes full of questions.

"It's called a handshake," Lane said. "Where I come from, when you meet someone for the first time you extend your hand, and the other person grabs onto it and shakes it."

Tora shrugged her shoulders and reached up to his hand. Her fingers were tiny compared to his. She grasped the end of his index finger with her right hand and shook it back and forth with all her might.

Lane chuckled, and Tora gave him a sheepish smile. "It is very nice to meet you, Pleroma," she said.

Tora's successful encounter with him encouraged the other children, and they moved in closer to his face. He stayed bent over in order to be closer to them.

"We were wondering, sir," Tora continued, a little less confident than the first time, "since this is your first night of training…" She paused and looked down at the ground. She drew lines in the dirt with her bare toe.

The smallest boy stood next to her. When she paused, he reached over and poked her in the side. She understood his message and continued.

"We were wondering if it would be all right with you if we came to the Great Hall and watched you train?"

The small boy nodded his head quickly and looked up at Lane with wide, hopeful eyes.

Lane looked over to see how Jethro felt about the suggestion. Jethro grunted. His dark eyes peered out from under thick, black eyebrows. He looked at the swarm of small children and then at Lane. After a moment of thought, he shrugged his shoulders and rolled his eyes.

"If you must," he said, and then walked away toward the edge of the village circle.

Squeals of delight pealed from the children.

"All right then," Lane said. He began to stand up, but then the smallest boy ran over to his calf and pulled frantically on his pant leg.

Lane stopped halfway up and then settled back down to the ground, resting on one knee.

"What's this about?" Lane asked.

Tora spoke up. "His name is Trik. He cannot speak."

"Do you know what he wants?" Lane asked.

She paused again, and Trik looked back at her. He looked up and pointed to Lane's shoulders.

"He wants to know if he can ride on your shoulders. I know it is a lot to ask, but I promised him that I would at least mention it. You do not have to, of course."

"No, it's fine." Lane rescued her from the awkward apologies.

He looked down at Trik. The pupils in his golden brown eyes had expanded wide enough to look almost circular. Trik smiled and begged with every ounce of body language he could muster.

"I'd love to give you a ride, Trik."

A wild smile expanded his face and he bounced up and down.

Lane stood quickly and lifted Trik to his shoulder. The little body was incredibly light and wiry, like a kitten, bristling with energy. Overwhelmed by the quick acceleration of his lift-off, a frail but happy chirp squeaked out of Trik's throat.

Everyone laughed, and soon Lane led the procession of tiny children toward the edge of the village circle. Jethro waited impatiently and disappeared into the shadows as soon as Lane approached. He followed Jethro and marched with exaggerated steps, lifting his knees high into the air and thrusting his elbows up like a drum major leading a marching band. He did this partly to entertain and partly to slow down his pace so that the tiny legs of the pursuing children could keep up with him. The children sang and laughed as they fell in step behind him.

Eventually the long procession wound its way down the forest path and came to the entrance of the Great Hall. The room that had housed Lane's reception feast the night before was now transformed. All of the tables and chairs had been pushed aside to the outer edges to make a great open space in the middle of the room.

Lane headed straight across the floor to the platform and ceremoniously disembarked his little passenger. All of the other children filed up the two staircases and plopped themselves along the edge of the platform, pushing and shoving for the privilege of hanging their feet over the edge.

Jethro was already in the Hall. He stood beside one of the fireplaces, next to a pile of weapons. A scowl distorted his face.

"Hmph! Children. What are we doing here, training a warrior, or a clown? Children do not belong in the battle training."

"Oh stop your whining, Jethro," Lane said. "It's good for them. They need to have something to cheer for. It'll give them hope—something to smile about."

"I wonder how much they would be smiling if they saw the real battle, when that monster comes out and tears your arms off. You are filling their heads with fantasies, Lane."

"Oh that's a lovely picture. And very encouraging. Thank you very much. Can we just start training, please?"

Jethro growled again and then surveyed his armory. He grabbed a mace with a spiked ball that was larger than his head. Barely able to lift it, he dragged the weapon to Lane and thrust it out for him to grab.

"Tonight we learn to wield the mace!" Jethro explained.

The children watched with wide-eyed expectation.

This nightly routine went on for many weeks. In spite of his gruffness and his propensity to growl at Lane and the children, Jethro proved to be a good trainer. Lane imagined that in his prime Jethro must have been a formidable warrior. When they sparred, Jethro was still very nimble on his feet, and Lane had difficulty keeping up with him. With every session Lane's confidence grew and his body became stronger and more responsive to his thoughts.

Some nights the sessions went extremely well, and Lane felt like he was getting a handle on things. Other nights he stumbled over himself and felt like a bumbling idiot. It was difficult to tell how he was really doing because Jethro always had the same stern expression on his face, regardless of Lane's performance.

One night the session was particularly difficult. Lane felt like he had no coordination and nothing was going right. He threw himself into a chair and buried his face in his hands.

"This is pointless, Jethro! I've been doing this for weeks now, and I'm still stumbling over myself. I'm never going to beat the Bellator."

Jethro looked nervously at the group of stunned children. He looked back at Lane, and a flicker of compassion lit in his eyes.

"Children, perhaps it is time for you to find the way to your huts on your own tonight," Jethro said. His voice was less rough than normal.

Instinctively, the children complied without objection. They quietly slipped out the door.

The Great Hall was silent, except for the crackling of the fire and the heaving of Lane's exasperated breath.

"Jethro, be honest with me," Lane sputtered out between breaths. "You've seen me train. You've seen the Bellator fight. Do I stand a chance at the Festival?"

Jethro did not respond right away. He walked over to the fire, picked up the stoking rod, and poked the logs, making the sparks dance and shoot up the chimney. His face glowed in the firelight, eyes peering deeply into the flames.

Lane stared at the ground, chest heaving. Sweat dripped off the end of his nose and splashed on the wooden floor between his feet. Jethro's silence was telling.

The air grew still and heavy.

Jethro broke his trance and moved away from the fire to face his young apprentice.

"Lane, you have done well."

"Stop it, Jethro. Kindness doesn't look good on you. Just cut to the chase."

"All right," Jethro said. "Spoken like a brave warrior." He cleared his throat. "Lane, your heart is big, and your will is strong, but your body is no match for the Bellator. I am afraid it does not look good for you. I am going to submit to the council that they reconsider…"

"No!" Lane stood up and the chair flew backwards, crashing to the ground. He paced around the room. "Don't do that. You can't do that. They're counting on me. It means so much to them. Don't you see? I have to do this!"

"Why, Lane? Why do you have to do this? What is at stake for you? You do not belong here. This is not even your battle."

"That's where you're wrong, Jethro. I have to fight the Bellator. It's complicated. I don't expect you to understand, but you have to believe me. I have to find a way to defeat him."

Jethro rubbed the back of his neck and let out a long, breathy whistle.

"Lane, I have no idea what you are talking about, but the one thing I do know is that if you face the Bellator, you will die!"

What do I do now? Jethro's words echoed in his head… "your heart is big, and your will is strong, but your body is no match…" *Heart…will…body…* There was one thing missing…

"Jethro, we forgot one thing. We forgot the one thing that has always been my strength. My *mind*!"

Jethro blinked in astonishment, confusion clouding his eyes.

Lane continued. "I know I can't outfight the Bellator, but perhaps I can outwit him. He has to have a weakness of some kind… a blind spot. Jethro, we need to spy on the Bellator. You and I, we need to go to Altania and find out the Bellator's weakness."

Chapter 10

"Absolutely out of the question!"

Gustov's normally bright, impish face steamed red with indignation.

"There is no way that we will allow the Pleroma to go sneaking around in Altanian territory. That is...that is..."

"Gustov, perhaps we have not thought through this completely," Thoraline said. "Perhaps the Pleroma has a point. Would it not be just like the Father to overcome the tyranny of the Altanians with weakness?"

"Yes," said the woman at the end of the table, "imagine how inspiring it would be if intellect prevailed and peace ensued."

"No!" Gustov slammed his fist on the table. "The prophecy clearly states that the Pleroma will come and defeat the Bellator...defeat him...and we would walk by the light of the Father once more."

"Remember, my friend," the man next to him said, "defeat can take on many shapes. How do we know that this is not part of the plan?"

Reticent flames cast varied shadows from the wall sconces, morphing and masking the expressions on the council members' faces. Lane and Jethro stood before them, unable to discern their thoughts in the shifting shadows.

Why was this such a big deal?

After several moments of awkward silence, Gustov spoke again.

"Jethro. Pleroma. Please excuse us. We must invoke the

pa'nay tonight before a decision can be reached."

The word sent a ripple of surprise and concern through the council members.

"You may not attend. The Father is difficult to consult when he wrestles in the underworld. It is often unpleasant. Return tomorrow night and we will deliver our decision."

"Yes, of course." Jethro seemed tense.

He backed slowly out of the room. Lane mimicked his actions.

Jethro carefully closed the wooden door behind them. It trapped the heavy air inside the council chamber and allowed them to breathe freely again.

"What was that all about?"

"It is not good, I am afraid."

They walked toward Jethro's hut.

"The pa'nay is a ritual that I have only heard about. I do not know the details, but I do know what it means."

Inside the hut, they settled themselves in front of the fire, and Jethro stoked its flames.

"So," Lane said, "what does it mean?"

"The council is divided. They are unclear regarding the Father's will."

He stroked his beard.

"I must confess, I have never seen Gustov like this. He is usually so confident about the ways of the gods."

He slapped Lane on the knee.

"You certainly have them guessing."

"Yeah, I'm sorry about that. I'm not trying to be difficult."

"You do not have to apologize to me. I think it is quite entertaining. All we can do now is wait."

The rest of the night crept slowly forward. Jethro filled the air with coarse snoring that aggravated Lane's raw nerves.

Inky darkness in the window slowly gave way to the gradual waves of morning's light.

Jethro went out to the fields and left Lane alone again in his daylight cell. A shaft of sunlight poked through the window and etched its path across the floor and up the wall.

Burning eyes longed for sleep, but the agitation in Lane's gut would not allow them to close. He waited and watched as the sunlight finally faded along the edge of the ceiling.

Jethro burst through the door and heaved his tired body across the threshold.

"Come, we must get to the council chamber before the Switching Hour begins."

A more reddish hue glowed from the sconces this evening as the shadows played their games with the council members' features. Vacant, distant eyes stared out from the weary faces that lined the council table.

Lane's chest burned from holding his breath. He slowly let out the air to relieve the pressure.

"It has been decided," Gustov's voice was flat and empty. "You, Pleroma, will travel to the temple of Amo, in the Altanian Mountains, and seek the knowledge of the Bellator that you desire. Jethro will accompany you. Go now."

That was it. None of the others spoke. They only stared at Lane with hollow eyes.

What happened to them? This was not exactly the send-off he hoped for. However, he was still given permission, and for that he was thankful.

"The council is wise and gracious," Jethro's gruff voice came from behind him. Jethro tugged on Lane's shirt sleeve. It was time to leave... graciously and quickly.

Once outside the council chambers, Jethro moved quickly.

"We must ready our things and be gone."

"Now!?" Lane exclaimed.

"Yes, now. We will gather up some supplies and leave at once."

Jethro accelerated. The time for talking was over, and the time for action was at hand.

When they entered the village circle Jethro darted glances

and head motions to several of the villagers, and they each disappeared into their huts. He ducked into his hut and motioned for Lane to follow. His intense expression told Lane to not ask questions and simply follow his lead.

They threw a change of clothes in a bag, doused the lamp, and stepped back out into the circle. Three women greeted them, each one carrying a sack. One sack had bread, another had cheese, and the third had fruits and vegetables. With a rough-edged graciousness Jethro accepted the packages. He handed two to Lane, leaving the one from inside his hut and the last of the women's sacks for him. They were ready.

With no fanfare, no goodbyes, no ceremony at all, the two travelers simply vanished into the shadows of the outer ring.

Chapter 11

Jethro was surprisingly nimble moving through the dark woods. Even with a longer stride, it was difficult for Lane to keep up with him.

After what seemed like several hours of hard marching, a low tone hummed directly ahead. A ghostly blue wall stood behind a row of dark tree trunks. As they reached it and stepped past the last tree, a blast of cool, moist air washed over them. The humming wall was a river.

Its gray-blue water stretched wide. The slivered Sister fractured her light into hundreds of tiny sparks that danced and flitted along the water's surface. Across the bank a thick, black band of trees stood dark and flat against the slate blue of the night sky.

"This is the Great River." Jethro broke his silent vigil with a hoarse whisper. "We will follow the fisherman's trail along the bank."

Jethro headed down a small path along the river's edge. Cool moist air invigorated Lane, and he pressed on.

Pale gray light tinged the tops of the trees behind them. Jethro stopped and took a quick assessment of his surroundings, then broke from the trail and shot up into the thick forest, snapping branches back into Lane's legs. They disappeared into the dark shadows of the woods.

"We will camp here," Jethro whispered.

Dawn's light poked tiny holes through the densely gathered trees, but the weariness of Lane's journey overcame his body and pulled his eyelids shut before he could enjoy it. He would have to wait another day to see the light of the Father in the open air.

The warm air hung heavy over Lane's body. Buzzing flies filled the stillness. He opened his eyes and dark streaks scratched across his vision. Startled by the canopy of spiky branches, he sat up quickly. The sudden motion made his head spin and left him disoriented. Jethro's chuckle and the smell of fish roasting over an open fire cleared his head, and he remembered where they were.

The river roared in the distance. Between the densely packed trees, like chinks in a shanty wall, glowing orange vertical stripes revealed the setting sun.

"When will I be able walk outside in the daytime?" Lane asked.

"We cannot risk you being noticed on this journey. I am sorry, but it is much better if we travel at night. The Altanians do not travel either the fisherman's path or the main commerce trail while the Sisters dance in the night sky. I think they are afraid of the lowlands at night. Stupid people." Jethro jabbed at the coals beneath the roasting fish.

"Lane, come, sit. The fish is ready. We must gain our strength for tonight's journey across the Lower Mountains. It will tax our legs, so we need all the help we can get."

Jethro had portioned off a piece of hard bread for each of them, and he handed it and the fish to Lane. They sat beside each other on a log and ate in silence.

Out of the corner of his eye, Lane noticed that Jethro kept stealing nervous glances at him.

"What?" Lane said. "Why do you keep looking at me like that? Is something crawling on me?" He swatted around his head and slapped himself, hoping to be rid of the possible intruder.

"No, no, you are fine." Jethro flushed slightly. "It is just that...well...bah, it is silly."

"What's silly?" Lane pursued. "What's going on?"

"Oh, all right. There is something I have been meaning to

ask you for a long time."

"Go on."

"Does it help you eat?"

"Does what help me eat?"

"Your saliva, being so hot and all."

Lane shook his head. "What are you talking about?"

Now Jethro looked a little confused. "Do you remember the first night we met, as we were walking along the ridge? You were ranting to Gustov something about having 'hot spittle' and you started barking at the sky. I had no idea what you were talking about, since I did not really care that night and was not paying much attention, but the words 'hot spittle' stuck in my head. I thought that perhaps it was something that helped you eat. Maybe it melted the food."

Lane racked his brain, trying to figure out what on earth Jethro was talking about. Hot spittle. When had he ever said those two words together? He scanned the conversation of that night. Hot spittle. Hot spittle.

"Oh! Not 'hot spittle,' you strange little man. *Hospital*. That was the night I told you my theory about this place. I said I was lying in a bed in a hospital and that all this wasn't real."

Jethro stared down and picked the remaining meat off the bones of the fish. They sat in awkward silence.

"Well," Jethro said, "what do you think now? Am I real?"

Lane stared into the dying flames of the fire and did not respond.

Jethro waited a few moments and then continued. "What would you say if you knew that some of us do not believe you are real?"

Lane looked at Jethro with wonder.

"It is true," Jethro explained. "We talk during the workday, out in the fields, when the councilmen are not around. Some of us do not believe in you. There are different theories. Some say that you are not real at all. They say you are a ghost or a phantom. They think that when we march toward the mountains for the Festival that you will vanish and leave us without a warrior and worse off than we are now.

"Others say that you are the same as the Bellator. They think that Amo sent you to us, just like she sent the Bellator to the Altanians, but that you are a cruel trick for us. They think you are here to spy on us and betray us in the end. They do not trust you."

"What about you?" Lane questioned. "What do you think?"

Now it was Jethro's turn to stare into the flames. He poked the embers with a long stick and worked his mouth back and forth as he considered the question.

"Jethro! Do you think I'm a traitor? Do you think I would turn on your people, after all the good they have done for me?"

Jethro's chin sank into his chest. Then he cocked his head, squinted his right eye, and peered sideways at Lane from beneath his bushy eyebrows.

"Lane..." He paused, weighing his words carefully. "You have worked hard over the past few weeks. Much to my surprise, I have grown to...well, I have grown accustomed to you. I know that most of the people believe in you. I know the council thinks you are the Pleroma. I also know that my people are desperate. We have known nothing but pain and suffering since the Invasion. When you arrived it was the first glimpse of hope that they have had. Desperate people will believe in almost anything. People who believe like that are generally setting themselves up to be terribly disappointed."

Jethro looked fully at Lane.

"I do not want my people to be disappointed again."

The conversation ended. Jethro stood up suddenly and began gathering his provisions.

Lane sat, stunned.

Jethro's voice startled him. He called over his shoulder, "Come, it is time to go," and then disappeared into the woods.

Lane scrambled to follow him. The fading sunlight had been replaced with cold twilight.

They walked in awkward silence, together, yet somehow apart.

Chapter 12

Jethro did not lead them down to the fisherman's path this time. Instead, they scrambled through thick underbrush, dodged around trees, and clawed up a steep incline. After a long while on this difficult trek, they finally reached level ground. With chest heaving and skin scratched and stinging, Lane stepped out from the woods onto a wide, well-beaten path.

The sky above it was torn in half by a jagged edge of darkness: the setting sunlight on top, the contours of mountain peaks below. The path disappeared into the inky, ominous shadow at the base of the mountains.

Engulfed by darkness, Jethro and Lane followed the path into a canyon and wound their way along its floor in wide, swooping turns. The crooked gray sky that marked the canyon ceiling melted into a river of inky black, and thousands of stars shimmered and pulsated in its current. The path rose under their feet, and walking became more difficult. Then it turned behind a jagged wall and began a series of switchbacks that cut up the side of a mountain, gaining elevation with every pass.

After many monotonous hours, Jethro took a hard right and seemed to dive into the canyon wall. Lane stopped and, at first, could not see where Jethro had gone. He bent over and looked more closely. A small path slipped through the scrub and led directly into the stone wall. Not wanting to be left behind and lost, Lane pushed through the bushes in pursuit.

This new path led to a rocky wall. They climbed and scrambled up the face of a cliff for quite a while. Lane was so intensely focused on gripping the rock wall and not falling off that he had not noticed that the sky was changing. It widened out to its normal half-dome.

The path flattened again. Jethro was now a small silhouette against of field of stars. Cut in half by the jagged horizon, the dancing Sister was making her way down to the underworld once again. They had been walking and climbing all night.

Jethro stopped, and for the first time on this mountain journey, he faced Lane. Barely visible, he didn't speak, but looked up at Lane and then motioned with his eyes to turn around.

Lane slowly turned. A wave of tingles sparkled up his body, starting at the back of his feet and washing up his legs, across his back, out his arms, and over his scalp. Even in the blue-gray shadows he could see the mountains fall away behind him and cascade down to the plain below. The flat plain shot forward and collided with the starry sky in a perfectly horizontal line.

Along the line a faint white glow emerged. It grew slowly at first, and the white light kissed the edges of the rocks and shrubs around them. Quicker now, the white turned to yellow, and its intensity grew until there, on the horizon, it happened. Like a white-hot flame burning a hole in the center of a canvas, the edge of the sun rose above the horizon.

Lane stood in awe as he watched the Great Father climb up over the edge of the world, victorious once again over his struggles in the underworld. With every step he grew in brilliance and splendor. The darkness fled from his presence and his aura painted the landscape with brilliant colors. It was no wonder that the people worshipped this great sphere of power and light.

The great orb's ascension began in the sea. A bright path of shimmering water spilled out directly beneath him and came forward to meet with the edge of the land, flooding into the mouth of the Great River. The river flowed through the fields and the woods and disappeared at the base of the mountain.

As the sun continued to climb, Lane turned around to comment, but the words caught in his throat when he saw a new vision. Another plain sprawled out to the west. It was very different from where they had just been. The place they had come from was full of trees, fields, water, and life. This new place was a desolate wasteland. Twilight shadows revealed a massive field of rocks and an occasional scrub brush.

This desolate valley spread to the left and the right along the base of the mountains as far as the eye could see. On the far edge of the desert stood another ridge of mountains. It was a muted purple silhouette against the gray morning sky.

Lane turned again to comment, but stopped short. Jethro stood with his eyes closed, his face glowing in the light of the rising sun, hands fully raised above his head. At first it seemed strange to see his usually gruff and skeptical companion in such a posture of reverence and serenity, but as Lane turned to face the eastern sky he understood. The Great Father was fully aloft in the morning sky. As the landscape ignited with brilliant color and long shadows, it seemed that everything bowed before the great orb of power. Lane closed his eyes, raised his hands, and let the warm rays of the sun caress his face. He had forgotten how much he missed the light of day.

"Are you hungry?" Jethro's voice broke the silence.

He didn't realize how much he had missed Jethro's voice until he heard it just then. He was afraid Jethro had abandoned him.

"Yes."

Jethro held out a piece of cheese and some bread. The look on his face, and the tone of his voice, said that it was time to forget what had happened back by the river and just move on. Lane gladly accepted his offer, and the two sat in sweet silence and watched the sun continue its regal climb into the morning sky.

"So, what's the plan now?" Lane asked as he brushed the breadcrumbs from his hands.

"I have taken us away from the Main Trade Route." Jethro turned toward the desert plain and pointed south. "Do you see where the road comes out from that valley? It is difficult to stay hidden when we cross the Waste. We must avoid the main route and cross through the desert itself. It is more difficult, but we will not be noticed.

"Do you think you have enough strength to make it down to the bottom? There is a cave down there where we can rest before we set out."

"I guess so," Lane lied. His body hurt so badly that he just wanted to lay down right there on the rocky summit. But he didn't want to give his newly mended relationship with Jethro any reason to go bad again, so he dug deep for a burst of strength and followed his leader down the mountain face.

Going down in the daylight was much easier than climbing up in the darkness. After a couple of hours they reached the edge of the desert.

"Here." Jethro ducked into a small hollow in the rock wall, "We will sleep in here for a little while to regain our strength."

"A little while?" Lane said. "Don't we need to sleep until sundown?"

"No. We must walk during the daylight through the Waste."

"What?" Lane was confused. "I can already tell the sun is way more intense up here than it was near the coast. Wouldn't it make more sense to walk at night and sleep during the day?"

Jethro was already lying down. He propped himself up on one elbow. "I did not want to alarm you."

"What?" Lane sat next to him.

"It's the *skuli*. They only appear at night."

"What are the school-ee? Is that another tribe? Do they live in this desert?"

"No, I wish that were the case." Jethro was sitting up now. "The skuli are terrible creatures. They roam the Waste in packs at night. They hate light, so if we walk during the day, then we do not have to worry about them. At night, as long as we build a perimeter of fire around our camp, we should be safe. Now lie down and get a little sleep."

"Oh, that's wonderful," Lane said. "Our choices are get burned alive in scorching sunlight during the day, or get eaten by vicious creatures during the night. This ought to be a fun trip."

"Sleep!" Jethro plopped on the ground and turned away from Lane with a huff.

Lane curled up in the corner of the cave, images of strange creatures racing through his mind. Soon the exhaustion of his mountain pass took over, and he quickly fell asleep.

CHAPTER 13

The sun blazed high in the sky when they woke from their nap. It was time to head out across the Waste. The ground was hard and made up mostly of gravel and sand. Everything had a rusty orange hue. There was very little vegetation, at least compared to the lush valley they had just left behind. Every ten feet or so, spread out in a fairly uniform pattern, a little cluster of tough-looking plants huddled together for survival. Most of the plants were very low to the ground and bore menacing spikes and brambles. Peppered across the landscape were larger bushes with two or three long branches that fanned out from one central point on the ground.

The terrain rose and fell in gentle swells. The hard ground and the sparse vegetation made for fairly easy walking. After a while they came to a large crevice in the ground. It was about ten feet deep and thirty feet wide, and it ran to the right and left as far as Lane could see. When they came to the edge, Jethro did not hesitate but jumped down into it, slid his way down the wall, and began walking along the bottom.

Lane followed his lead, and soon the two of them were walking along the bottom of a crevice with walls on either side.

"What is this thing?" asked Lane.

"It is a river, can you not tell?" Jethro smirked and looked up to see Lane's reaction.

"A river? What do you mean?"

Jethro chuckled, paused, and then became very serious.

"There was once a time when this river basin flowed with cold, sparkling water, and its banks were full of lush trees and plants. Fish swam through the river. Animals lived in the forest. It was a beautiful valley, very much like our own. This was the home of the lost tribe."

"What happened?"

"*She* happened." Jethro pointed up and over toward the mountain range that was hidden by the crevice wall. "Amo. Legend has it that the people of this valley angered her. In her anger, she sent down fire from the mountains and scorched the earth. She killed all the animals, burned away all the plants, and dried up all the rivers and lakes. She wiped out the tribe and erased their name from history. That is why we call them the lost tribe; we don't even know who they were. In order to ensure that no one ever lived in this valley again, she buried the Great River below the plain so that it flows from the Upper Mountains, under the Waste, and comes out at the base of the Lower Mountains into our valley, leaving the Waste parched and barren forever."

"Wow, she sounds so nice." Lane said, "I like her more and more every time I hear these lovely stories."

Jethro stopped and looked up at him in shock.

"I'm kidding!" Lane backed away with his hands up in surrender. "Come on Jethro, don't you recognize sarcasm?"

"Hmph." Jethro shrugged it off and continued walking. "There is no room for joking when it comes to Amo. She is devious and treacherous. Every step that takes me closer to her mountains makes my heart grow more sour."

"Did you ever think," Lane ventured cautiously into this topic, "that there might be another explanation for the Waste?"

Jethro looked up in puzzlement but did not object to Lane's offering.

"Yeah, I mean, think about it. You have the sea to the east. The moisture from the sea rises into the sky and moves over the land. When it reaches the mountains it rises quickly and cools off, causing the moisture to condense into water droplets, and rain dumps out onto the plain. The Lower Mountains wring all the moisture out of the air and leave nothing for this plain up at the higher elevation. It's called the water cycle. Come on, I learned that in second grade."

Jethro thought for a while. "So, you are saying that the mountains reach up into the heavens and steal the water from the air, so that the Waste gets nothing? Does that not seem a little strange to you? Mountains cannot do that."

Jethro marched on, shaking his head at Lane's crazy ideas. Lane decided it would be best to drop the subject.

They walked along the winding course of the dry river all afternoon and late into the evening. When the sun slipped behind the Upper Mountains, they found a place along the wall of the crevice and made camp for the night.

Jethro chose a spot that had a high wall above them and an indentation deep enough for the two of them to lie down.

"This will be perfect," Jethro said. "Now go and find as much dry brush as you can and bring it here. We must get a fire started before the last light is gone."

The urgency in Jethro's voice motivated Lane to search quickly.

"Pile it here." Jethro pointed to the gap that formed the entrance to their nook in the wall. "We need enough fuel to keep the fire burning all night."

Once the flames were kindled, Jethro relaxed and leaned against the wall. "This is a perfect spot. There is only one way the skuli could get to us, and it is blocked by the fire. This way we do not have to be surrounded by light and use up excess fuel. It is so hard to find things to burn in this cursed place. We must consider ourselves fortunate tonight and get good sleep."

"If you say so," Lane said.

After eating a little, making sure to ration their food, they lay down. Sleep came quickly. The cool air of the desert night and the crackling of the fire made it a pleasant slumber.

Chapter 14

The sound woke Lane. His eyes opened, but his body lay stiff in alarm. Something scraped through the rocks on the bottom of the crevice, opposite from where they were sleeping. Thin wisps of smoke lifted from the remnants of the fire and filled the entrance to their alcove, clouding his vision. He quietly breathed a sigh of relief when he saw that it was only a small rodent of some kind. It had the ears and the hind legs of a jackrabbit, but its face was wide and squared-off, and it had a long tail.

Just as Lane was about to sit up and greet the furry creature, it shot straight up on its hind legs in alarm. Sizzling cracks, like the sound of electric sparks, popped on top of the ridge. The rodent's long ears swiveled like little radar dishes, scanning for possible intruders. It became agitated, and its head jerked to the right. A dark figure appeared on top of the crevice wall, a black cut-out against the pale morning sky. It walked on four legs, but its silhouetted shape was unrecognizable.

For a split second the hunter and the prey made eye contact in a frozen gaze. Then, in a flash, the rodent ran, and the dark creature plunged down the wall and across the crevice floor. The chase was on.

The features of the mysterious creature were now visible. Blue, scaly spines covered the majority of its body. They shimmered in iridescent waves with every move of its long and slender but well-muscled form. It was difficult to tell if this creature was mammal or reptile. A long tail flowed behind it, accentuating its elegant lines. Razor teeth flashed and purple saliva frothed from its gaping mouth and splattered through the air as it ran.

Directly ahead of the terrified rodent grew a small cluster of plants. Most were small bushes, but off to the edge of the cluster two tall bushes grew side by side. Their branches shot up from a center stalk and arched outwards. One branch from each bush bent toward the other and joined to form an arch-shaped opening.

The rodent sped toward the arch. The creature pursued, hot on the rodent's heels and gaining quickly. Just as the creature's jaws were about to snap down on its hind quarters, the rodent passed through the arch... and disappeared. Vanished. The creature chomped down onto nothing. Its momentum sent it into a summersault, its head pounding into the gravel and its back legs flipping over the top, tail whipping through the air. It was stunned.

It shook its head. Three flaps on each side of its face opened and closed quickly, like the gills of a fish deprived of oxygen. Regaining its senses, the beast sniffed furiously around the base of the bush. It went in front, it sniffed in back, it looped back and forth through the arch. The rodent was gone.

Lane blinked. What just happened? He sat up, and his movement caught the creature's attention. Several eyes blinked in staggered cadence on its thin head. Lane froze, wondering whether human flesh was on its preferred diet and how willing it would be to attack someone his size. He stood slowly, keeping a confident stare fixed on the set of eyes.

Lane took a few steps toward it and the gills flared wide. The bottom row of eyes narrowed. Snarling teeth dripped purple ooze. Lane stopped and tried not to breathe. The air around the creature distorted, like heat waves rising from hot desert sand. Electric sparks flashed around its head and startled the beast. It turned, clawed its way up the side of the crevice, and disappeared over the edge.

I hope he's not going to find some of his friends.

With the creature gone, Lane was free to approach the bush and investigate the missing rodent. The top of the bushes reached the height of his head. Three long, straight branches grew from a central spot at the base of each one. The branches flared out in different directions like a palm tree. Each one sprouted smaller branches covered with small leaves, each rimmed with pointy, scalloped edges. Spread throughout the bush were clusters of tiny, green berries.

The archway formed where two of the branches, one from each bush, came together and twisted around one another, as if the two bushes were shaking hands. It was tall enough that, with a slight bend at the waist and a tuck of the head, Lane could easily walk through it.

At the base of the bush and around all the clusters of vegetation the ground was covered with soft sand that revealed the footprints of the animals. On the front side of the arch there were clearly two sets of prints; the smaller set of the rodent's tracks and the larger set belonging to the creature. Lane crouched down on his heels and looked closely at the threshold of the arch. Just where the arch formed, the rodent's prints stopped, and the blue creature's continued.

What is this? What happened to that furry little guy?

He stood up and looked closer at the berries, reaching out to touch one.

"Do not touch that!" Jethro's voice made him jump. "Move away from that bush. Now!"

Jethro was dead serious. Lane obeyed and slowly backed away from the bush.

"What's going on, Jethro? Did you see what happened? That little rabbit-thing just vanished into thin air when it ran through this arch."

"Numa," Jethro spoke the words in a dark, mysterious tone.

"Numa?" Lane repeated.

"Yes. I had hoped we would not see one. I did not notice the bitter bush when we camped last night."

"The bitter bush? Do you mean this thing?" Lane pointed at the bush with the berries.

"Yes. The numa love to eat the bitter berries. They are the only creature that does. Strange and troublesome little pests."

"Not as strange as that blue, spider-eyed, dog-lizard thing,"

Lane said.

The blood drained from Jethro's face. He stood motionless and stared at Lane.

"What," Lane asked, "what's the matter?"

"Did you say blue?" The words barely escaped Jethro's tight lips.

"Yeah, it had bluish scales all over its body, a long tail, and nasty teeth with purple spit everywhere. And all those eyes really freaked me out."

Jethro staggered backwards and fell to a sitting position on the ground.

"Jethro!" Lane reached to catch him, but was too late. "What is it? What was that thing?"

"It is not possible," Jethro muttered to himself, "They have never been seen in the daytime before."

Lane shook Jethro's shoulders and yelled, "Tell me what you're talking about!"

Jethro looked up at Lane, "Skuli. What you described is a skuli."

"That night-crawler beast you told me about?"

"Yes. Up until this moment, there has never been a sighting during the daylight."

Lane dropped to the ground next to Jethro. "So, what does that mean?"

"I honestly do not know." Jethro stared up at the sky where the top of the earthen wall met it. "The only defense we have ever known against the skuli is light. If that did not stop this one, then I have no idea what will.

"Did you see any others?"

"No, it was all alone. Something weird flashed around its head that seemed to scare it. Then it ran off over the wall that way." Lane pointed to the top of the ridge in the direction from which they had come the night before.

"At least we will be traveling the other direction," Jethro said. He stood up. "We need to gather our things and move right away."

They returned to the campsite and gathered their bags. Jethro raised his water flask to his mouth. Nothing came out. He tipped it higher and craned his neck as far back as he could, but only a small dribble remained. Panic tinged his eyes. He shook the flask and searched the outside. At the base of the flask there was a small hole that looked like it had been chewed out.

"Numa!" Jethro slapped the flask. "Lane, check yours."

Lane shook his. Nothing. It had been chewed through as well.

"This is not good." Jethro rubbed the back of his neck. "Without water it will be very difficult to make the journey. We cannot turn back, especially if the skuli went that direction. We are closer to the Upper Mountains than we are to the Lower at this point."

He looked up at Lane with grave eyes. "We have no choice. We must continue, and quickly. Are you ready?"

"Like you said, we have no choice, right? Let's go."

They started walking along the base of the crevice, past the bitter bush. As they passed, Jethro gave it a menacing, sideways glance.

"Numa," he muttered under his breath.

"OK," Lane said, "you have to tell me what's going on. What is it with these numa and skuli?"

"Yes, the numa. Cursed creatures in a cursed land. Do you remember I told you that Amo cursed this valley and destroyed an entire tribe? The numa are the spirits of those tribesmen. The skuli are Amo's dark minions, sent to hunt and torture them forever. The numa are cursed to walk between the worlds for eternity, hunted by the skuli, always foraging for water, always eating the bitter berry."

After a moment of soaking in this tale, Lane said, "So, the little rabbit-thing is really a tortured spirit that bounces back and forth between this world and the afterlife, right? And the skuli are night creatures, sent by Amo, to torment them?"

Jethro shrugged his shoulders. "You asked. That is the truth. This is a cursed and wretched place. Is that any harder to believe than mountains that reach up and grab water from the sky?" Jethro lifted his eyebrows and looked at Lane with an "I got you on that one" expression.

"Right." Lane rolled his eyes.

"Oh, by the way," Jethro continued, "What is a rabbit-thing?"

"Never mind."

The conversation ended, and the long, hot, dry journey began.

As the sun rose in the sky, so did the temperature. Lane's dry tongue stuck to the top of his mouth.

The crevice turned a corner and opened up to reveal the Upper Mountains. They were much larger on the horizon now. The foothills at the base of the range rose from the desert like a pile of rocks with red-and-yellow stripes angled across them.

There were three distinct levels of mountains. The highest level loomed misty and purple above the two rockier levels below it. It appeared to be covered with trees.

The mountains bobbed up and down along the horizon with each step that Lane took. He and Jethro were too tired and parched to talk. They simply trudged on, trying to strike the right balance between the speed they needed to make it to the mountains by nightfall and the efficiency needed to not overheat and pass out. Every sound they heard from the desert floor above alerted them to the possibility of the skuli. Heat, fatigue, and fear were an exhausting combination.

The heat swirled the air as it rose from the rocky ground, creating distortions that looked like dancing specters. Tiny pools of imaginary water formed and vanished, lasting only long enough to remind Lane of how thirsty he was. They vanished with mocking laughter. This truly was a cursed place.

The rhythmic walking and the pulsing heat lulled Lane into a trancelike state. His body clicked into autopilot, and his mind turned inward. *What's happening to me? Let's be logical about this. What does a desert represent? Lack of water. Desperation. Dehydration. A time of testing. Maybe my mind is getting discouraged and my hope is drying up.*

But what about those numa? Where did those come from?

I don't remember reading about anything like that or hearing about them in any of the stories Mom read to me. Well, I guess rabbits are often used in stories. Alice followed a rabbit, didn't she? But why would the rabbit steal my water? Why am I so thirsty? And what are the skuli?

It seems my only hope is that mountain in front of me—that mountain that is crawling with Altanians. I have to keep going. If I lie down and die right here...maybe I'll really be dead out there.

Josh! What's happening to Josh right now? How long have I been unconscious? I have to wake up and be there for him.

Several popping sounds startled him from the trance. They came from the top of the ridge. A few more sparks popped. Jethro looked wild-eyed at the top of the wall.

"Skuli. Run!" Jethro shouted, then sprinted ahead, sending dust and gravel spitting from his wide feet.

Lane turned to look down the river bed. About a hundred and fifty yards away, five dark figures appeared on the top of the ridge. The now-distinctive form left no doubt. Skuli. A pack of them. As Lane turned, the pack noticed his presence. They paused for a moment, and then, as one body, broke into a full run toward him.

Jethro was already several paces ahead of Lane when he turned back around and began to run. Within a few strides Lane closed the gap between them. There was no way Jethro could match Lane's pace in a full-on run. Lane glanced back over his shoulder. The pack pursued with great speed, closing the distance between them.

Slowing only slightly, Lane reached down, scooped Jethro up, and threw him onto his back. The dense body weighed more than he expected, and the weight threw him off balance. He stumbled sideways and nearly lost his footing.

"Go, go!" Jethro shouted in his ear, like a little jockey urging his thoroughbred from the mount.

The riverbed took a turn and widened out. Not far ahead, clusters of large rock formations formed a jagged wall. One gap in the rocky wall led to a flat bed of rocks.

PLEROMA

"There," Jethro shouted, his voice surging with the pounding of Lane's gallop. "That is the entrance to the mountains!"

Lane accelerated. He stole a glance over his shoulder. The skuli rounded the corner, much closer now. It was a dead sprint to the rocks.

Loose gravel, peppered with larger stones, made running difficult. Every third step turned an ankle or shot a painful rock edge into the sole of his foot. Jethro's body weight slammed into his back, making each stride an awkward maneuver.

Raspy snarls filled Lane's ears. The skuli were almost upon them.

"Run, Lane!" Jethro beat Lane's shoulder.

They passed the first rock cluster, and Lane's foot caught on a larger stone. He lurched forward, stumbled, and sent Jethro flying over his shoulder. They both skidded along the rocks.

Lane instantly rolled over onto his back and clawed backwards in retreat, expecting to see a skuli clamping down on his throat. When he turned he did see the skuli, but they were not on top of him. Less than five feet from him, the entire pack darted back and forth along an invisible line that ran between the rocks that formed the gap. Their gill flaps flared, and all the sets of eyes narrowed and expanded wildly. Purple froth flung from their mouths as they wagged their heads in protest.

"What just happened?" Lane asked.

Jethro stepped up next to him, blood dripping from scrapes on his hands and arms. "I am not sure. I know this gap marks the beginning of the Upper Mountains. The skuli must be confined to the Waste, somehow."

Lane laid his head back against the rocks and started to laugh, chest still heaving from the sprint.

"Oh man," Lane said, in between laughs, "I thought that was it."

"As did I," Jethro agreed, "although, I do not see the humor in it. We need to get as much distance between us and those creatures as possible."

"You're right." Lane stood and took a long look at the pacing, frothing pack. "Not today, boys. Better luck next time."

He turned and walked with Jethro toward the mountain. Each step revealed a new sensation. First was the stinging in his hands and arms. Like Jethro, he was bruised and bleeding from his fall into the rocks. The bright blood glistened in the sunlight. Next it was the stinging in his throat. The footrace had sapped every last ounce of moisture left in his already parched mouth. Then, the weight of exhaustion. The sprint had drained all the energy from his legs, making them feel like large sacks of rocks dragging along the ground.

All they could do was press on.

The dry riverbed wound its way into the hills. They followed it between walls of coarse sandstone. Along its edge, new kinds of bushes appeared.

They kept walking. The bed made another turn and, as they cleared the large cliff wall, they saw it. Lane couldn't believe it. Water. As soon as it registered, his body reacted automatically and he ran straight toward it. In the middle of the rocky riverbed, surrounded by a cluster of bushes, a small spring bubbled down into a pool of clear water.

They plunged their faces into the pool and let its life-giving power run over their tongues and down their throats. Lane drank and drank until he felt full.

Leaning down on hands and knees, with water dribbling down his beard, Jethro looked like a strange child to Lane. The cold water sent an impish impulse through him, and he reached down and splashed Jethro in the face. At first Jethro looked up in shock. After a brief hesitation, his countenance changed as the impish impulse infected him. Jethro stood and kicked a wave of water at Lane. Before long the two of them were running, splashing, and laughing like a couple of children in the backyard sprinklers on a hot summer afternoon.

When they had run and splashed the impulse out of their system, they stood side by side, hands on their knees, panting to catch their breath. They looked at each other and laughed. It was good to be alive. They had crossed the desert without water and survived.

With thirst quenched and a quick bite of bread and cheese

PLEROMA

in their bellies, both travelers lay down under one of the larger bushes. Lane's legs felt like they were made of lead, and his feet throbbed. His entire body was being pulled into the ground by the weight of his exhaustion. Although he was physically spent, his mind was now at ease. The skuli were behind him. Their water was replenished. He would not die today. Now, he would sleep.

Chapter 15

A sharp pressure pressed into Lane's ribs. He moaned and turned onto his other side, eyes shut fast. There it was again, this time in the middle of his back, then again in a different part of his back. This time it came with a whizzing sound and a sharp crack on his rear.

A strange sensation rushed over him, like he had been at the bottom of a deep pool and was suddenly pulled upwards toward the surface. His mind splashed out of the waters of sleep and into consciousness. He sat up and shook his head.

It was still dark, but Jethro was visible in the moonlight. The little rim-lit figure held a long, thick stick in his hand and a smirk on his face.

"Ow! Thanks a lot, man," Lane said. "What are you doing? It's not even light out yet."

"Yes, I know. We must move now. We have a difficult journey today, and we have to get to the trail before the Great Father emerges."

"Right," Lane answered, "I suppose there will be Altanians around now." He rubbed the remaining sleep from his eyes, and they made preparations for the hike.

Jethro plunged his flask into the pool of water.

"Jethro, won't that water just spill out where the numa ate it?"

"No, before we went to sleep last night I took some sap from that tree over there and patched the holes. It is wonderful stuff. Good as new."

Lane was impressed. How did he know about that?

Fully replenished with water, and having taken a few bites of cheese and a few berries that Jethro had collected from some nearby bushes, they were ready to head out on their mountain trek.

One of the Sisters still danced in the dark sky and kissed the edges of the rocks and trees. Her light revealed that they were walking along a rocky riverbed that ran along the bottom of a canyon. The bare rock walls glowed brightly in the moonlight. Along their base grew more shrubs and trees than in the desert. It was still a fairly desolate valley, but at least a small stream ran through the middle of the rocky bed.

They followed the winding riverbed for a while. It was on a noticeable incline. As they crept upwards in elevation, more and more foliage grew along the edges. Now the dark shapes of trees speckled the rocky wall. High above the canyon floor the dark silhouettes of mountain peaks blocked out the stars behind them.

The riverbed came to a large group of trees and made a sharp turn to the right. Jethro left it and headed straight into the trees. Now it was very dark, and Lane found himself once again scraping through tree branches and pulling himself up an incline. They were definitely climbing the mountain now.

After a lot of scraping and ducking and climbing, they came down to a more gradual incline. Directly ahead, gray sky peeked through black trees. Lane stopped in awe to observe. The trees at the edge of the woods stood black against the lightening sky. The ground dropped off just past them, and another ridge rose up again in the distance. The face of the ridge was flat and bluish-gray at first. Slowly, as if a broad paintbrush moved back and forth in even strokes, the trees along the top of the ridge came alive. Colors emerged like a rainbow of pastels—soft purples, greens, yellows, and pinks—and as the light came down the ridge they all took on a warm, golden glow.

Jethro stood beside him. "Ah, the Great Father has quite a knack for painting these mountains." He sighed.

They stood in silent reverence and marveled as the colors cascaded to the bottom of the ridge. With a great heave of his chest and a deep sigh, Jethro pressed forward. They stepped out of the trees and onto the top of the ridge. Its glory had faded, and now it was just an ordinary ridge among many.

Lane and Jethro walked along the top of the rocky ridge, just along the edge of the trees.

"Jethro," Lane asked, "the way you talk about these mountains...I don't know...it seems like you've been here before. How do you know your way around here?"

Jethro did not answer right away. He just looked up to the top of the mountain.

"Yes, I know these mountains. I know them very well. I used to live here."

"What? Are you telling me you're an Altanian?"

"No, no. I am not an Altanian. Bite your tongue! No, a long, long time ago, when I was a boy, before the Invasion, my father was in charge of the trade route between the Upper Mountains and Deltonia. I would spend my summers here in the mountains. My father and I would hike through all these bowls and ridges and hunt and fish together. If you can believe this, I even had friends here..."

His monologue stopped suddenly and his gaze dropped to the ground. Even from behind, Lane could tell that a dark cloud had just descended over Jethro's fond memories. He was left to fill in the gaps for himself. The Invasion. Betrayal. Slavery. These mountains were no longer a place of serene retreat. They were the citadel of the enemy. A chilling thought reminded him of where they were headed. The Bellator.

They climbed all day. Sometimes along a ridge, other times on a small forest foot trail. The path rose and fell, but overall it was always up. As they scaled the side of the tallest peak, two things became apparent. The first was that it was becoming increasingly harder to breathe. The second was that it was getting colder. How far had they climbed?

After several hours, they came to a ridge and Jethro stopped. He turned away from the mountain and looked back toward where they had come. Lane turned and took it in. The mountain fell away below them, and its furry spine of pine trees rose and fell as it descended. The contrast between the strata of life-zones was obvious. Directly below them was the pine forest that they had just passed through. Below that was the transitional zone of scrubby trees and bushes interspersed among the mostly rocky hills and valleys. And then, sprawling out away from them, like a large, dried and cracked piece of old, bleached clay, lay the Waste. In the far distance, purple against the eastern sky, the Lower Mountains tore a jagged horizon. He wasn't sure if it was the shock of the vision or the high altitude, but Lane lost his breath as he realized how far they had come.

Above them stood one more stratum of life-zone. It was more like a non-life zone. The trees stopped growing, as if someone had taken a giant knife and scalped the top of the mountain, leaving the stone skull of its ancient head exposed to the sky.

They stood on a rocky ridge that ran along the top of a steep cliff.

"Are you ready for this, Lane?" Jethro looked up with a serious expression. "There are two dangers in front of us, the least of which is that nasty drop. I have taken us up the back side of the mountain, where few people travel. When we clear the other side of this summit you will finally see the real Altania. That is where our danger lies. Whatever we do, we cannot let you be seen."

Chapter 16

The ridge ascended quickly above the tree line. At times it was only slightly wider than Lane's feet, forcing him to grip the rock wall with his back and shuffle sideways, inch by inch. Loose rocks shot out from under his feet, plunged over the edge, and fell and fell. Dark, gray clouds gathered low in the sky and swirled around them. With no tree cover, the winds picked up, adding to the tension as certain gusts seemed intent on prying him from the wall. It was little comfort to know that this was the least of the dangers.

As the ridge tucked around one last turn, they finally came to a large, level area where they could walk freely. As soon as Lane started to walk, however, Jethro pulled him to the ground and whispered harshly, "Get down! We must crawl from here."

Jethro motioned with his eyes for Lane to look across the ravine to the base of the summit. For the first time in a few days they finally saw civilization. At the base of the summit, beginning at the tree line, rows of buildings stood side by side. Each row was stacked on top of the other and set back against the rock wall like steps leading up the mountain. The structures were built out of the rock that was so prevalent in this area, blending them into the mountain like natural formations. The steps were connected by a series of wooden ladders that looked like stitches holding the patches of a quilt in place.

Just above the rows of buildings, nestled in a hollowed-out part of the rock, was a large, clear lake. Its water was channeled down to the buildings by a series of stone aqueducts that switched back and forth along each step.

Slightly higher than the lake, on the flat summit of the mountain, rose a large stone structure. It formed an oval and looked like a stadium or a circus from ancient Rome. At one end of the oval wall, rising like a spire on the top of the mountain, a round, stone tower loomed over everything beneath it.

"Is this where the Altanians live?" Lane asked.

"No. Their villages are further down the mountain, along the Main Trade Route and below the winter snows. This is the cloister for the priests of Amo. That tall building at the top is her temple."

"Where are the people?" Lane asked.

Jethro looked toward the summit. The sun was barely visible through the gray clouds as it began to set into the western sky.

"It is sunset. All the priests are gathered in the temple for their evening vigil. That is where we must go. If I am correct, that is where we will find the Bellator. It is good that they are all there; perhaps we will not be so easily noticed."

Jethro motioned for Lane to follow, and they crept along the final section of the ridge and over to the lake. As they approached the temple, the sound of beating drums grew louder.

"This is good," Jethro said, "They are all in there for the vigil. This is our only chance to get to the temple without being noticed."

The summit was completely exposed. There were no trees to hide behind and no rock walls to slink against. The mountain fell away from them in every direction. They stood on top of the world and, with the low cloud-covering, felt like they were scraping the bottom of the sky.

Lane marveled at the sight. "It's no wonder someone would build a temple up here."

Jethro motioned for him to follow. They moved quickly across the rocky plateau, toward the stone temple. If one priest happened to be looking over the wall that very moment, they would be discovered for sure.

He focused on the temple wall and ran as fast as he could. His longer legs brought him to the wall far ahead of Jethro. Lane slammed his back against the wall and tried to disappear against it. Jethro's little legs pumped as fast as they could. His eyebrows were stern and focused, and his cheeks puffed in and out with the exertion.

Jethro made it to the wall. They stood frozen. No sound except the drumming. Good. As they inched their way around the wall, shouts erupted from inside the temple. Then it sounded like rocks beating on stone. The noise clamoring over the wall was deafening, but served as a convenient cloak, allowing them to move freely.

The wall stood about fifteen feet tall. It was built out of rough-hewn stone blocks, and its protrusions and seams made easy handholds. Quickly they climbed the wall and came to the top, where a row of carved stone figures looked on as eternal spectators. Hidden behind the statues, they quietly observed.

It was an oval stadium. Rows of stone benches filled three quarters of the walls, like bleachers at a ball field. The field itself was made of smooth dirt. At the far end of the oval, in the one place that had no benches, stood the stone tower, rising another fifteen or twenty feet above the wall. The top of the tower, which rose above the wall, was an open room facing the stadium. The base of the tower was built into the wall and had a large metal gate that opened to the stadium floor. Two doors sat beside the large gate, one on either side.

People filled the far end of the stadium bleachers. All men. Altanian men. The Altanians were halflings like the Deltonians, but they had unique features. They were slender and lanky, and their feet were much smaller. There were perhaps a hundred of them, fifty on each side of the tower. Along the top of the wall, in front of the open room of the tower, ten priests rhythmically beat on tall drums.

In the middle of the drummers, above the gate and directly in front of the open room, stood a priest who was different from the rest. He wore a long, white fur robe that hung to his feet. Twisting up from his head, he wore a headpiece made of antlers and tree branches.

All the priests shouted and howled, pounding staffs on the stone floor. The robed priest allowed the cacophony to continue until he raised both hands and brought the din to a sharp stop. He pointed to the large doorway beneath him on the left. A gate inside the door opened, and a creature that looked much like an antelope was released onto the stadium floor. It bolted into the ring, terrified and bleating. It ran around in circles for a while and then stood panting and frozen with fear.

The horned priest raised both hands again and the drumming began. The beats fell faster and faster until the mallets were a blur of motion. Suddenly, the priest brought his hands down in a jerk, and the drumming stopped. The large metal gate below him lifted.

Lane's stomach fluttered, and a wave of nausea swept over his body. The gate opened, slowly revealing a lone figure. It filled the entire doorway, standing three times taller than any Altanian. His body was thick and muscular, and naked except for the fur loincloth that hung around his waist. No hair. None. Not even eyebrows. Only mottled skin that stretched across its muscles like raw bacon, marbled and smooth. The grotesque strips covered most of its body, severely contorting its face into a snarling grimace.

There was no question about it. This was the Bellator. Where were the long talons, the sharp fangs, and the one eye? Where was the shining armor and the caricatured upper body? Any ideas that Lane had once held of the creature were gone. The reality was worse.

His very essence oozed power and violence. The creature peered out from inside the dark opening and focused on the frightened animal that stood in the middle of the ring. They stared at each other in a long, dead silence. The Bellator's fingers twitched. Then, in a surprising flash of agility and speed, he bolted out of the doorway.

The priests went wild with cheers, clapping, hooting, and pounding. The hunt was on.

The Bellator headed straight for the antelope. The slender creature ran to the right. With quick reflexes the Bellator adjusted and created a cut-off angle. The antelope made a counter move. The hunter and the prey parlayed like this for a long while, running and twisting around the ring, carried along by the cheers of the priestly crowd.

With each lunge and miss, the antelope slowed from exhaustion. It was cornered. The Bellator closed in. With one swift pounce the slender creature was in his grasp.

Icy chills ran through Lane's bones. The Bellator carried the struggling and bleating creature out into the middle of the ring and faced the high priest. He raised the creature above his head for a moment and then brought it down to waist level. Slowly, with an intense glare, he panned the crowd, which now stood in eager anticipation. After a moment of frozen silence, he raised his right hand and plunged it into the animal's abdomen, shoved it up into its rib cage and, in one bloody swoop, pulled out its heart and hoisted it up in the air like a trophy. The bloodthirsty crowd went wild with delight.

Lane felt the blood drain from his face. His knees turned to rubber, and the stadium swam in his vision. Jethro dropped his head and slowly shook it back and forth. Lane knew that look. Jethro had seen this disgusting display before. Except, it hadn't been an antelope.

Fear wound its way up Lane's body, first wrapping its icy fingers around his ankles, then shivering itself up his legs, his back, his arms. He was frozen in panic and dread.

His paralyzed state forced him to watch as the Bellator dismembered the creature, piece by piece, with his bare hands. The muscles in his back bulged and flexed as he performed the brutal surgery. Dark blood spattered the stadium floor, which bore the rust-red stains of previous hunts.

After the Bellator had finished his display and eaten his fill of raw, bloody meat, he dropped the remains of the carcass and moved toward the door next to the gate, opposite the one from which the antelope had been released. At the top of the door there was a small inset window. The creature's bulking body, still dripping with the blood of the slain animal, stood before the door as he stared at the window. He looked up at the high priest. Then he stared at the window again, then back up at the priest. This time he cocked his head like a dog waiting for its master to act.

The window opened, and a wooden cask poked partially out of it. The Bellator lunged for the cask, but it disappeared just as he got to it. The momentum of his lunge threw his body against the door. He looked up at the opening and the cask peeked out once again. He reached up for it, but was too late. It disappeared. With this second disappearance the crowd erupted in laughter.

The icy grip that held Lane slowly melted. They were taunting him. They were laughing at him.

After a few more rounds of cat and mouse, the Bellator turned and faced the high priest. His body slumped in humiliation and defeat. The priest stood regal and tall, high above the gnarled beast, and pointed to the ground.

The Bellator wagged his head in abject defeat, and, with a momentary pause, dropped to his knees, then to his face, and lay prostrate before the priest. The crowd doubled over in gleeful delight. They heckled and mocked the hulking mass whose face was in the dirt.

The small window opened again, and the cask dropped through it and fell to the dirt with a thud. The Bellator sprang to his hands and knees and crawled over to it. He swung himself to a sitting position with his back against the wall, ripped the top of the cask completely off, and lifted it to his mouth to take a deep drink. His thick throat pulsated as he sucked the liquid from inside the cask. Within a few moments, the contents of the cask had been emptied; some ran down his face, but most went down his throat, into his stomach and, from the expression in his eyes, straight to his bloodstream. Whatever was in that cask had a dramatic and apparently pleasing effect on him. Almost immediately his eyes glazed over and fell to half mast as his shoulders rounded in relaxation. With a deep sigh he slumped down against the wall, oblivious to the mockery directed at him from the grandstand.

Lane blinked in disbelief. The Bellator wasn't the mighty war leader of the Altanians. He was their slave.

Chapter 17

Lane's mind raced wildly as he tried to reorder the pieces of this puzzle. Jethro was engaged in the same kind of paradigm reshuffling. What were they going to do now? More importantly, how were they going to get out of there without being seen?

The deep moan of the heavy metal gate recaptured their attention. The Bellator's lair was closing. Lane looked up just in time to see the massive beast hoist himself from his sitting position and drag his thick, muscled body back into the black hole. Now he looked more like a trained circus gorilla than a mighty warrior. Still, circus gorillas were dangerous and could rip your arms off just as easily as a warrior. One way or the other, Lane was going to have to face this pitiful creature in battle.

The gate clanked and locked in place. Several priests emerged on top of the wall, just above the room from which the cask had appeared. Each priest carried a large serving tray loaded with goblets. They filed out among the stands and dispersed the goblets until each priest held one in his hand.

While the goblets were being served, two priests walked up to join the high priest at the base of the tower. They approached from either side and stopped to bow their heads to him. The three figures turned and faced into the open, hollow chamber. Two stone slabs lay at the base of the cavernous room. The two priests headed toward these slabs, one to the left, the other to the right, and laid down on them with their heads facing into the darkness. Once they were situated, the high priest walked over to the one on the right and waved his hands, palms down, just above the priest's face. His mouth formed words that did not reach Lane's ears. He repeated these actions on the other priest.

A priest who had been serving now stood in the center of the platform and held one last goblet on his tray. The high priest took it, and the server made a quick exit. The drummers pounded in unison. The high priest raised his goblet in the air, and all the priests hoisted theirs upwards in response.

"Amo ap opthalmati!" they shouted in unison, then lifted their goblets to their mouths, tipped their heads back, and emptied the contents in a few quick gulps.

The high priest turned and faced into the dark void of the tower and raised his hands in the air. He swayed back and forth, repeating the phrase, *"Amo ap opthalmati."*

A dull murmur of deep voices accompanied him from the priestly crowd. His long, bony arms swayed back and forth against the dark background.

Lane stared into the blackness of the tower. The drone of the chanting and the rhythmic movement of the arms pulled his mind into the void.

A spark popped. Then another. Lane rubbed his eyes. Perhaps his field of vision was starting to fade because he had been staring so long. It didn't work. More sparks of white light popped and multiplied like kernels of popcorn suspended in midair. A fuzzy, static glow engulfed the sparks of light.

Suddenly, a bright string of light stretched up and down from the center of the cluster and then widened in a brilliant flash.

As soon as it came it was gone, and, standing in its place, was the figure of a woman. A human woman. Her body filled the entire tower. Lane guessed she was at least fifteen feet tall. She was not solid. Her body shimmered and fractured as if she were a film being projected onto a wall of mist. The image was overexposed to the point where all of her features were blown out by light. She was a bright, white silhouette. All white—her empty face, skin, long flowing robe—except for her hair, which was jet black, blending in with the dark room behind her.

She was tall and slender, and even though he could not see

the features of her face, Lane found her to be beautiful and soft. At her appearance the priests fell to their faces and began chanting, "Amo, Amo."

Lane knew that the Altanians worshipped a goddess named Amo, but he always imagined it to be like every other god of primitive people—just an anthropomorphism of the forces of nature that helped them to deal with the cruelties and the vastness of life. Now, to see this woman standing in front of him in her ethereal glow, he didn't know what to say or do.

The woman's body swayed back and forth. She raised her hands out in front of her, as if she were reaching for something. Then her face panned back and forth along the bleachers of the stadium. Her gaze started at Lane's right, swept past him, and fell on the cluster of priests on his left. Then it swept back toward him and stopped. Her body leaned forward. Her arm thrust out in front of her. She was pointing...at Lane.

She looked directly at him. He lost his balance and leaned into the statue that was hiding him. It scraped and wobbled just enough to push a loose piece of stone free from its mortar. The stone crashed down to the bleachers below. The sound echoed throughout the stadium. Every head turned toward the noise.

The two priests that lay on the stone slabs sat up, and the vision of Amo instantly vanished. Every eye in the stadium was focused on Lane and Jethro. Now what? They looked at each other and then looked across the plain toward the ridge that had brought them there. The last flickers of twilight barely lit the ground. They had to run for it.

Quickly they slid and scraped down the wall and hit the ground running. Everything seemed to move in slow motion. Stone scraped on stone, and clashing voices sounded from the other side of the temple. The priests were exiting the stadium in pursuit. Lane and Jethro ran full speed toward the lake, but Lane outran Jethro's short strides. He stopped, turned back, and flung Jethro over his shoulder like a sack of potatoes.

He ran around the edge of the lake and came to the narrow ridge. He set Jethro down and they inched their way around the rocky lip. The sun was gone now. It was almost black. The sound of an angry mob approached the ridge.

"Jethro, we have to move faster!"

A large cracking sound popped from the wall behind them. The small ridge beneath them started to crumble. Lane turned and reached up, but the smooth wall offered no handholds. As he turned he saw a dark shadow fall away and looked to see Jethro disappearing in the blackness below.

The ridge broke free. Lane began to slide. He grasped for a handhold. Every rock he touched pulled away from the wall. His body slid down the face of the cliff. Now he was in free-fall. Blackness.

Chapter 18

Pain. That was the first thing that registered in the darkness. Over the past day or so, the pain in Lane's head had faded into a constant and dull companion. Now it throbbed and spiked with a new intensity. Pressure pushed on his face from the inside out. His arms were raised above his head.

I'm upside down.

He opened his eyes but saw nothing. It was still night. He swung his arms around. Leaves. Branches. He was tangled in a tree, and his leg was wedged in the crotch of two branches.

"Jethro! Where are you?" He arched his head back to look "up" and scan the ground beneath him. The meager moonlight revealed a fuzzy black spot on the ground that had the right size and shape to be Jethro's body. It lay still and lifeless.

"No, Jethro!" Lane swung his arms and grabbed a branch big enough to pull him into an upright position. He worked his leg free. It was sore, but did not seem broken. He quickly climbed down the tree.

The dark form was definitely Jethro. He lay facedown, chest rising and falling slightly. His right leg bent in the wrong place. It must be broken. This was not good.

"Jethro." Lane carefully grasped Jethro's shoulder. No movement. "Jethro!" He spoke louder, but kept his voice to an intense whisper for fear that the Altanian priests might still be looking for them. He shook Jethro's body this time. "Wake up, man. I need you."

A deep moan escaped from Jethro's body. His eyelids fluttered and then opened. Pain registered instantly in his eyes.

"Jethro, what is it? Where does it hurt?"

"My leg. I do not think I can move it." He tried to flip his body over, but pain contorted his mouth into a grimace, and his torso fell back to the ground with a thud.

"Here, let me help you." Lane carefully lifted the broken leg as Jethro twisted his body around so he was lying on his back. Lane scanned the dark ground and gathered a large pile of pine needles to make a pillow under Jethro's head. "Here, rest your head on this."

"You know I have to try to straighten this leg, right?" Lane studied the twisted limb for a moment, then reached for a stick that lay next to them. "Here, you should bite down on this."

Jethro placed the stick in his mouth and dug his teeth into the wood. With a firm nod, he was ready.

Lane placed his left hand on Jethro's thigh and grasped his ankle with his right hand. A quick twist, a pull, then a *pop*, and it was done.

The stick snapped in Jethro's mouth. He arched his back and swallowed a scream. His hands dug into the ground.

After a moment his body relaxed.

"Good job, Jethro. That should hold until we get home."

They sat in silence for a while. A single tear escaped and ran down Jethro's face.

"This is a fine mess, eh?" Jethro said. He tried to smile, but the pain masked his failed attempt. "What happened?"

"As far as I can tell," Lane explained, "the section of ridge we were standing on broke free. We fell down the side of the cliff into a patch of trees. I have no idea how far we fell or where we are. All I do know is that if those trees hadn't broken our fall we'd have more than a broken leg and a headache."

"How long have we been here?" Jethro asked.

"I really don't know. It's obviously the middle of the night. My guess is that I couldn't have survived very long hanging upside down in that tree. It's probably only been a few hours."

Jethro rubbed his eyes. "The guards will be swarming the mountains at daybreak. They know you are here now, Lane. You did not happen to have a back-up plan did you?"

Lane looked to the forest, but the darkness flattened everything into a wall that penned them in on all sides.

"Do you have any idea where we are?" Lane asked.

"Hmmm." Every sound was a painful effort for Jethro. "If we fell straight down the cliff," he paused and studied the map in his mind. "There are only two ways to get down from this mountain. We can follow the base of the cliff until we find the ridge and then go down the way we came up, or..." He placed the palm of each hand over his eyes and pressed in.

"Or what?" Lane said.

Jethro extended his left arm to the side and pointed, "Or we can follow the hunter's trail to the upper village and take the trade route down the mountain."

"Go right through Altania?!" Lane said. "That would be suicide."

"The ridge or the route," Jethro said. His words were heavy with pain. He took in a long, deep breath that erupted in a cough. "Lane. Find the ridge, you are smart, you can retrace our steps. You do not need me anymore. At this point I am putting you, and our hopes of victory, in danger. Just leave me."

"No way. That's not an option." Lane was on his feet now. He paced back and forth. His head throbbed with intense pain.

Think, man. There has to be another way.

The Bellator must be my coma. I have to defeat him. I spied on him and discovered two things. First, he's a slave and he kills to get that liquid. What was that stuff?

"Jethro, what was in the cask that the Bellator drank? What was in that room?"

Jethro's head fell back into the pillow of pine needles, and he let out a deep sigh. "That, Lane, is our shame."

"What?"

"Locked inside that room is the very symbol of my people's shame and disgrace. It is the fruit of our labor and the evidence that we are weak and defeated."

"What are you talking about, Jethro?"

Jethro propped himself up onto an elbow and looked directly at Lane.

"It is the nectar. What the Bellator drank. What the priests drank. What is in hundreds of casks locked in that room. It is the nectar. It is what my people work to produce every day. We grow the flowers. We harvest them. We extract their nectar. We refine it. We put it in the casks...and then they take it from us.

"The Altanians crave it. They cannot get enough of it. They take what they want, and they kill us if they do not get it. All because of that wretched beast."

"But Jethro, didn't you see what they were doing with the Bellator? He's not the leader of their war band. He's like a trained animal. He does whatever they want him to do because he wants the nectar. Did you see how they taunted him? Did you see how he cowered to that priest with the weird hat? Did you see how he melted into a lump of putty when he drank the nectar? That guy is an addict!"

Jethro's brow furrowed. He had no response.

Lane continued pacing.

The second thing I learned about the Bellator is... I didn't find his weakness. He's huge. He's ugly. He's brutal. And he's an addict, so he will stop at nothing to get what he wants. Great. How am I supposed to defeat this guy?

He sat down at the base of a tree and leaned his head back against the trunk. Thoughts of his life and home tumbled around on each other. He thought of Ms. Mitchell and how nice she had always been to him. Heather's face appeared: a twinkle in her eye. Had she really said he was her hero? He drifted further back, to the days when he was little and his mother was alive. She was always so kind to him, and gentle. He missed her deeply. Then Josh's face appeared. His big, blue eyes stared at Lane. Just behind Josh's face, growing larger, his deep, angry glare superimposed over Josh's innocent eyes, the face of his father grew larger. *Josh, no!*

Lane sat up straight and startled Jethro.

"What is it, Lane?"

"Jethro, I know what I have to do. I've been going about this all wrong. We have to get to the trade route."

"Lane, what are you talking about? Did the fall make you

crazy? You said it yourself, that would be suicide."

"No, Jethro, I don't think so. I need you to trust me right now. I know what I'm doing. Just lead me to the village."

Jethro tried to move, but winced as the pain of his leg shot through his body.

Lane looked at the leg, then back at Jethro's face. "Right. You can't walk."

He paced a little more, then stopped.

"I can carry you. I'll put you on my back. Now I know this is the right plan. You'll never be able to make it home going the way we came. We have to get to the trade route, and we have to get home fast."

Chapter 19

Jethro groaned when Lane slung him over his shoulders like a backpack.

"Sorry. I'll try to be careful," Lane said. "Now show me where that path is."

They set out toward a small clearing that was barely visible in the first pale light of dawn. A chorus of birds sweetened the morning air. First one song called out. Then another answered from the other side of the path. Soon the whole forest burst into song as light sparkled off the mist that hung low to the ground.

The path was nothing more than a footpath that cut its way through the undergrowth on the forest floor. Lane allowed the fresh, crisp air to fill his lungs and splash over his face. It invigorated him to feel the breeze and to hear the crunching of the pine needles under his feet.

"Lane, what in the name of the Great Father are we going to do when we get to the village? This is insane!"

"I know it sounds crazy, but I have a plan. Trust me. Just tell me what to expect when we get to the village. Will there be guards everywhere? Who's in charge?"

"To be honest, I do not know," Jethro paused a moment. "I have not been to an Altanian village since the Invasion. Except, of course, when we march through them to attend the Festival, but that does not count. Everyone lines the road and jeers at the visiting tribes, and the villages are all chaotic. The only thing I can tell you about the villages is what I remember from when I was a child.

"I remember that they were peaceful places. They are very

different than our villages. They do not have a central fire or concentric circles like we do. They are mountain people. Their huts are built out of stone and are cut into the side of the rock walls. The trade route runs through the center of each village, so if we are going to use that route to get home, we are going to have to face every single Altanian. This is insane."

"Relax, Jethro, just keep talking," Lane assured his skeptical friend as he tried to also convince himself that it would be fine.

"Well, I think the most important thing is to know that each village is controlled by the priest. Every village has a priest that lives within it. Those priests answer to the high priest that we saw in the temple. Whatever the local priest says, the people do."

"What about guards?" Lane asked.

"Back then they did not have guards to speak of. During our time of peaceful trade we did not have war. Usually, the men would train for competition at the Festival, but there was no organized military. But, since the Invasion, having seen all the wretched guards they have posted in our villages, I have no idea what to expect up here."

They fell into silence and continued along the path. It curved around the base of the rocky cliff and headed south. The eastern sky grew brighter as they walked, and the morning sun sparkled off the craggy rocks of the mountain wall to their right.

"Stop," Jethro whispered in Lane's ear. "Look straight ahead. Do you see through those trees? Do you see how the sun seems brighter there?"

Lane squinted. "Yes, I see it."

"That is where the village is. We need to be careful here. We may run into some early morning hunters. Whatever your plan is, you had better get it going...now."

Lane pressed on toward the clearing and coached himself along the way. *You can do this, man. Stay focused.*

They approached the bright patch and stopped to observe from behind the cover of some bushes. At first glance, it did not seem like a village at all. It appeared to be a small valley with steep, wooded slopes that rose up either side. At the base of the valley, where you might expect to see a stream, there was a wide, smooth path paved with large, flat stones. The valley walls were peppered with piles of gray stone.

"Where's the village?" Lane whispered. "There's nothing there."

"Look closer." Jethro pointed toward a cluster of rocks across the path.

Something moved beside it. A halfling. A woman. She walked in front of the rocks. They were twice her height. Then she vanished. Lane blinked and looked closer. She hadn't vanished. She walked into the rock.

"Where'd she go?" Lane asked.

"Keep your voice down," Jethro said. "Keep looking. Do not assume you know what you see."

Now he saw more people moving in and out of the rocks and trees. These were not naturally occurring outcroppings. These were their houses. With his new realization, the houses started popping out all over the hills. They were everywhere. Little fires flickered in front of some of the rocky huts and small tongues of white smoke licked the pine branches that towered above the village. Together, the smoke and trees reached high up into the clear morning sky.

"That was weird."

Lane let Jethro down off his back.

"Lean up against this tree," he told Jethro. "Look mean, follow my lead, and, whatever you do, don't move."

Lane searched the underbrush around them until he found a large stick. He handed it to Jethro and said, "Here, hang on to this. You'll need it. Just be ready."

Jethro winced at the pain of being set down on his leg, but nodded in agreement.

Lane took a deep breath, then stepped out onto the stone path in the middle of the village. A tiny ball rolled from the side of the path and stopped at his feet. A small child chased it. She was so intent on retrieving the ball that she didn't notice the giant at first. The girl pounced on the ball and then stopped suddenly. First, she noticed Lane's feet, scanned up his legs and torso, and then arched her back to see into the giant's face. She was frozen in fear for a moment, then dropped the ball and screamed.

A woman appeared in the doorway of the closest stone hut. She stopped suddenly at the sight of Lane. In fear, she looked at him, looked at the child, and then bolted from the doorway, scooped the girl up without stopping, and ran to the other side of the path.

"Aldo, Aldo!" she screamed as she ran.

At her voice, several other women appeared in dark doorways, each wearing similar expressions of shock and fear. More children appeared and huddled at their mother's feet. From one hut an old man, hunched over with age, shuffled out, looked up at Lane, and staggered backwards.

Eventually the stone path in front of Lane was filled with a sea of Altanian women, children, and old people.

He stood motionless, allowing the tension of his presence to sink deeply into his audience.

It's show time.

First he leaned back and stretched out his arms, as if to gather air into his lungs. Then with a lurch forward he let out the deepest and gruffest growl that he could muster.

"Aarrrrr," he roared, "I am the Pleroma of the Deltonians. I have come to deliver a message to you, the Altanian people."

He picked through the crowd to find a worthy representative and landed on a woman who looked like she was one of the more matriarchal of the group. He pointed at her and glared with fierce eyes and clenched teeth, trying to exude as much anger and wrath as possible.

"You!" he yelled.

Terror filled the woman's eyes.

"Where is your priest, woman?" Lane questioned. "Bring me your priest, now!"

She quickly obeyed, running up the path and disappearing behind a group of trees. While she was gone, Lane leered at the crowd and tried to be as intimidating as he could.

Soon the woman reappeared with a man who looked very

similar to one of the priests that had been in the stadium the night before. He was a slight man. The top of his head was completely devoid of hair, and the sides of his head sprouted strands that spilled down in gray waves over his shoulders. A long, thin beard converged in a wispy point at his waist. He wore the white fur robe of the Altanian priests.

At the sight of Lane, he stopped, and his face turned the color of his white robe. His steps seemed forced as he came closer.

When the priest joined the crowd, Lane continued.

"Listen to me, people of Altania! I am the Pleroma," Lane shouted and motioned with his arms and body in overly large dramatics. "I am the long-awaited deliverer of the Deltonian tribe. The Great Father has tolerated your insolence long enough. Now, he has sent me to bring deliverance for his people and justice and wrath on you."

On the word "you" he leaned into the crowd and swept his pointed finger across them in accusation.

"Look up to the hillsides." He pointed to the forested slopes that surrounded them. "Hiding in these hills, right now, is the Deltonian war band that I have assembled and trained. With my signal they could swoop down and destroy you and your village in a matter of moments. Look, there," with this he pointed, with great emphasis, over at Jethro, who still stood by the tree on the side of the path.

"There is their leader now. Jethronius Maximus, the warlord of the Deltonian Hordes!" *Hordes?* Lane thought to himself. *Is that the right word?* He thought he remembered that word from one of those barbarian stories. "His fierceness in battle is surpassed only by the vengeance that fuels his fury."

The surprise on Jethro's face cast him as anything but a fierce warlord. Lane scowled at him.

Jethro understood and raised the large stick above his head and shook it, his face contorted in a snarl. For a moment he got caught up in the role and took a step forward. The scowl of false ferocity transformed into a grimace of concealed pain.

Lane noticed Jethro's mistake and quickly diverted the crowd's attention.

"Listen to me! Many years ago you invaded our lands with cruelty and demonstrated that you and your goddess are merciless and fierce. I am here today to show you that the Deltonians are different than you. Today, I will demonstrate to you the higher way. I could crush you where you stand." He slammed his fist into his hand to demonstrate this point, and the crowd flinched in unified horror. "And I would be vindicated in doing so. But that is not the way of the Great Father and the Deltonians. No, we follow a higher path.

"You have declared that whoever defeats your Bellator in battle at the Festival will win their freedom. I stand here today to deliver a warning and a promise. I will return at the Festival, and on that day I will deliver my people from your cruel hand and lead them into freedom!"

His hands were upraised now, and he called out his proclamation to the mountain tops. His speech, which had begun as a ruse, now filled him with excitement and, to his own surprise, gave him a sense of empowerment and courage.

He continued with increased enthusiasm.

"Now, as a gesture of goodwill, I will call off my war band and spare your lives, on one condition. You," he singled out the priest, "you must be my herald. You must walk before me as I go down this path and through the villages of your people and declare to them who I am and what will happen on the day of the Festival. If you do this, and lead me out of the Upper Mountains, my war band will melt away into the desert and leave you in your peace."

The priest sputtered and stammered. He glanced up to the summit where the temple stood. His brow furrowed deeply. Hatred oozed from his pores and blazed in his eyes. As he hesitated, Lane, battling his own fear that his plan might backfire, screwed up his face and cupped his hands to his mouth as if he was about to summon his mighty hordes to swoop down from the mountain side and rain terror down on the village.

Just as Lane was about to let out his battle cry, the priest shouted, "No! Do not call them. I will do it."

Jethro and Lane both let out deep sighs.

"Wise choice, priest," Lane tried to maintain the fierceness in his voice. It was harder now since every ounce of his body felt like Jell-o. He walked over to Jethro, picked him up, and slung him onto his back. The crowd seemed confused.

Lane quickly responded, "Jethronius is not as gracious as I. Unless I carry him he will not be able to restrain his fury. Keep back or he may become violent."

At this warning the crowd melted away from the path and opened up the way for Lane's escape.

"Nicely played, Lane," Jethro whispered into his ear. "Nicely played."

The priest walked several paces in front of them and led Lane, with his halfling backpack, along the path, out of the village, and around the bend. Lane motioned with his hands to the hillsides, instructing his imaginary war band to stand down and retreat.

Much to Lane's surprise and relief, the priest kept up his end of the bargain. With each new village they entered, the priest raised his hands without stopping his forward march, and shouted to the people, "Behold, my fellow Altanians, the Pleroma has come! Prepare yourselves for the day of the Festival."

As they walked through the villages, the people peeked out from inside the safety of their huts and watched as the strange parade marched along the path.

Chapter 20

The rest of the day progressed in an uneventful and regular pattern. They marched down the mountain path from village to village. During the time between the villages, Lane enjoyed the walk. The mountain air was fresh and clean. Unlike his journey to the Upper Mountains, this walk was smooth and easy because the path was wide and well-traveled. It flowed down the mountainside like a lazy river, finding the easiest path along the bottom of gullies and valleys, always edged by thickly forested slopes. The trees rose high above them on both sides, cutting a ragged slice of sky that shone bright blue as the day came into full bloom. The forest teemed with the sounds of life—birds sang to one another, small creatures rustled through the fallen leaves and pine needles, and the trees themselves seemed to whisper ancient secrets as the breeze tickled their branches.

Each village was the same. The path was lined with stone huts on either side. The handfuls of women, children, and elders who happened to be on the path shuddered in fear as they saw the giant approach. The priest cried out his proclamation of the Pleroma's impending day of reckoning, and the people melted away into their homes and allowed the threesome to pass through the village unhindered.

As the path descended and the sun rose in the sky, the air grew thicker and warmer. Directly ahead of them a large, rocky ridge descended to their right, and the path turned to meet it. The ridge ended with a steep cliff that came down to the edge of the path. The path rounded the rocky wall in a sharp turn, and a new scene spread out before them. They were at the base of the mountains. Sprawling out before them, cracked and desolate, lay the Waste. The pine trees were now sparse, and the majority of the foliage was mostly tough-looking bushes and scrub.

The path wound back and forth along the rocky slope until it came to one more village, which lay at the base of the mountain and the edge of the desert floor. From that village the trade route spread straight out across the Waste like a white chalk line in the reddish brown dirt. It vanished on the far horizon, where the purple outline of the distant Lower Mountains met the eastern sky.

They descended the last few switchbacks and approached the final village. The sun was hot on their backs, and the air was much thicker than it had been in the mountains. A fine layer of sand lay over the path and crunched under their feet as they walked. At times the sand caused them to slip as the path sloped down the final inclines of the rocky foothills.

Lane looked up to see where they had come from. The summit was now hidden by the lower ridges. He marveled at how green the mountains were and already longed for their shade and cool air.

As they entered this last village, Lane sensed an immediate difference from the others. Here there was a buzz in the air. The village bustled with movement and activity. The path was lined with carts and wooden booths housing vendors and merchants. The booths were covered with multicolored fabric, which was stretched over the tops to protect the inhabitants from the intense desert sun. The merchants sold different goods—some had vegetables, some pottery, others had jewelry or textiles. People moved back and forth on the path in a swarm of activity. The air was filled with the sound of people bartering and talking.

"Jethro," Lane spoke softly, "do you notice anything different about this village?"

"It is hot and dusty."

"Besides that."

Jethro studied the crowd from his perch on Lane's back. "I am not sure what you mean."

"Men, Jethro. There are men here. Why would they concentrate all their men in this nasty village?"

They walked further into the village.

"There is the answer," Jethro motioned forward.

A group of people entered the village from the Waste. Six soldiers marched in front, and six marched in the back. In between these two groups of soldiers, two Deltonians pulled a wooden cart. The cart carried a large load of casks that looked just like the one served to the Bellator.

"They bring a new batch of the nectar," Jethro said, his voice heavy.

"When you make deliveries, do you ever go any further than this village?"

Jethro thought for a moment. "No. I do not believe so."

"I get it now," Lane's voice was now an intense whisper. "The Altanians aren't strong. They don't have a large war force. This is all smoke and mirrors. They put all of their soldiers in this one village because it's the gateway to the mountains. Do you see it? By concentrating all the activity in this one place they can appear strong and demand respect. These people rule through a façade of fear and intimidation and the threat of the Bellator. Nothing more."

Jethro stuttered, "I...I suppose you are right."

Lane's resolve to free the Deltonians deepened.

Façade or not, there was still a strong concentration of soldiers in this village. As they stepped into the crowd, Lane tensed. He could also feel the muscles in Jethro's body tighten as they pressed against his back.

Lane took a deep breath. The recognition of their presence swept through the crowd like a wave. First there was a gasp, then silence. The silence washed over the crowd and splashed against the garrison of soldiers as they raised their spears in alarm.

Lane's herald-priest climbed onto a stone bench along the side of the path, faced the crowd, and lifted his hands. He did not speak at first. In the silence he glared at Lane. His hesitation sent a ripple of panic through Lane's body. What was he doing? Was he going to call his bluff? They stared intently at one another and the priest looked deeply into Lane's eyes. Lane returned the penetrating glare with equal intensity, then slowly turned his gaze up into the hillside, as if to say, "My army is still there, and still waiting for my call." The priest's eyes fell on Jethro's face. Jethro clenched his jaw so the muscles on the side of his face bulged, and he snarled and growled at the priest with the fury of a warlord.

The intensity of the priest's eyes shut off as if someone had flipped a switch, and he quickly turned to face the crowd.

"My fellow Altanians, do not be alarmed. You are safe. I present to you the Pleroma of the Deltonians."

The two Deltonian cart-pullers had paid no attention to the activity in the village. At the priest's proclamation they snapped to attention. When they saw Lane and Jethro towering over the crowd, their faces beamed with amazement and delight.

The priest continued, "The Pleroma has promised us that no harm would come to us if we allow him safe passage through our land and back to Deltonia. But be warned. He will return to face our Bellator at the Festival. May Amo have mercy on us all."

The priest stepped down from the bench and walked up to Lane. He bowed his head slightly and with reluctance said, "I have done as you requested. I have given you safe passage through our villages, and you have kept your war band at bay. Our agreement has been fulfilled." He held out his hand in the direction of the path that led into the Waste.

Lane scanned the crowd and tried to read into the priest's statement. *Something isn't right. Is there a trick or a trap in this somehow? What will happen if we walk through the Waste alone? There will be bands of soldiers on the path and then guards in Deltonia. What was I thinking?* This plan seemed to be backfiring and disintegrating in front of him. The priest had a new look in his eye, like he was beginning to sense the panic that was quickly bubbling up inside of Lane.

"Guards!" Lane shouted.

The priest looked surprised at this outburst.

"I need your guards for the path," Lane continued. "Yes, you have kept your part of the bargain, and I have kept mine. But once I enter the Waste, my war bands will be watching. If I have a band of Altanian guards with me, leading us along the path, then that will be their signal to hold off their attack. You must transfer your heraldship to that band of guards and command them to lead us safely to Deltonia and to pass the message on to the guards posted there."

He pointed to the band of soldiers that had just led the procession in from the Waste. The look on their faces showed their disappointment at the prospect of turning around and heading straight back across that desolate stretch of road.

The priest looked hard at Lane once again. Lane came closer and towered over him. He looked down with Jethro's angry face peering over his shoulder like a parrot on the shoulder of a marauding pirate.

"I suggest you comply if you value the lives of your people." Lane slowly and deliberately uttered his final threat.

The priest wilted away from Lane in timid concession and quickly walked over to the soldiers. He spoke to them and motioned with his hands. The expression on the soldiers' faces told Lane that the priest was ordering them to take them home. His great masquerade was working.

"But, Lane, the Great Father is nearly ready to dive behind the mountains!" Jethro was now sitting on a bench against the wall of a hut that sat along the path. Long shadows stretched across the ground and reached out into the Waste, pointing the way home.

"We have been traveling all day. Do you think it is wise to venture into the Waste right now? What about the skuli?"

"I think we're pushing our luck as it is," Lane answered. "I have a funny feeling about that priest. I'm afraid that if we stay in the village overnight he might change his mind. I'd rather risk being out there with a handful of little soldiers than sleeping in the middle of a swarm of Altanians. Hey, if we're lucky, the skuli will eat the soldiers first."

"That is not amusing." Jethro scratched his beard and crinkled the bags that hung under his eyes. He rubbed his leg and tried to hide the pain that was throbbing and radiating through his whole body.

"I suppose I do not really have to complain too much, you are carrying me," he managed a slight chuckle and a half smile. "After all, you are the Pleroma, right?"

Lane detected the tone in Jethro's voice that said, "I know you are not, but you sure have fooled them." Lane was surprised at how that tone affected him. It sat sideways and burned a little around the edges. He had always known that Jethro did not believe in him, but now something had changed. Was it possible that Lane was starting to believe in himself?

"Come on, you little skeptic. Let's get moving." Lane hoisted Jethro up onto his back once again. He felt heavier this time. Perhaps skepticism weighed a few pounds.

Chapter 21

The setting sun ignited the desert floor with deep reds and golds. Long purple shadows stretched from the occasional patch of vegetation or a large boulder. The jagged, muted-purple skyline of the distant Lower Mountains seemed clear in the dry air. Lane knew it would be a new sun before they reached those mountains.

The unlikely band of travelers set out on the trade route. Four soldiers marched several paces ahead of Lane. He quickened his pace so he could catch up to the soldiers and ask a question. As the gap between him and the soldiers closed, they sped up and widened the gap again. *That's weird.* Lane sped up more. The gap began to close, and then the soldiers increased their speed even more. They were nearly trotting to maintain the distance. Lane slowed down to an easy gait and the soldiers did the same. No matter how slow or fast Lane walked, the soldiers matched his speed.

An impish grin spread across Lane's face. "Jethro," he whispered, "watch this."

In a sudden burst, Lane walked in long, fast strides toward the soldiers. Their armor rattled and they broke into a flustered trot to keep away from him. Jethro snorted in delight.

Lane slowed down again and watched the soldiers breathe sighs of relief. He leaned his head toward Jethro.

"This reminds me of chasing cockroaches on the sidewalk when I was a kid."

"What is a cockroach?"

"Oh, it's a nasty little bug that lives in dark shadows. They're almost impossible to get rid of."

Jethro chuckled. "An appropriate analogy. It is nice to see them scurry in fear for a change."

The amusement of the game eventually wore off and they all fell into a steady and deliberate march. The path was straight and flat. It had been built on the top of a man-made ridge that smoothly spanned the little hills and valleys of the desert floor. Occasionally it ran across a bridge over a dry riverbed. This way was definitely preferable to crossing the Waste the way they had come.

As the last light began to fade, Lane stayed alert for the skuli and continually searched the landscape.

"Jethro, I'm curious. Why aren't there any of those bitter bushes around here?"

The soldiers cocked their heads and tensed their muscles.

"What was that?" Lane whispered to Jethro.

"They are deathly afraid of the bitter bush. If you want to get a real rise out of them, just say 'numa.'"

"Really? The numa? Don't you mean skuli?"

"Well, of course they are afraid of the skuli. You would have to be a fool to not be afraid of those vile creatures. But the Altanians have a particular fear of the numa and the bitter bush."

"Why?" Lane asked.

"One can only guess." Jethro continued in a lower tone. "I do know that when this path was built, many generations ago, the Altanians hired Bedite workers to fan out on either side of it and burn out any bitter bushes they found. The Altanians did not want to get near them in case a numa might drag them into the other world. And, just in case burning the bushes angered Amo, she would get angry at the Bedites and destroy their tribe instead of the Altanians'. Very thoughtful of them, was it not?"

"Yeah," Lane echoed sarcastically, "they're always looking out for their neighbors. That's what I love about them. It just warms my heart."

Darkness was fully upon them. The cool desert air filled Lane's head, and the weight of the past day's journeys caught up with him. They had to stop.

The soldiers were thankful for the halt and quickly made camp. Each of them produced two stones from the pouch that hung from their belts and placed them in a circle that filled the width of the path. The lead soldier opened a small, metal box that revealed a glowing stone. He touched it to each of the surrounding stones, passing its radiance to them. Within moments they were encircled by a wall of light.

"The glowing stones," Jethro anticipated Lane's question. "They have been blessed by the priests of Amo to ward off the skuli."

Lane motioned to the soldiers, "I guess you guys have done this before."

They did not respond, but huddled closer together, as far from Lane and Jethro as they could get while still remaining within the circle's protective light.

Lane shrugged at Jethro and lay down.

Something flashed through Lane's eyelids. It startled him, and when he opened his eyes the light burned. He had looked directly into the sun just as it peeked over the edge of the Lower Mountains. He turned over to face the other direction and looked down the long path. The Upper Mountains now seemed far away. He marveled at how far they had traveled in such a short amount of time.

The morning sun quickly drove the purple and gray away from the desert floor and painted it once again with deep reds, yellows, and browns. It was time to go. Lane poked one of the soldiers with his toe. At first the soldier simply flinched and didn't rouse. Lane kicked him slightly harder, and the soldier raised his head in tired protest, his eyes still stuck shut with sleep. He pried his eyes open and looked up at Lane, who now towered above him. Sight of the giant jolted the soldier into action. He flipped onto his belly, scrambled to his hands and feet, and slapped his comrades as he stood. He staggered backwards, away from Lane, as if he were trying to avoid a person who carried a highly contagious disease.

PLEROMA

An impish urge crept up the back of Lane's mind and, without thinking, Lane lunged toward the soldier, with hands outstretched…"Boo!"

All of the soldiers reacted in fear to this childish motion. A cackle of laughter broke out from behind Lane. He turned around to see Jethro sitting on a small rock, holding his stomach in laughter.

"Oh, great Pleroma!" Jethro said in between loud chortles, "Now, that was not very nice. Ho, hooo!"

Lane flushed with embarrassment. That wasn't like him. He remembered the crows who used to taunt him on his way to school and felt ashamed that he, with a small taste of power, could act just like them.

His face turned stone serious. "You're absolutely right, Jethro. It wasn't."

He reached down, picked Jethro up, and threw him onto his back. With steady determination he walked over to the group of soldiers, looked them square in the eye, and said, "I'm sorry, please forgive my rudeness. Let's go." He walked down the path toward the Lower Mountains and didn't look back.

The soldiers were dumbfounded at first and stood motionless as he walked away. They quickly realized that they needed to be with him and marched in double time to catch up.

Soon their parade was back in line, and they marched toward the rising sun. A small black smudge appeared on the path ahead of them. The smudge grew larger and separated into several smudges casting long shadows. As the gap between them grew smaller, the clear outline of a small caravan appeared. It was a column of soldiers leading a wagon.

"It must be another shipment of the nectar on its way to Altania," Lane said. "That means Deltonians will be pulling the cart."

"Perhaps." Jethro responded. "There will also be more guards."

At the first sight of Lane's band of soldiers, the oncoming Altanian guards were visibly shaken and called to alert. They stopped their own procession and waited for Lane's parade to approach.

As they drew closer, Lane saw that his assumptions were wrong. This was not a Deltonian shipment of nectar. There was a cart, but instead of large wooden casks it was filled with bundles of large leaves, wrapped in cloths. The cart was pulled by halflings unlike any Lane had seen so far. They had the same goatlike eyes as the other tribesmen, but all four of these men had leathery, bluish-gray skin. The lower halves of their bodies were covered with green leather pants adorned with colorful feathers hanging from the waist. Their torsos were naked, covered only by long necklaces weighted down with bones, claws, and smooth stones.

"Jethro," Lane whispered over his shoulder, "who are those men? I haven't seen anything like them before."

"Those are Bedites. They bring fruits and vegetables to the Altanians. Ah, the fruits that grow in their forests along the sea are some of the sweetest things you will ever taste. They are a delicacy. They used to bring a high trade, but, of course, now the Altanians just take what they want."

The moment of truth had arrived. The two caravans met, and the Altanian guards faced one another. Lane tensed and readied himself for anything.

The leader of Lane's guard spoke loudly in a strange, robotic voice. "Behold, the Pleroma of the Deltonians. He has come to bring justice to the Altanians. Prepare yourselves for the day of reckoning."

Up to this point the Bedites had been staring at the ground in dejected resignation, paying no attention to the encounter. At the sound of the passionless recitation, their heads popped up. With wide eyes they looked at Lane. In amazement they glanced back and forth at each other and then back at Lane. Like a blossom greeting the morning sun for the first time, smiles spread across their faces. Small sparks ignited in their eyes. Their backs straightened in the yokes that held them bound to the cart.

That was it. Three simple sentences, and then Lane's group of guards marched on with no further expression or exchange. As Lane and Jethro walked past, the Altanians' and Bedites' eyes were all glued to them. The Altanians looked at him with both fear and disgust. The Bedite eyes, however, called out to him, their souls pleading through oval pupils, "Save us. Deliver us. Please be the one."

Lane and his troop moved on, leaving the caravan behind them. This encounter left Lane with a new set of emotions. Up to this point he had only known the plight of the Deltonians. The other tribes were nothing more than names to him. Now, to have seen the strange, blue-gray Bedites, to have looked into their golden eyes and felt their pain—the enormity of the task that lay ahead of him weighed heavily on his shoulders. The outcome of the Festival would not only affect the Deltonians, but it would have implications for all the tribes that felt the oppression of the Altanians.

They passed many other caravans along the path. Most were carrying shipments of Deltonian nectar. Some were large caravans with many wagons and many slaves. Others were simply comprised of two soldiers heading back to their home village for leave. All of the encounters were the same. Lane's guard would recite his passionless proclamation, and the listeners would react in turn. The Altanians would be concerned and alarmed, and the slaves would beam with hope and delight.

These encounters helped to break the monotony of the path and mark the day as they traveled. The journey was much quicker than the clandestine route they had taken to get to the Upper Mountains. Soon they left the desert and headed into the mountain pass that led down the Lower Mountains into the fertile plains of Deltonia.

The path turned behind a large stone cliff and revealed a deep, narrow canyon that cut into the rocky mountains. The desert came to an abrupt end and fell hundreds of feet straight down a sheer cliff wall forming one end of a narrow canyon. About a hundred feet below the desert floor, water gushed out of a cave in a ferocious roar of power. Its force caused the spout of water to run nearly horizontal for several feet before gravity pulled it down into a long, narrow waterfall that poured into the canyon floor below. At the base of the cliff, wedged at the bottom of the narrow canyon, the water met the ground in a billowy cloud of mist that shrouded the point of impact in mystery. Out of the base of the cloud a river rushed along the canyon floor and flowed around a bend.

"This is the headwater of our beloved river," Jethro explained to Lane. "Do you remember when I told you how Amo buried the river under the Waste as part of her curse? This is where it reemerges and fills the valley and the plain, then runs to meet the sea. It is our lifeblood. I never tire of seeing this blessed sight."

Lane was amazed at the reverence he heard in Jethro's normally skeptical voice. Jethro's awe was contagious, and Lane joined him in his adoration of the spectacular display of raw power. The driving sound of the rushing water and the smell of the mist rising from the canyon floor were intoxicating, and Lane felt that he could stand and stare at that sight forever.

"Well," Jethro snapped out of his reverie, "we have a long way to go before we get home, and I would like to get there before the evening fires are lit. Shall we?"

Lane agreed, and the march continued. The path followed the river as it cut through the mountains. It rose and fell in a smooth and steady pattern as it followed a natural ridge in the canyon wall. Soon the canyon opened up and revealed the sprawling Deltonian plain.

Vibrant greens shouted up at him from the fertile fields and forests below. The symphony of color was a loud and welcome contrast to the stark brownish red of the desert they had just left behind. The river rushed out of the mountain canyon with a bubbling fury but then widened and slowed into a lazy, life-giving, pastoral ribbon of blue that wound its way through the countryside and, in the far distance, emptied into the misty sea on the horizon.

They followed the path into the forest, where tall, leafy trees lined it on both sides. These trees were very different from those they had seen in the Altanian Mountains. Those were sparse and rugged mountain pines. Here, in the lush plains, the trees were rich with broad leaves that waved their fanfare as they passed.

Chapter 22

The path gently wound its way through the woods, following the course of the river. They passed several more groups of travelers along the way and exchanged the same mixed messages of warning, alarm, and hope.

Eventually they came to a large clearing. To the right ran the river. A rocky shore stretched from the edge of the water, flowing across the grassy plain and to the path.

The soldiers stopped and stared at the river. The leader looked at Lane, then back at the water with longing in his eyes.

"What," Lane said, "do you guys want to go for a swim?"

The soldier did not speak, but looked relieved at Lane's acute perception.

Lane looked over his shoulder to find Jethro's opinion. Jethro shrugged, "I suppose it would not be a problem. Perhaps they could wash the stench from their bodies."

"Yes," Lane said to the soldiers, "in a further demonstration of how different the Deltonians are from the Altanians, I will grant you this gracious gift. Go, but don't make me regret this."

Without hesitation the men moved toward the water's edge and found a place behind a row of trees that blocked them from view.

On the other side of the path was a large, open field. Several piles of stones lay around the field and formed a circle. They were strewn in a haphazard pattern and infested with tall weeds. A wide path, similar to the one they were traveling on, started at the other side of the circle, flowed north, and then disappeared into a patch of woods.

"What is this place, Jethro?" Lane asked.

Jethro stared at the grassy field and released a deep sigh. He seemed heavier on Lane's back.

"This is the old Festival Grounds. Before the Invasion, this was the crossroads of the tribes. The Bedites and Erles would come up the river and dock their boats there on the shore. The Gamordines would march down from the north on that path. The Altanians would come down the route we have been taking, and we would come up from the east on this same path.

"I was just a small boy then, but oh, Lane, you should have seen it. It was a glorious sight—definitely the highlight of everyone's year. Each tribe would come together with great pageantry and celebration. Their flags and colors flew high in the air. They would set up their tents on the outside of this field, and this whole plain would be transformed into a marvelous carnival full of music and dancing and food...and games. Yes, the games! There would be tests of strength, speed, and skill. They even had a portion of the contests just for the children. My favorite was when they would tie a ribbon around the body of a young boar and release it in the middle of the ring. All of us children, from every tribe, would swarm around that scared little creature and try to grab that ribbon from off of its back. Whoever was the lucky child was allowed to sit there, on the main platform, next to the master of the games, for the rest of that day. It was a great honor."

Jethro was no longer in this space and time. He had been transported to another time as he looked through the eyes of a child and relived a treasured memory. For that brief moment he seemed to be weightless on Lane's back. Lane tried to borrow Jethro's magical lenses and imagined what this place must have looked like during those days of old.

With a sniff, Jethro concluded, "Those days are gone." He melted into Lane's back and seemed to weigh even more than he had before. "Look at this place now. It is nothing more than a heap of rocks and a weed-infested field. During the Invasion the Altanians destroyed the Festival Grounds and moved them to their accursed mountain. Now, every year, the four defeated tribes meet here and march together in sorrow across the Waste and up the mountain to the stadium where we saw the Bellator. We do not bring our colors or our music. We bring only our pain, and our one poor soul who has been chosen to fight the Bellator. It is not a Festival anymore. It is more like a ritual sacrifice."

A choking sound came from Jethro's throat, and his body convulsed. This startled Lane, and he arched his neck around to get a look at Jethro's face.

"Are you OK?" Lane asked.

The pain in Jethro's eyes shot a wave of emotion through Lane's body. Lane tried to speak, but his voice caught in his throat. He wasn't sure exactly what triggered this display in Jethro, but the depth of his feeling was tangible, and Lane was caught up in its intensity.

Blinking away a tear that escaped his attempt to block it, Jethro was finally able to speak.

"Lane," he choked out, "do you know how many men I trained, only to send them to their deaths? I cannot even count them anymore. The Altanians would grab me and force me to watch as the Bellator ripped them apart, limb from limb."

Jethro howled this time. The pain of these accreted memories wrenched up from the depths of his bowels and released in a sound that chilled Lane and broke his heart. Lane's knees went weak, and he had to sit down in the grass beside the path.

The two of them sat next to each other and cried. Jethro's body heaved up and down in uncontrollable movements as the names and faces of those lost men marched across his memory.

After a while the tears dried up and the convulsions abated. Jethro, eyes clear and moist, looked up into Lane's eyes.

"Lane, this year will be different. This year we have you. I do not want to send you to that kind of fate. I do not know what I would do if I was forced to watch that happen to you as well."

He paused again and looked deeply at Lane. His oval pupils dilated to nearly full circles, giving them a more humanlike character. It was as if he was looking past the surface of Lane's eyes and searching deeper for something. This scrutiny made Lane a little uneasy, but somehow he knew this was a safe moment.

"Lane, you have to be the one. Whether you are the Pleroma or not, you have to be the one. You must defeat the Bellator. You must free my people. We must restore this field and bring things back to the way they were. Please be the Pleroma."

Now it was Lane's turn to be overwhelmed by emotion. He was transfixed on Jethro's gaze. It felt like Jethro was trying to pass something to Lane through that stare; trying to pass to him power, or strength, or confidence...or hope.

Lane fought through the fear and doubt that tried to capture his words and hide them from Jethro, and he was finally able to speak.

"I will, Jethro. You have my word. The Pleroma will appear on that day."

They stared at each other for another moment. A smile spread across Jethro's face. For a fleeting moment his face was no longer that of an old, weathered, and defeated warrior, but was instead the soft, hopeful face of a young child who watched the Festival on these grounds and basked in the glory of those peaceful times.

A scraping sound startled Lane and Jethro. The soldiers returned from the river. They had missed the displays of emotion. Lane realized that these emotions could be counterproductive to the façade they were displaying for the Altanians, so he flipped a switch in his mind and tried to become the mighty Pleroma once again. He reached down and flung his fierce warlord back over his shoulders, shouting at the guards.

"You've taken long enough with your foolishness. Let's get back on the path!"

The guards looked scared and slightly scolded as they stepped back in line on the path and began to march double-time toward Deltonia.

PLEROMA

Chapter 23

The Deltonian plain spread out before them like a patchwork quilt. The vast fields of green and yellow glowed with rich, warm tones in the golden light of the setting sun and opened their arms to welcome them home. The villages spread out amongst the fields and the patches of forest. Each village formed the familiar circle, surrounded by a ring of trees. They were all linked by paths to the central ring, where the Great Hall sat.

This was the first time Lane had seen Deltonia in the daylight. His heart warmed and beat a little faster as he watched the small figures moving through the fields toward the circular villages after a long day of work.

A dark thought invaded this beautiful scene.

This isn't real.

All of this—Jethro, the people, the village, the Pleroma, the Bellator—is a figment of my imagination. No.

The dark shadow-thoughts chilled him. His father. The bed. The accident. *Josh! I have to wake up.*

Lane's heart wrenched. Not only was he worried about Josh, but now he mourned the loss of the Deltonians. He felt accepted and part of this tribe. But they weren't real.

Lane stopped and looked back toward the west and the setting sun. The ragged line of the Lower Mountains was dark against the blaze of the Father's glory. Beyond that lay the Waste, the Upper Mountains, and the Bellator. Somehow he knew that the Bellator was his coma. He had to face it, and he had to win... for Josh.

He had to win for Josh and the Deltonians.

That's it! The connection snapped together in his mind. *The Deltonians are Josh.*

He faced the village again. He didn't have to feel sad that the Deltonians were not real. He just had to remember that they represented Josh. He was protecting them. With this realization, the bounce returned to his step and the dark cloud fell away. The golden sunlight penetrated his eyes once again, and he was caught up in the glory of this return after all.

Lane's caravan entered the village ring just as the people were returning from the fields. They dragged their tired bodies to the huts. The Switching Hour was nearly upon them.

The crowd stood in hushed suspense as they stared at Lane, Jethro on his back, and the four Altanian guards. Lane's band slowly moved to the center, next to the fire pit, and the guards stood back to back, facing out to the encircling crowd.

After a moment of tense silence, one guard shouted to the crowd, in his dead, robotic voice, "Behold, the Pleroma of the Deltonians. On the day of the Festival he will administer justice. Altania, beware."

With no expression or emotion, the guard said no more and stood like a stone statue, staring just above the crowd, avoiding eye contact.

The people stood in shock.

Lane sensed the confusion, so he carefully set Jethro on the edge of the fire ring to address the crowd. The Altanian guards who worked this village gathered around the outer edge of the circle like a pack of wild dogs getting ready to close in for the kill. He knew why they were there. The Switching Hour was about to begin. Lane was glad they were there. He stood up taller and loomed over the halfling crowd.

"Yes, my people. Your Pleroma has returned. I have been to the mountain. I have seen the Bellator. The Altanians have been warned. On the day of the Festival, we will be victorious and freedom will be ours."

The crowd went wild with hoots and shouts. They raised their hands and hugged each other. Some of the older women even broke into dance. They swarmed Lane and smothered him with hugs and adulation.

The Altanian guards looked like children who had been denied their dessert.

Lane pushed his way through the edge of the crowd of villagers and walked toward the group of guards. The ones who had been his traveling companions were now standing with the others. Lane stood in front of them, tall and heroic. With both hands outstretched in front of him he pointed at each guard. He took the time to stare each one of them in the eyes. One by one he worked his way down the line, blasting holes through the back of their heads with his stare.

"Tonight," he shouted with all the fury and power he could muster, "there will be no Switching Hour. There will never be another Switching Hour. In fact, there will be no more of you at all. In this moment, I will demonstrate the benevolence of the Deltonians one last time. I, the Pleroma, the mighty warrior of the Deltonian tribe, give you a choice. Either you leave this place right now and run back to your precious mountains, never to return…or," he paused to let the impact of his next words build strength, "I will tear your limbs from your body one by one in ways that would make your Bellator seem merciful."

With his last word he lunged toward them and snarled, trying to look as much like a crazed homicidal maniac as his smooth, teen-aged face would allow.

The soldiers scattered like cockroaches when the lights turn on. They tripped and clawed over one another to make sure they were not the last one in the ring. The group of them sprinted as one man out of the village circle, into the ring of trees, and toward their guard post.

As the clanging of their armor faded away, the village circle was left in silence. The villagers stared at Lane in wonder, speechless.

Lane gave a sheepish smile, all mock fierceness completely erased, and with his boyish demeanor, he extended his arms to the people.

"I'm home."

A sigh of relief swept over the crowd and they rushed in on

him once again. They swarmed him with a village-sized group hug. The children climbed on him like he was a tree. Soon he had two children on each shoulder, three hanging from each arm, and Trik perched right on top of his head.

Lane looked over at the fire ring and saw Jethro sitting on the rock.

"Hold on! Hold on, everybody," Lane shouted above the noise of the crowd. "We need help. Jethro is hurt."

He moved toward Jethro, peeling the children from his body. The medicine man came forward from the crowd.

"He broke his leg. I've been carrying him for the past two days."

Lane picked Jethro up and carried him to his hut. The crowd followed a few paces behind, visibly concerned for their friend. As Lane stooped to enter the hut, he stopped and called back to the people, "Ready the fire. I'll be out shortly. Jethro will be fine." With that he ducked into the hut.

The medicine man lit the lamps as Lane laid Jethro on his cot. The sun had set, and it was dark in the room. In the dim lamplight, Jethro's face looked tired. It had been a long and painful journey for him. Now the exhaustion of it overtook him, and he looked older than he had ever looked to Lane.

Jethro fought the exhaustion as his eyelids fluttered and tried to close. He struggled to keep them open long enough to look at Lane as he spoke.

"Lane," he said, his words slurred with fatigue, "you have done a great thing tonight. You have set my people free. Thank you…Pleroma."

His eyes shut, and Jethro lay motionless. Lane stared at him and fought back the lump that had risen in his throat. Jethro didn't move.

"Jethro?" He shook Jethro gently. No response. Lane shot a glance to the medicine man.

"Is he…" Lane couldn't bear to even think the word. *This can't be happening.*

Lane and the medicine man stared at Jethro's lifeless body.

Suddenly Jethro's chest swelled up and the most horrible

sound came out of him. The sheer volume of the noise made Lane jump. Slowly, as the sound resonated from Jethro and reverberated throughout the room, a grin spread across Lane's face. He recognized that sound. Jethro was snoring.

"Sleep well, my friend. You deserve it." Looking at the medicine man, Lane said, "Take good care of him. He's been through a lot."

The man smiled and nodded his head.

Lane got up from the bedside and walked to the door. With one last look back over his shoulder, he gave a knowing smile to Jethro and stepped out into the light of the blazing fire.

Chapter 24

From that day on the guards did not return. They had abandoned their guardhouse and fled for the mountains. The Deltonians were now free to live and move without the overbearing eye of the guards. For the first time, Lane was able to live with the Deltonians in the daylight.

Over the next two months, after the hilarity of the initial celebration died down, the village fell into a regular—and wonderful—routine of life. The people worked in the fields during the day. Only now they did it because they wanted to. Harvesting the nectar had always been part of their culture. Now they were able to regain the pride they had lost under the forceful hand of the Altanians. They also enjoyed the freedom to cultivate their other crops and ensure a proper harvest to feed themselves well during the lean months.

While they worked, Lane trained in the Great Hall. Jethro's leg was splinted, and he coached from the sidelines as he ran Lane through the paces of battle training. The children loved to snuggle next to Jethro, who was now a much more pleasant character, as they watched their champion train. They would "ooh" and "ahh" as Lane wielded his staff in an overly dramatic flourish of legs and arms. Lane loved entertaining them. In the evenings, the villagers transformed the training facility back into the Great Hall, and they feasted, and danced, and laughed. Gustov captivated the people with the stories of the tribe. When the firelight faded the most glorious thing of all would happen. The people would go to bed…and sleep through the night. No longer were they the split personalities that Lane had originally encountered. Once again they were the people of the sun. The Great Father had shined down upon them and blessed them with their champion. The Pleroma had come.

The Great Father began to grow old. His path across the sky was losing ground, and he was being pulled closer to the southern horizon, where he would eventually succumb to the powers of darkness and die. His light shone less each day, and the cold winds crept their way into the villages each evening. Fall was upon them.

One day, after a particularly invigorating workout, Lane returned to the village. Gustov stood outside the Great Hall and greeted him.

"Pleroma," Gustov said with a smile, and his eyes twinkled. Lane didn't mind being called Pleroma anymore. He had become accustomed to it. It felt especially good when he heard the title flow from Gustov's mouth. "May I join you along the path?"

"Of course, Gustov."

"Wonderful!"

Gustov fell in step beside his long-legged champion. Lane slowed his pace so that Gustov would not have to overexert himself just to keep up with him. Even with the slower pace, Gustov's cheeks flushed and his breathing became a little more deliberate as he walked with a quick, full stride. He tried to mask the exertion with his smile.

"Pleroma, as you know, the Festival is next week. Since the day you drove the guards out of our village, life has changed so dramatically. For the first time we have begun to feel like our old selves again. Most of our people have never known life without slavery. Only the oldest of us can remember the terrible days of the Invasion. We were only children then."

Gustov paused and began to trail off in his mind, back to those horrible memories. He caught himself and recovered quickly.

"Forgive me," Gustov continued, "that is not what I came to talk about. Since you drove out the guards, and we have been living in the light of the Father once again, we have been rediscovering our traditions.

"I have come to invite you to the council chambers this evening. We have a special session planned that I think you will enjoy. When you are ready, please come."

"That sounds great," Lane replied. "But I don't have anything to wear."

Gustov looked puzzled. "You have clothes on right now, Pleroma."

"It was a joke, Gustov. Don't you get it?"

Gustov's blank expression showed that he did not.

"Never mind. Of course I'll be there. Just give me a few minutes to get ready."

"Very well. The council will be ready. We will see you there."

The conversation carried them into the village ring. Lane peeled off to the left and went inside Jethro's hut to prepare himself for the meeting.

A little while later Lane arrived at the council chambers. Most of the villagers were gathered, filling the small room and spilling out the door. The warm faces and smiles of the people drew him into the room. His heart warmed as he entered.

"Ah, Pleroma," Gustov stood as Lane entered. Gustov was at his normal place at the council table, flanked by the other members. The sconces burned brightly on the wall behind them and sent shadows dancing through the room in a delightful celebration of Lane's arrival.

"Come in, come in."

Lane stood before the council. Children gathered around his legs. Trik tugged on his pant leg and begged with his big eyes. Lane picked him up and perched him on his shoulder. Trik beamed. The energy of the crowd in the room was tangible and excited Lane with anticipation. What was going on? Obviously everyone was in on it but him.

"Pleroma! Great people of Deltonia!" Gustov addressed the

crowd with his oratory voice, "we are gathered here this evening for a very special occasion. As you know, since that blessed day when our Pleroma drove away the Altanians, we have entered into a season of rebuilding and new visions. Our scholars have been studying our ancient texts and familiarizing themselves with the ways of our ancestors—the practices that we had not been able to follow under the occupation. We have made many wonderful discoveries, all of which will be revealed in due time.

"Tonight!" he thrust this word forward with special enthusiasm and a broad smile on his face, "Tonight, we will institute an especially wonderful tradition in honor of our Pleroma.

"In times past, on the eve of a great battle, it was a common tradition for the king to lead all the men of the village down to the woods along the shore, and..." Gustov paused for dramatic emphasis, "hunt the great boar!"

The crowd cheered with delight. The men clanged swords and tools on the floor, and the children giggled and danced around Lane's feet. Trik nearly fell from his perch, he was so excited.

Lane didn't know how to respond. To be honest, this was a little anticlimactic. They got all hyped up...to hunt a pig? First of all, he had never hunted anything in his life. He usually liked the idea that other people killed the animal, deep fried the meat, froze it, put it in a box and called it a TV dinner. Secondly, it was a pig. Couldn't it be the White Stag, or the elusive long-horned beast, or something really exciting like that?

The excited crowd didn't seem to notice Lane's ambivalence. Lane looked around at the people as they celebrated. Gustov, the leader who had believed in him since the moment they met in the field. Jethro, whose leg had healed nicely. He looked happy, no longer the skeptic who was so rough around the edges. He had truly become a friend. Then there were the children—his little fan club.

The enthusiasm was contagious. Lane couldn't help but put his anti-swine prejudices aside and get caught up in the excitement. He was going to hunt pig.

"This is a grand occasion," Gustov called out above the

noise. He gathered the crowd's attention once again. "I declare tomorrow to be a holiday. The warriors will travel together to set out on the King's Hunt, while the others prepare the Great Hall for the King's Feast on our return."

The crowd once again responded with cheers and exhilaration.

"Now, my friends," Gustov concluded, "go back to your huts and get some rest. Tomorrow will be a day we will not soon forget."

Everyone left the chamber and made their way back to the circle in a festive parade. Many gathered around the central fire to discuss what had happened, hanging on to the moment as long as they could. Slowly, one by one, everyone made their way to their own huts and the village became silent. Tomorrow would be a momentous day.

PLEROMA

Chapter 25

Pain again. Voices all around. A bright light seared through his closed eyelids. Beeping sounds. Metal clinking. Lane slowly opened his eyes, and the world seemed different. Everything was distorted, like he was looking through clear gel. Four bright white lights hung directly above his head, nearly blinding him. Their light obscured the rest of the room in total darkness. The beeping. The clinking. Where was he?

White. He was covered in white sheets. Four people approached him, two from either side. They materialized from the shadowy ring just outside the bright lights and approached his bedside in unison. They were tall. White masks. Safety goggles. Distorted. Fuzzy. Their forms swirled and oscillated. The one closest to his head held metal utensils. A knife and fork? No, smaller. A scalpel?

The one with the utensils stepped behind him, just outside his field of vision.

The beeping. The clinking. Now a voice. It was low and distorted.

"We will have to make the incision here, and then drill. Be sure he has enough anesthetic. Watch his vitals. Are you ready?"

All the white-masked heads bobbed in unison. Pain shot through the top of his head.

Lane sat up quickly and banged his head on the low ceiling of Jethro's hut. The bright lights were gone. Morning sunlight streamed through the windows and hung in the morning air. He spun around, panicked. Where were the masked people?

He could still hear the clinking. What was going on? His heart pounded and his head throbbed.

"You really banged your head. Are you all right?" Jethro's voice came from next to the small cupboard on the other side of the room. "Why did you sit up so fast? Did you have a night vision?"

A night vision. A dream. The details of Jethro's hut materialized before Lane's eyes, and the shadowy distorted images he had just experienced melted away like fog before the morning sun. That was it. He had been dreaming.

The clinking continued. It came from outside. Lane went to the window. The village circle was filled with people. Some wore armor—a breastplate here, a metal helmet there—none of them had a full set. Others of them wore only a loincloth, and their upper bodies were painted in bright colors. All of them carried some sort of weapon—a sword, a spear, a bow and arrows. Some sharpened their swords while others sparred with one another. Metal clashed against metal. Clink, clink.

Lane retreated from the window, still disoriented from his "night vision," and sat back on the bed.

"Lane, are you ready for the hunt?" Jethro inquired. "Almost everyone has gathered, and we are about ready to leave."

Jethro made his way to the door. He carried a long spear in his hand and wore a simple leather breastplate. He opened the door, then stopped and looked at Lane.

"I have something special for you. Do not be long." Then he left the hut.

Lane was alone with his thoughts. His head throbbed. It hadn't hurt this badly in a long time. *Wait a minute.* A burst of adrenaline shot through his system. *Maybe that wasn't a dream. Could it be? Did I just see a small glimpse of my reality? Did I wake up for a split second? Oh no. They're operating on me. This must be bad. I have to hold on. I have to fight. I have to protect the Deltonians...I mean Josh.*

He looked out the window at the beautiful morning sun. The sound of the warriors talking and laughing outside his hut filled him with a sense of familiar security. Children's laughter mingled with their voices like bubbles in soda, adding vitality to a heavy drink. How he had come to love these people.

A pang shot through his heart. *These people aren't real. But I love them so much.*

They are Josh, they are Josh. Lane repeated the mantra in his mind. *I have to keep focused. I must save them. I must seal their freedom by defeating the Bellator. I must wake up.*

His long body unfolded from the door of Jethro's tiny hut. The morning sun washed over his face and effectively counteracted the brisk fall morning air. Puffs of steam billowed from the mouths and nostrils of the crowd and caught the morning sunlight, like little spirits dancing around them, enticing them to the hunt.

All eyes fixed on Lane—eyes bright with excitement, and thirsty for adventure.

"Pleroma," Jethro greeted Lane in an especially robust voice, "you finally emerge."

He held a small bowl in his hand, filled with a blue, pasty substance.

"Come down here," Jethro instructed. "Come down to where I can see your face."

Lane got down on his knees and sat back on his heels, bringing him eye to eye with Jethro.

"Oh Great Father," Jethro stared into Lane's eyes, but was obviously not speaking to him. Was he praying? As he spoke he plunged his right thumb into the blue substance and spread it across Lane's face. First he made a swatch under his left eye, then under his right. Next he made a circle on his forehead with rays shooting out all around it, like a simple sun. With each new stroke he put the same stroke on himself, alternating back and forth between their two faces.

While he painted he said, "Great Father, prepare us this day for what we are about to do. Quicken our minds and senses. Strengthen our bodies. Give us fleet feet and sharp aim. In the forest there is a beast who is preparing himself as well. We thank you in advance for this beast. Go before us now and lead us on a fruitful hunt."

His timing was perfect, and he finished the last stroke as the final word faded from his lips. Jethro stopped and stared at Lane. His old, wrinkled eyes glistened with the moisture of a memory.

With a deep sigh of satisfaction, Jethro said, "I have not seen this ritual performed since I was a child. I watched my father perform this with my oldest brother when they set out on the hunt together.

"I never had children...," he paused to catch his emotion and keep it under control, "...the Altanians took my wife when we were only newly married. I have never known the joy of having children. I never thought that I would be given that privilege. Today, Lane, it is an honor to share this with you...my son."

Jethro grasped the back of Lane's neck and drew their foreheads together.

It had been so long since someone spoke to him like that. To have a man call him "son" and treat that word with such reverence. Words escaped him. He placed his hand on the back of Jethro's neck and pulled him closer.

The warriors encircled them and watched in reverent silence.

"Warriors of Deltonia!" Gustov's voice rang out from the central fire pit. He stood on the pit's stone wall and addressed the people. The hunting party gathered around him, bristling to begin. The rest of the village circled around the edge.

"On this day," Gustov continued, "we initiate the King's Hunt. We go together, as free Deltonians, into the forest to hunt the Great Boar, as did the kings of old. You have fasted; you have prepared your spirits, your minds, and your bodies. Now, are you ready?!"

They shouted and raised their weapons to the sky.

Not wanting to squelch the battle cry, Gustov motioned with his hand and shouted at the top of his lungs, "Let the hunt begin!" The volume increased and the mob of hunters moved out.

Lane stood in the middle of the wild pack. They hooted and hollered and brandished their weapons and flashed their painted bodies, calling out to the woods that they were coming. It was an exciting moment. Something like Lane had never experienced before.

They marched down the path that led to the Great Hall. This time, instead of going into the Hall, they marched past it to its far eastern side. Lane had never really paid attention to the circle where the Hall stood. It was surrounded by trees, just like the village. Paths radiated out in all directions like spokes shooting out from the hub of a wheel. The hunting party entered the circle from the western path, then marched out on the other side.

The path led through open fields, up and down hills, and through patches of woods. A large, bluish-gray wall rose up from the grassy field in front of them. The top of the wall was perfectly flat and ran at eye level to the left and right as far as the eye could see. There was something strange about this wall. Its texture seemed rough and uneven, moving somehow, as if it was alive. As they passed the trees and came closer to the wall, Lane noticed that its top stayed level with his eyes, but the grass along its foundation bounced up and down in sync with his steps.

He squinted and looked harder at this massive blue obstacle in front of them. Suddenly, a bird screamed across the surface of the wall. It was obviously a huge bird, yet it was tiny, like it was miles away. As Lane focused on this mystery, he stepped forward...onto nothing. For a split second his foot hung out over emptiness. He lurched back to counteract his forward momentum, arms flailing. Teetering over the edge of the precipice, the reality of what he saw flooded into his mind. This was not a wall at all. It was the ocean. A hundred feet below his extended foot, at the bottom of a rocky cliff, waves crashed against the rocks. The bird he had seen was far in the distance, flying above the surface of the water. The top of the wall was the horizon where the sea met the sky.

Lane stood on one foot, swinging his arms, trying to catch his balance. Suddenly he was pulled backwards and came crashing down on his rear. Three goat-eyed faces stared at him in amazement.

"Pleroma!" a painted woman said, "what were you doing?

If we had not grabbed you just then, you would have fallen and died."

"I don't know," he said between quick breaths, "I guess I just wasn't expecting it."

He paused and looked out over the vast ocean that roared below the cliff.

"It's funny how things can appear to be something completely different when you aren't expecting it to be what it really is," he said, shaking his head in embarrassment. "I'm not sure if that made any sense."

Grinning at his rescuers, he said, "Thanks, guys. I don't know what I would have done if you hadn't been there. I guess even the Pleroma needs saving once in a while, huh?"

He laughed and bounced back to his feet. He turned to face the stunned warriors.

Lane raised his hands above his hands like a gymnast after a dismount. "I'm fine. Just thought we needed a little entertainment before the big hunt, you know."

They laughed and the tension of the moment quickly faded.

"Now, Pleroma," Gustov spoke loudly for all to hear, "if you are through with our entertainment, we can begin the hunt."

Lane bowed and extended his hand to Gustov, "It's all yours, sir."

"Very well," Gustov continued. "You all know the members of your small hunting parties. We will spread out from here and enter the forest at different points up and down the cliffs. When the Great Father has nearly reached the edge of the sky we will regroup here and carry our trophies back to the village. Are you ready?"

They raised their weapons in silence. To raise a battle cry at this point would alert the animals that danger was near.

Everyone weaved in and out as they met up with the two or three others in their small band of hunters. One by one, the clusters separated evenly along the edge of the forest and disappeared into the shadows.

"Come, Lane," Jethro stepped up beside him, "I have the perfect spot for us. Today you and I will catch the prize."

PLEROMA

He led Lane into the wall of trees. Lane's heart beat faster as they passed out of the morning sunlight and into the shadowy canopy. Fallen twigs and leaves crunched under their feet. Birds sang back and forth to one another. The air seemed colder, heavier, and sweeter. It wrapped around their bodies, and whispered, "Welcome."

Jethro moved slowly and deliberately a few steps ahead of Lane, trying to make as little sound as possible. After a long period of walking and weaving through the web of trees and branches Jethro stopped and froze. He pointed to a small bush. Lane looked at it, then pantomimed to Jethro with an expression that said, "What are you talking about?"

Jethro mouthed the words silently, "the branch is broken."

Lane's expression said, "and this is important because...?"

Jethro shook his head and dropped the subject. His large, inexperienced partner had no clue about hunting.

They continued, more slowly now. Jethro hunched over and bent forward, listening intently. He stopped again, frozen, with one foot still in the air. A twig cracked just a few feet away from them, and Lane saw the branch of a bush swish in the air. Jethro's focus locked on to the moving branch.

Lane found himself hunched over and bending forward just like Jethro was doing. He didn't know why he was doing it, but it seemed like the right thing to do.

Jethro waited, motionless.

Suddenly, a grunty squeal came from behind the bush and a large mass darted away from them. Jethro's face lit up, and he burst forward in a full sprint, high-stepping through the undergrowth.

Lane fell into step behind his short-legged friend and trotted along. The large object shot out from behind a bush and into a small clearing. Ugly. Ugly and big. The creature ran on four legs, and its shoulders were as tall as Jethro. It looked like a large, muscular pig with long hair, a curly tail, and long, sharp tusks jutting up and out from either side of its lower jaw.

It shifted left. Jethro ran and motioned wildly for Lane to pursue. Lane made a hard turn to the left and ran on a parallel course with the boar. His long legs were the advantage they needed. He was able to run past the boar and veer to the right, cutting off its angle.

The boar grunted in fear and disgust when it realized Lane had impeded its escape. It doubled back to run away from Lane but was surprised and very irritated to find Jethro closing in from the other direction. It cut a hard left and bolted at full speed. The muscled flank opened directly in front of Jethro. Without missing a stride Jethro lifted his spear above his head and thrust it forward, toward the beast. The shaft flew through the air and found its mark. As the metal point sunk deep into the beast's heart, the boar let out a wild screech, took two more steps, and then dropped in its tracks, dead.

Jethro's momentum brought him to the fallen beast. He breathed wildly and looked up at Lane with wide eyes.

"Well done, Lane, well done. That was exactly what I hoped would happen. Without the advantage of your long strides we would have had to pursue the beast all afternoon. Ha, ha!"

Lane was excited to see Jethro so happy. By the time Lane reached the hunter and his kill, Jethro had already taken out his knife and begun to disembowel the creature. Lane looked down just as the abdomen split wide open and the entrails burst out onto the ground in a flood of blood and fluid. Lane wasn't prepared for that sight, and his stomach instantly convulsed. He gagged and reeled back, staggering backward and bumping into a tree trunk.

"What is the matter, Lane? Have you never cleaned an animal before?"

"Cleaned an animal? Well sure, I gave the neighbor lady's dog a bath once. That's cleaning. What you're doing is…is…disgusting."

Lane slid his back down the tree trunk and sat on the ground, head between his legs.

Jethro chuckled and continued his work. After he had gutted the animal and cleaned his hands with some leaves, he walked away, searching the ground. He was not gone too long before he returned with a long, thick branch dragging behind him. He laid the branch along the boar and then pulled some rope out of the pouch at his waist. Soon the boar's feet were tied onto the pole.

"There," he announced with great pride in his accomplishment, "it is ready to take back."

Jethro looked up at Lane who was still battling the churning in his stomach.

"Lane, are you ready to be a hero?"

"Huh?"

"When we march this beast back to the camp we will be heroes. Everyone will want to hear our tale of how we chased down the Great Boar. It will be glorious to stand at the King's Feast and spin this tale. Can you not see it now?"

Lane had to admit, that did sound fun. The thoughts of glory and hero status at the King's feast helped to settle his stomach. He was able to stand and join Jethro.

"Now, just pick up that side of the branch."

The branch extended a few feet on either side of where the boar's feet were tied. Jethro stood at one end and Lane at the other. They each lifted their end at the same time. Jethro strained to hoist his end up to his shoulder. The boar's head barely cleared the ground. Lane had to hold the branch at his waist in order to keep it level.

The two victorious hunters carried their trophy back to the rendezvous point, picking their way through the branches and the undergrowth. Soon they stepped out from the edge of the forest and were back on the grassy field that lined the top of the cliff. They walked along the rim toward the mouth of the path as the sea breeze blew through their hair. Some large gulls circled around them, calling out with loud squawks, heralding the heroes as they returned from victory.

They were the first to return to the rendezvous point. A little outcropping of rocks along the edge of the cliff made a perfect perch for their mounted boar. They hung the beast on the rocks and found a nice patch of tall, green grass in which to sit down. Side by side, they lay on the grass and stared up into the blue sky, breathing in the deep satisfaction of a successful hunt and of being the first to claim a prize. With a sense of serenity they both drifted into a well-deserved nap.

Voices in the distance woke them. The sound of laughing and singing carried over the breezes from both directions along the forest edge. The Great Father was quickly making his descent toward the western horizon, and it was time for everyone to report back. Hunting parties arrived one by one. Some carried long poles with beasts slung beneath and beamed with the glory of victory. Other parties walked with shoulders slouched, carrying the disappointment that they would not have a tale to tell at the Feast that night.

 Soon everyone had returned. After much congratulation and exchange of stories, the party was ready to march back to the village. They formed a glorious parade. Everyone agreed that Jethro and Lane should lead the procession and be the first to announce the great victory to the village. They marched along the path with chests puffed out, full of pride and excitement.

 The anticipation of the Feast shortened the distance between the cliff's edge and the village. They all spoke of how wonderful it would be to see the children run to greet them and to hear the cheers of the villagers as they entered the circle.

 Finally, they approached the village. No children came. Odd. They moved closer and stepped on to the outer edge of the circle. A strange feeling swept over the parade. Instantly they all felt it. Quiet. It was too quiet. Dread flushed over them and no one knew exactly why.

 Lane and Jethro were the first to enter the circle. The silence was broken with a high pitched sound. It was not the cheering they had expected. Was it a bird calling out to them? No. It was… the sound of wailing. Another sound joined it. Crying, sobbing. As they moved into the village circle they saw a group of people gathered around the fire pit. Some were on their hands and knees, rocking back and forth. Others embraced one another, their backs heaving up and down. Others just stood, staring toward the eastern rim of the village.

 One of them noticed the hunting parade enter the village. It was Nalin, one of the matriarchs. Upon seeing Jethro and Lane

PLEROMA

her face contorted in pain, and she let out a wail that chilled Lane's blood. Her hands flew out toward them and she rushed to Jethro. She was sobbing and unable to speak.

"Nalin," Jethro grabbed her shoulders and tried to calm the hysterical woman. "What is happening? Why is everyone wailing?"

It took several moments for Nalin to calm down enough to speak. Through tears that streamed down her face, trembling, she said two words that darkened the skies, "the children."

Lane's heart jumped into his throat, and a deep sense of foreboding crawled up his back. His mind whirled as he listened to Nalin's tale.

"This evening," Nalin continued, between gasps for air, "after we had finished preparing to receive your trophies, we all gathered in the circle to play games with the children..." She paused and seemed like she couldn't breathe.

"Go on, Nalin," Jethro prodded.

"The guards, Jethro. The guards returned. There were more of them than I had ever seen. They rushed in on us from every side of the village. Without notice they surrounded us. We were helpless."

She stopped again and started weeping, burying her face in Jethro's chest. Jethro patted her back, then gently, but firmly urged her to continue. "What happened, Nalin?"

Forcing the words out of her mouth, she said, "They...took...the...children. Before we knew what was happening they had gathered all the children, put nooses around their necks, bound their hands together, and tied them in a train. Oh Jethro, they marched our babies out of the village like they were animals!"

Jethro's eyes blazed. His nostrils flared and his chest heaved. By this point all the hunters had abandoned their meaningless trophies along the edge of the circle and gathered around Nalin. The consoled one another as they all stood in stunned silence and waited to hear the rest of the story.

Nalin stopped and looked up at Lane. Her face was sunken and grave.

"Pleroma," she said, staring intensely at him. Lane wasn't sure if she was accusing or pleading. "They gave me a message to give to you. They said that they know you. Your presence here has shifted the balance of power. You are a threat to them. They have taken the children to ensure that you will do what you have said. On the day of the Festival, you must fight the Bellator, as planned, or they will kill the children." With those last words she fell apart in Jethro's embrace.

Lane stumbled backwards in shock. He had to sit on the rock next to the fire pit. Trik. Tora. The children were gone. Their lives were in his hands. What could this mean? His head began pounding. Pain and confusion swarmed in his brain like a flurry of hornets. What was he going to do?

"We have to go after them. They can't have gotten far!" a young man called out from the back of the crowd. Several voices agreed.

"No!" Nalin shouted. "They said that if we tried to follow them they would kill the children before we reached them on the path." A gasp rippled through the crowd as their rising plans deflated. "We must follow through with the Festival if we have any hope of saving the children," Nalin collapsed once again with the weight of the terrible message she was forced to deliver to her people.

Gustov paced back and forth through the crowd of bewildered villagers. He scanned up and down the scene and rubbed his face. On the edge of the circle several boar carcasses lay in the dirt. Gustov stared at the boars, and then looked back at his people. His eyes filled with pain. Slowly he looked to the west, where the Great Father dipped below the horizon and the afterglow of his daily glory burned orange in the sky. Darkness was setting in once again.

"My friends," Gustov addressed the crowd, "this is a grave situation. We have much to do. At this point we have two choices. We can either sit here and stew in our misery and worry about the children—this option will not get us anywhere, it will not bring the children back. Or, we could focus our energy toward preparing for the Festival. We must ready ourselves.

"Tonight was supposed to be the King's Feast. We were going to prepare the boars and dance and sing while we told the tales of the hunt and prepared ourselves for the march to the Festival tomorrow. This turn of events must not dissuade us from the feast."

The people reacted in shock to Gustov's suggestion.

"Calm yourselves," he continued, "these boars will spoil if we do not prepare them now. We have a long journey tomorrow and we need our strength. We will not celebrate the King's Feast. Instead, we must gather together in vigil to prepare our hearts and minds for the Festival and to lift up the Pleroma before the Great Father. He is our only hope.

"Come, let us get to work...together."

The people stared at him with blank eyes, frozen with shock and indecision.

Jethro shot a glance to Lane from across the circle. With a quick flip of his head he motioned to Lane towards the boars. Lane understood and jumped to his feet.

"Yes," Lane said to the crowd. "Gustov is right. We must prepare. Tonight is our last night together before the Festival. Come!"

He moved toward the boars and met Jethro at the one they had carried into the village. They each took one end of the pole, hoisted the beast off the ground, and then marched their game toward the Great Hall.

Slowly, the people brought their animals to the Hall. Soon they all slipped into preparation mode. They did not regain a sense of festive joy, but the mood of the villagers improved greatly as they busied their hands with preparation for the meal.

The Hall was filled with the smells of roasted meat, boiled vegetables, sweet cakes, and nectar. Musicians found appropriate music and washed the souls of the people with ballads that recounted great deeds of old and conjured up memories of past victories.

The council sat on the platform with Lane in the center. They ate in relative silence, with only the soft sounds of music and clinking of dishes. It was a hollow silence. Something was missing. There were no children.

When everyone had finished eating, Gustov stood at the edge

of the platform, directly in front of Lane, and faced the people.

"It is with a heavy heart that we gather tonight. A terrible violation has been wrought against us today. As we all ate in silence a thought occurred to me. I was wrestling with the Great Father, asking how he could let something so terrible happen on the eve of our greatest victory. Then it hit me. I am actually grateful that this happened."

The people were visibly shocked by Gustov's statement.

"Let me explain. For several weeks now, we have enjoyed a freedom that we have not known in ages, thanks to our Pleroma and his boldness." Gustov turned around and extended his hand to Lane in recognition. Lane blushed.

"This freedom, however," Gustov continued, "has been artificial and premature. We have always known that the only way we can be truly free is if the Bellator is defeated at the Festival. Only then will the balance of power be restored to the tribes, so that we will be able to live in true freedom once again.

"During these weeks of false freedom, I believe we have grown lax in our focus on the real issue. The Altanians do not realize this, but by stealing our children and holding them captive they have done us a great service. By taking them they have shown us two things. First, they have reminded us of our slavery and oppression. They have brought to the forefront of our memory the bitterness of the forced labor that we have endured throughout this generation. Secondly, they have betrayed themselves and demonstrated that, in truth, they are weak. They are afraid of the Pleroma. They have seen that the gods have shifted their favor, and the age of the Altanians is coming to an end. Only a desperate people would do such a cowardly thing as taking innocent children captive. Their only hope for maintaining power is if the Bellator can defeat our Pleroma."

Gustov stepped to the side to reveal their great hero.

"You, Pleroma," Gustov looked intently at Lane, "are our true hope. Tomorrow we will march in victory toward the Upper Mountains. You will lead us into a new era. May the Great Father shine upon you and fill you with power as you take us to victory and to freedom."

PLEROMA

The crowd rose to its feet and roared with applause. Gustov motioned for Lane to come forward and to get on his knees. Sitting on his heels, Lane was the same height as the council members. They encircled Lane and began chanting. Lane didn't know the words they spoke, but he guessed their meaning.

As they circled around him, Lane projected his vision into the coming days. Soon he would be standing in the arena to face the Bellator. He still didn't know how he was going to defeat him. He could see the faces of the people from all the tribes staring at him, eyes full of hope. He could see the children, staring out from behind the bars of a cage, begging him to set them free. It was all too much. Why couldn't he just wake up right now? Or, perhaps better, why couldn't he just never wake up? Either way, all of this would go away. His head pounded, and the circling elders made him dizzy. Lane's heart thumped in his chest, and his throat was getting dry.

Then his vision changed. The children trapped in the cage came to the forefront. Trik reached out to him through the iron bars. His huge eyes, filled with terror, pierced Lane's heart. For a split second his little face blurred, then it swirled and changed. Now it was the face of Josh. Josh's big, blue eyes stared at Lane from behind the bars. Josh just stood there, grasping the bars on each side of his head, looking deeply and longingly at Lane, eyes full of sadness and pain.

The vision changed again, and the caged children pulled quickly away as an ominous shadow fell across them. A bulky shape filled Lane's field of vision. The Bellator. Now the monster's disfigured face was all Lane could see. His red eyes fixed on Lane and burned into him. Anger and violence seethed from the Bellator. No words were spoken, but Lane's mind flooded with dread and the impression of a single syllable…death.

"Lane! Pleroma!" Jethro's voice shattered the vision. "Lane, are you all right?" Jethro grasped Lane's shoulders and stood before him.

Everyone gathered around Lane, looking on with concerned and questioning expressions.

Lane shook his head to gather his senses.

"Lane, can you hear me? It was like you were in a trance."

He realized that that the vision had removed him from the moment. Now the faces that stared at him were real. They were present. They were looking to him for answers…and for hope.

He quickly gathered his wits, rose to his feet, and addressed the crowd. The last thing they needed right now was to know the truth of his vision.

"My people," he said to the group, "I have received a vision." He paused and carefully weighed the next words. Which was more important right now, truth or hope?

"Victory! Tomorrow we march to victory." He held up his hands in the air, and the people went wild with applause. Hope had won the day.

Chapter 26

The morning chorus of birdsong finally arrived. Lane hadn't slept at all. At the first sight of pale gray light in the window, he was up and out of the hut. Apparently he was not the only one who couldn't sleep. Half the village was already up and moving.

The cold, crisp autumn air quickened Lane's mind and body. There was very little talking in the circle. The people busied themselves with preparations for their annual journey into the mountains. The silence was odd and disturbing. No sounds of children. No laughs and giggles. No padding and scuffling of little feet. Even incessant crying would have been welcome right now. Instead, there was only the sound of men and women cinching leather straps around packages and loading supplies onto wagons.

Soon everyone was up and loaded for the trip. Lane noticed something different about them. They seemed more serious, more regal than he had yet seen them. Some wore brightly colored shawls around their shoulders. Some had feathers in their hair. Others had multicolored paint on their face. Toward the front of the group a few people carried long poles flying colorful banners that bore the symbol of the Great Father, a simple circle surrounded by radiating lines. Intense determination filled the air.

Without a word, everyone fell into line. Gustov stood at the front, next to Jethro, and motioned for Lane to join them. He led the procession out of the village circle toward the Great Hall. Similar processions flooded in from all the surrounding villages. Hundreds of Deltonians now filled the circle, each carrying banners that marked their own village as unique from the others but united under the banner of the sun.

Once the circle was completely filled with villagers, Gustov climbed onto a platform at the edge. The usual mischievous twinkle was absent from his eyes as he addressed the crowd.

"This morning we begin what will be one of the most important marches of our people's history. Each step that we take along this path will lead us closer to our new dawn of freedom and prosperity. A heavy and dark cloud hangs over this march as we feel the loss of our children and pray for their safety.

"My friends, I urge you to use this journey to prepare your hearts. We will be entering the land of our oppressors. Year after year we have made this journey, and each time it has felt to us like a funeral march as we took one of our own and sacrificed him to the Bellator. This year it is different. This year we do not march to certain doom. In spite of the dread we feel for our children, let us not forget who goes before us! This year we march behind our champion. This year the prophecy is fulfilled. This year we have the Pleroma!

"My people, reach deep inside yourselves, right now. Find the last ounce of joy and hope that you have and bring it forth. I urge you to throw your joy and hope up into the air as we march along this path. Send your praises and song to the Great Father as he passes over us and makes his journey behind those cursed mountains. Give him our songs and praise to carry with him and deliver to our enemies a message that reminds them of their doom. We will not be discouraged or dissuaded from our hope."

He smiled, and the twinkle returned.

"Come with me now. March with me in song. Let me hear the drummers drum and the minstrels play. Let us sing the songs of our people as we go. Let us hear the praises to the Great Father and encouragement to the Pleroma. Come, let us go!"

Small sparks flickered through the crowd. One by one, their icy stares melted as a small glimmer of hope was fanned into a flame by their leader's inspiring oration.

The drummers were the first to dislodge the procession from

its parking space. Their rhythmic beat was joined by lofty pipe tones that propelled the crowd forward.

As they marched, the elders of each village took turns leading the people in songs. Most of the songs recounted ancient stories of triumph or lessons learned by those who had gone before them. Some were lighthearted tunes with a quick tempo that livened up the pace of the procession. Others were dramatic and intense, instilling a sense of determination. Lane did not recognize the people or the stories that most of the songs referenced, but the spirit was contagious.

They left the last ring of villages and fell into stride along the Main Trade Route. It rolled along the hills, sometimes flanked by wide-open fields, newly harvested, and at other times cutting a swath through a patch of forest. Eventually they came to the old Festival Grounds.

Even from a long distance away it was evident that a great number of people were gathered there. Many multicolored banners flourished above the swarming mass of people.

"Lane," Jethro said, "do you see it?"

"See what?"

"That!" Jethro pointed toward the quickly approaching mass of people.

"Sure, I see a bunch of people waving banners just like we're doing."

"Yes, but do you not know what this means?" Jethro was a small boy again, looking through eyes of wonder. "The people are displaying their colors. This has not happened for ages. It usually feels like a funeral procession."

Jethro's pace quickened as they came closer to the people.

"Look at these colors. There are the Bedites. Over there are the many colors of the Erle villages. Oh, look," he was very excited now, almost skipping as he surveyed the throngs of people, "the Gamordines are just arriving." He pointed to the path that led from the north.

Many of the tribes and clans had already encamped around the ruins; they appeared to have been there for a while. Others were just arriving. A fleet of boats pulled up to the river's edge carrying the blue-skinned Bedites.

The Deltonians were almost upon them. The other tribes faced them. Lane noticed that they were not just looking at the Deltonians, they were looking at him. Two people stepped out from the masses and walked up to Lane, Gustov, and Jethro. The man on the left was a Bedite, there was no mistaking that. His dark hair was interwoven with colorful feathers, and an elaborate beaded necklace hung over his brightly painted torso. A woman stood next to him. She looked very similar to the Deltonians, except for her clothing. It was made from a rough, burlap-type cloth that hung stiffly from her shoulders.

Jethro leaned over to Lane, "She is an Erle."

"Ah," Lane nodded in appreciation.

The Gamordine procession marched into the ruins, and one man stepped forward to join the other two in front of Lane. He was a Gamordine warrior. A dark, dense beard framed his pale face, and his thick, broad shoulders were draped with fur.

The mass of people encircled the six figures. Everyone jockeyed for position to get a good view.

The Erle spoke first. "Welcome, my brothers." With arms outstretched toward Lane, she said, "Welcome Pleroma of the Deltonians. We have been awaiting this day for many weeks now."

Gustov blew out his cheeks in amazement. "I am overwhelmed, Oliphar," Gustov presumed to speak in place of Lane, "What has happened here? How is it that everyone is dressed in full Festival regalia?"

"Word spreads quickly," the Bedite spoke, now addressing Lane directly. "Pleroma." He bowed his head to Lane, "As you came down from the mountains, you encountered many people along the way. When our people returned from their delivery and told us a tale of a giant who had told them of a day of justice coming to the Altanians, we were overwhelmed. We did not believe them at first, but the tale intrigued and inspired us. The idea that there was another giant among us, like the Bellator, ignited something that had not been present for a very long time. Our elders began to search the ancient texts, and in the

PLEROMA

secret of the night we began to retell the tales of old."

"Yes," a robust voice from the Gamordines interjected, "it was the same for our people. When the news reached us in the north we, too, began to look into these things. We discovered a prophecy that there would be another that would come and deliver us from the Bellator."

The Erle continued, "It is apparent that a similar thing has happened in each of the tribes. When the news spread that the Pleroma had driven the guards out of Deltonia, our spark of hope was fanned into a full flame of passion. We rose up against our guards and drove them out ourselves."

"That explains why the guards suddenly left our villages," the Gamordine interjected.

"And ours." The Bedite beamed with the realization.

Oliphar continued, "You have brought us victory, Pleroma. We have spent the last few weeks preparing ourselves to march up to the Altanians and claim our independence once again. No more will we sacrifice our warriors to the goddess. We have all converged here to march behind you to proclaim our victory to the Altanians!"

Gustov's face fell as he listened to Oliphar's bold proclamation.

"What is it, Gustov? What is wrong?" Oliphar asked.

"Then you have not heard," Gustov spoke slowly. The excitement in the crowd settled and a hush rippled from the inner ring outward.

"Of course you have not heard. It only happened yesterday. I am afraid your celebration of victory is premature, my friend. The Altanians must have sensed the insurgence building among all the tribes and became desperate. They came yesterday, while our warriors were off on a hunt, and stole our children. They told us that if we do not follow the rules of the Festival and present the Pleroma to the Bellator, as planned, then they will kill the children."

The three tribal leaders lowered their eyes to the ground. Their chests heaved.

"This is a tragic turn of events," the Bedite said. His nostrils flared, and the muscles in his jaw and temple bulged.

"It is not surprising, though," the Gamordine added. "The Altanians have known power by intimidation for so long. They have much to lose. With the Pleroma attending the Festival this year, they stand to lose everything that they have gained during the era of the Bellator. A people in that position are desperate enough to do whatever it takes to preserve their way of life."

There was a long, haunting silence. The birds in the nearby trees sang a chilling melody, calling back and forth across the clearing, "The children, lost are the children...save the children."

Gustov broke the silence.

"My friends, look around you. Do you not see the amazing things that are happening today? How long has it been since the tribes have gathered in this sacred place, flying our banners proudly, without the Altanian guards lording it over us? How long has it been since our four tribal leaders stood face-to-face and openly discussed the affairs of the world?

"This is not a time to feel defeated. This is not a time to allow a bully to strongarm us into submission. That is exactly what they want us to do. Yet, that is exactly what our children need us *not* to do.

"It is a time like this that we must unite. We must come together as a family of tribes and march up the mountains in strength. The Great Father has given us the Pleroma. He will deliver us. We must have faith. Now is the time for courage. Let us come together and march to our freedom, once and for all!"

Gustov's words worked their magic on the crowd. As in a body that had been resuscitated, a breath of hope filled the crowd once again. Banners thrust into the air, and the colors of all the tribes danced and flapped in the breeze. Cheers rose to the heavens and music flowed from the minstrels.

"We will follow you as the Pleroma leads us to victory," Oliphar said. She stepped to the side of the road and motioned with her hands for the Deltonian tribe to proceed. Quickly the mass of people parted along the path and made room for Gustov, Lane, Jethro, and the Deltonian tribe to lead the way.

Over the course of the next two days the tribes marched toward the Upper Mountains. They crossed over the plains of Deltonia, up and down the rolling hills, through open fields, and through forests ablaze with colorful leaves. They wove their way up the Lower Mountains, along the edge of the deep canyon that cut its way through the rocky mountain cliffs.

By nightfall they reached the edge of the Waste and made camp. As the majority of the people slept, some priests performed a night vigil to ward off the skuli and to ensure a clear passage through the accursed Waste.

As the first light of the Great Father's face kissed the sleeping tribes, the people began to stir. Soon they had breakfasted and were underway on their journey across the Waste. The long purple shadows stretched out in front of them, angling to the north into the barren plains of the desert. The shrinking shadows marked the time as they walked. The tribes took turns leading in song as they marched, each offering their own unique style to the procession.

The Great Father descended toward the top of the Upper Mountains as the procession approached the gate village of the Altanians.

Gustov stopped to confer with the other leaders. "We must be cautious at this point," he warned. "Anything could happen when we enter the village. This is where they place most of their guards."

The leaders agreed, and the procession moved cautiously, yet courageously toward it. What they found surprised them. Nothing. No one. The village was deserted. A small creature scurried across the road, fleeing from the intruding throng of people. A few birds called back and forth to announce their entry, but other than that there was not a sound in the village.

"Where are the Altanians?" the Gamordine spoke the obvious question.

"I smell fear in these mountains," answered the Bedite leader. "The Altanians have retreated from us."

With an apparently clear passage ahead of them, the long ribbon of people wove its way through the village and made the ascent up the mountainside. Each bend of the forested path took them higher, and revealed the repeated scene. Empty villages. There was not an Altanian to be found on the mountain path. The tribal leaders pressed on, each trying to suppress their increasing agitation.

Lane was the first to step around the final bend in the path. The other leaders were quick to follow. All of their fears culminated in that moment. A throaty gasp escaped from the Gamordine's mouth before he could suppress his emotions.

"Great Father!" someone breathed both an exclamation and a stifled prayer.

The sheer cliff loomed above them, riddled with cracks and streaked with bloody stains spilling down the face of its profane altar. At the base, spilling out and filling the valley, swarmed a mass of Altanians. Hundreds of men, women, and children filled the streets, sat on the roofs of the huts, and hung from trees to get a view of the incoming parade. A wall of guards stood in front of them. They spanned the road, standing shoulder-to-shoulder, four soldiers deep.

Lane stepped toward the guards, but Gustov and the other leaders stood frozen before the regiment. Lane turned to see why they hadn't moved and Gustov's expression told all. Fear. Intimidation.

Lane turned back and stepped in front of the four tribal leaders. Now he stood, a giant in a sea of halflings, and filled the gap between the oppressor and the oppressed.

For an intense moment Lane wrestled with fear. A voice told him that he was not strong enough for this. He needed to hide, to run away. Then another voice shouted louder in his mind. *They need you. This is your time to stand.*

The voices went silent. Lane stood tall and leaned forward, towering over the ranks of soldiers. The soldiers wilted.

"Altanians," Lane addressed the crowd in as dramatic and powerful voice as he could muster. "Do you dare to greet us with a posture of strength?" With this he lurched forward, and the already frightened soldiers broke ranks and stumbled backwards. The bumbling antics of the soldiers sent a wave of muffled laughter through the procession behind him.

"I have been gracious to you once by sparing your lives. I promised to you that I would return on the day of the Festival. How did you return my favor? When offered peace and grace, you returned it with treachery and cowardice. You have taken our children in a display of weakness and fear.

"Enough of this foolishness. Stand down from your empty posturing and allow us to pass. I demand to speak to the high priest himself!"

Lane's speech hit its mark, and the ranks of soldiers split down the middle and shuffled to the sides of the road like the doors of a large gate swinging open in front of them. The rest of the Altanians smashed along the side of the road and allowed Lane to lead his procession through the village and to the base of the cliff. The Altanians stared up at him with a mixture of fear and awe.

With no further hindrance, Lane led the procession up the narrow staircase that wound its way back and forth up the steep cliff toward the summit. Toward the top they encountered the stacked, stone buildings of the monastery. In order to ascend to the next row of buildings they had to climb the wooden ladders, one person at a time. Lane went first, and, one by one, the long parade of tribes inched their way up through the monastic village and to the plain of Amo at the summit.

The process took hours. Slowly the tribes trickled into the plain and surrounded the temple. The Deltonians, the Erles, the Gamordines, the Bedites, and the Altanians dispersed evenly around the temple and made camp. Thousands of small bodies crammed into the small acreage.

While the people were making camp, Lane and the tribal leaders went straight to the entrance of the temple. Two guards met them and stood as tall as they could in front of the gate.

"Stop trying to look strong!" Lane yelled at them. Their faces could not hide the shock. "Fetch the high priest for me at once, or I'll rip the doors off and get him myself."

The guards, still in shock, looked at each other, wondering what to do, and then quickly complied with Lane's wishes and vanished inside the gateway.

Jethro raised his eyebrows and gave Lane a nod. "I have never seen anyone treat the guards like that. I like it."

After a few minutes of waiting, the two guards reappeared from within the shadows of the gate.

"Come with us," one guard said. "The high priest will see you now."

Lane, Jethro, and the four tribal leaders followed the guards through the gate. It stood at the entrance to a long, wide hallway. At the other end of the hallway stood a large archway that opened up to the arena. The guards walked halfway down the hall and then stopped at a door in the right wall. They opened the door and motioned for the party to follow them in. It opened to a small, stone room, just big enough for the door to open, nothing more than a landing for a flight of stairs.

Lane had to bend over to enter the room, and the stairs were almost too small for him to walk on. Being inside this tiny stairwell reminded him of just how large he must seem to these people. He was a giant, and with each rising step his confidence increased.

At the top of the stairs, the guards led them through a door that opened into the side of a cavernous room. Lane immediately recognized it as the tower in which he had seen the vision of Amo. From their vantage point they could look out into the empty arena. A figure stood on the edge of the open wall, staring out across the empty battleground with his back to the newly arrived party. He wore a robe made of white fur. Long, white hair fell halfway down his back.

The guards motioned to Lane that he was free to approach. As he drew closer, the solitary figure moved.

His eyes were the first thing that Lane noticed. They burned bright yellow, slashed open across the middle with the distinctive horizontal pupil. Something about them was different. Deeper. Haunting. Knowing. Their flames burned holes in Lane's mind.

Even though Lane was twice the height of the high priest, he felt dwarfed and intimidated by this presence.

"The Great Pleroma," the priest spoke with icy articulation,

PLEROMA

"it is good to meet you. I must admit, you have given my people quite a scare. Very impressive."

"Where are the children?" Lane asked.

"Oh, yes. The children." The priest turned away from Lane and looked out over the empty arena once again. "They are safe and well-fed, if that is what concerns you. We do not plan to harm them. After all, we need the next generation to be strong workers for our fields. It would be shortsighted to harm them." He paused, then turned and looked directly at Lane. "Of course, much of that depends upon you, Pleroma. You must keep your end of the arrangement. You must face the Bellator, alone. And unarmed."

"Unarmed?" Gustov protested. "This is highly unusual."

"Well," the high priest said, "the wise Gustov has found courage to speak, has he? How wonderful. Are you displeased by the rules of the Festival this year, Gustov?"

The priest leaned in to his last words and locked his gaze on Gustov.

"No. No, of course not." Gustov melted.

"Well," the priest continued, "now that we are all clear on that, where was I? Ah yes, Pleroma, once the battle is over, the children will be released. One way or the other."

The priest paused. His eyes flashed again and he regained his hold on Lane. Icy fingers wrapped around the back of Lane's thoughts. It was unclear whether the next words that entered his mind were spoken and entered through his ears or thought and entered directly into his mind.

"I hope you are ready."

A cold sensation spilled out from his scalp, ran down his back, trickled down his arms, and sizzled with frost around his legs. A wide, sinister smile spread across the high priest's face.

Suddenly, with a quick spin, the high priest broke the connection and turned away.

"Guards, lead them away!"

Nothing more was spoken. The guards led them back the way they had come in. Down the stairs, out the wide hallway, through the large gate, and back out onto the open plain.

The scene outside the temple was fuzzy. The Great Father had just dipped below the farthest mountain on the western horizon. Fires now glowed in the camps that cluttered the open plain. The burning eyes of the high priest stayed superimposed over Lane's field of vision.

Mindlessly, he followed Jethro to a nearby tent that had been pitched for him. He entered in a fog and sat on the cot, staring into a distant place.

"Pleroma," Jethro tried to reach him. "Lane!" he raised his voice. The volume startled Lane and he returned to the present moment.

"Lane, are you all right?"

"Oh, yeah," Lane shook his head a little, trying to minimize the terrible battle that was raging in his mind. "I'm fine. I think the altitude is making me a little lightheaded. I think I need to get some sleep. Tomorrow is the big day, right?"

Jethro squared off in front of Lane, their eyes level.

"Look at me," Jethro said.

Lane found it difficult to obey. Something kept him from focusing on Jethro's eyes. Jethro put one hand on Lane's shoulder and, with the other hand, gently held Lane's chin and brought his face to center.

With a soft voice, he repeated, "Look at me."

Lane settled. The warmth of Jethro's hand on his face melted the ice, and he started to relax. The eyes that Lane looked at now were a stark contrast to the eyes that had drilled into his psyche moments before. Jethro's eyes were soft and kind. They welcomed him in and offered him safety. They offered him acceptance. Lane felt at home there.

"Lane, I know what must be happening to you right now. Tomorrow you will face the greatest challenge of your life."

Lane's heart beat faster again.

"Shhh..." Jethro quieted him. "Put that out of your mind. Right now I want you to focus on one thing. I want you to think about all the training we have done together. Think about all the good that you have brought to my people.

"Son, I want you to know this. When I first met you, I did not

PLEROMA

believe. But now, I know. You are the Pleroma."

Lane's heart flooded with emotion. Jethro's confidence and belief in him sparked a pulse of warmth that radiated out, shattering and melting the icy grip that the priest had placed on him.

"Now, my son... sleep."

Lane lay down on the cot and was amazed at the sense of peace he felt in that moment. Soon he was fast asleep.

CHAPTER 27

The hallway was long and dark. Several doors lined both walls, and a single door stood closed at the end. Pain shot through Lane's head. He was running. Running, but not moving forward. Heavy footsteps echoed behind him. They pursued him from the darkness. The more Lane ran, the longer the hallway seemed to get. The footsteps grew louder, and closer.

A boy's voice rang through the tiled hallway.

"Lane! Help me!" It was Josh.

"Josh, where are you?" Lane's voice seemed strange to his own ears. As he yelled, the pain intensified in his head. The voices and the footfalls reverberated in his brain as in an echo chamber.

He skidded to a stop and tried to open one of the doors. Locked. He flung himself to the other side of the hall and tried another door. It was also locked. He tried the next, and the next. They were all locked. Josh's voice kept calling, echoing from a distance. He had to get to Josh before the dark footsteps caught up to him.

Now the voice seemed to come from the door at the end of the hallway. He ran again. It felt like running through water. The footsteps were almost upon him.

Finally he reached the door. The pain in his head throbbed with every rapid heartbeat. He fumbled on the door handle. Josh's voice screamed from the other side. The latch opened, and he flung open the door. Looming in the doorway, eyes burning, teeth bared...the face of the Bellator.

Lane sat up in his cot as the scream caught in his throat and wouldn't come out. Heart pounding. Chest heaving. He looked around frantically. Inside a tent. It was only a dream.

The pain was the one piece of the dream that was real. His head throbbed.

Not right now! He rubbed both temples with his fingers.

Lane swung his legs over the side of the cot, placed his head in his hands, and rested his elbows on his knees.

Focus, man. Remember what is really going on here. This place isn't real. These people aren't real. It pained his heart to think that Jethro's strong kindness was just a facsimile that his own subconscious had constructed to help him cope with his coma.

His coma. That was the reality here. The Bellator was out there, waiting for him. Who knows how long he had really been unconscious? Every moment that he laid there on the hospital bed the Bellator grew stronger and Josh's fate grew more perilous. It was time to face his fears, to face the Bellator, to defeat him…or die trying.

He drew in a deep breath and then stood up. It was time.

He threw back the tent flap and walked out into the cold morning air. The sky was gray with cold clouds. Along the eastern horizon a bank of dark, ominous clouds churned and moved toward the summit. The cloud cover hung like a ceiling above the stark landscape of the summit plain.

Tents covered the naked summit like a patchwork quilt. Thin tendrils of smoke rose up from among them like hundreds of renegade strings that had come loose from the patches and blew in the wind.

The gray stone temple stood cold and ominous in the middle of the tents. People already streamed through the gate to find their seats.

Jethro squatted next to a fire just outside the tent. He cooked some meat over the small flames.

"Ah, Lane. Good morning. Here," he extended a stick with some roasted meat skewered on it, "you will need some nourishment for today."

"Thank you, Jethro, but I couldn't eat anything right now if

I wanted to." Lane's stomach churned.

"Pleroma!" a voice called out from a few tents over.

"Pleroma. The Pleroma is out!" another voice called out. Soon many voices echoed his name, and a crowd appeared in front of the tent. Lane scanned the beaming faces. He really had come to love these people. This was his family.

Gustov stepped out from the group and smiled his broad, cheeky smile. "Ah, Pleroma. You are awake! It is glorious to see you on this most auspicious day."

Gustov stepped beside Lane, took him by the hand, and faced the crowd. Now the group had grown to include more than just Deltonians. All the people who had not yet entered the temple flocked to him, trying to get a look at the Pleroma.

"My fellow Deltonians," Gustov raised his voice and spoke in his important dignitary tone, "my brothers and sisters of the Erles, the Gamordines, and the Bedites. It is appropriate that dark clouds are collecting above this summit today. Dark clouds have been hanging over our heads for far too long. For countless years we have gathered at this same spot and prepared to enter that temple. When we did, we knew what would follow. It was a somber occasion. We did not fly our colors. We did not gather with excitement. We were forced to come and to watch. We entered the gate with dread because we knew our warriors had no hope against the Bellator. We knew we would face another year of slavery."

Gustov paused, and the crowd seemed to soak in the grayness of the looming clouds above them as they remembered far too well the reality of Gustov's commentary.

"But today," Gustov's voice shot up and tore through the gray veil that had descended over them. "Today is a new day. Today we have a ray of light, as the Great Father has sent us his promise and his hope. Today we will enter through that gate with expectation, with anticipation, with celebration …and with hope. Today, we have the Pleroma!"

Gustov lifted up his hands, still holding Lane's in his. The crowd went wild with excitement. They hooted and cheered and jumped up and down.

PLEROMA

A loud horn blast from inside the temple interrupted the excitement. Another blast sounded. Several horns blew in unison. Everyone turned toward the gate and moved as one toward the temple.

Gustov and Jethro held Lane back.

"We will let everyone get in first, and then we will present you to the high priest." Gustov explained.

It took a while for the large crowd to file into the temple gate. Eventually the tent village was empty, and a low roar of noise and energy emanated from inside the arena.

"It is time," Jethro said and walked toward the gate. At first Lane's feet wouldn't move. Jethro walked a few paces before he realized that his large companion was not at his side. He stopped and looked at Lane. With a knowing look in his eye he extended his hand to Lane and gave him a reassuring nod.

At the first step his foot seemed to weigh a thousand pounds; the second was slightly easier, and eventually he found his feet carrying him toward the gray stone gate. They passed through it into the dark hallway. There were doors on either side that led up to the seating areas. Some faces poked out of the doorways to catch a glimpse of Lane.

At the end of the hall, a large iron gate blocked the entrance to the arena floor. Two guards stood in front of it and opened it for them as they approached. Within the threshold, just before they entered the arena, Gustov and Jethro stopped.

"We must stop here," Gustov explained. "You must enter the arena alone. We will take our places up there."

Gustov stood squarely in front of Lane and looked up at him with grave sincerity. "Pleroma. This is your day. May the Great Father shine upon you. May he light your way and strengthen your body for the fight."

Drums thundered as Lane entered the arena. The stadium seats pulsated with a sea of faces. The crowd leaped to its feet and roared with approval when Lane cleared the shadow of the archway and stepped onto the dirt floor of the stadium. The drumbeats and cheering of the crowd marked his steps as he made his way to the center and turned to face the tower.

The tandem priests had already assumed their prone positions on the stone slabs, and the high priest waved his hands over their heads. They were summoning Amo. The drumbeats grew faster. Dark clouds swirled overhead. They hung heavy, threatening to dump their watery cargo at any moment. Cold wind whipped through the stadium.

A spark flashed inside the tower shell, and the spectral image of the woman appeared. The crowd fell silent in her presence. Looking up at her from the stadium floor she seemed even larger than Lane remembered. Her body convulsed when she first appeared, as if she were struggling against something. She settled and her faceless head scanned the arena. When the blank face pointed toward Lane, her body convulsed again and she thrust both her arms toward him, fingers clawing. A gasp escaped from the crowd. Lane flinched and stepped backward.

The high priest seized this opportunity and stood on the edge of the platform, now able to loom tall above Lane.

"Amo has spoken. She is insulted at your presence. The time for reckoning has come." He thrust his arm out and pointed his bony finger at Lane. "You claim to be the Pleroma. Today all truth will be made known." Both arms went into the air as the high priest spun around to face the goddess. In a loud, piercing voice, he shrieked, "Release the Bellator!"

The latch on the large iron gate echoed. A flash of lightning ripped across the sky, followed quickly by a ground-shaking crack of thunder. The iron gate dragged open. From the darkness of the archway the Bellator emerged. He, too, seemed larger than Lane remembered. He was only a few inches taller than Lane, but he was at least three times wider and thicker. His hulking frame was pure muscle under gnarled and disfigured skin.

Blood-red eyes fixed on Lane. They blazed with rage. The huge chest heaved as he breathed heavily through his tightly clenched teeth. His fists contracted alternately, sending ripples of muscle up his massive forearms.

Lane thought of that poor, helpless animal he saw the last time he was here. Now he was looking through the eyes of that defenseless creature. It was his turn to be hunted.

A peal of thunder shook the walls, and the Bellator lunged toward Lane. The weeks of training that he had spent with Jethro now seemed meaningless. Nothing could have prepared him to face this massive killing machine. What was he thinking? How could he have believed that he could ever have a chance to defeat this beast?

There was no time to think. And no turning back. The beast was upon him. He moved with incredible agility. Lane shot to the side and rolled, barely escaping his first attack.

He scrambled to his feet and ran toward the center of the arena. He did not want to get pinned against the wall. The Bellator corrected his angle and ran straight for him. With only a second to think, Lane knew that strength had no bearing on his side. Speed was his only weapon.

The Bellator lunged again. He spun to the side and escaped his grasp. Another lunge. Another spin. The two giants played a game of cat and mouse as the world of halflings looked on from the stadium seats. Their voices rose and fell with every lunge and near miss.

Rain fell. Another flash of lightning splintered across the dark sky.

Lane's plan was not working. He had hoped to outrun his massive opponent and wear down his endurance. Just the opposite was happening. Lane was beginning to drag with fatigue, and the Bellator seemed to be fueled by every failed attempt to capture his prey.

Lane stood in the middle of the arena again. His side burned, and his chest heaved for lack of oxygen. His head pounded and felt like his brain was going to explode out the top of his skull. The Bellator paused for a brief second. He bared his teeth, narrowed his eyes, and glared as if to burn a hole into Lane.

The beast lunged again. Lane spun away, but this time his left foot caught on the back of his right ankle and he stumbled to the ground. The Bellator pounced. A heavy hand slapped on the back of Lane's neck, and thick fingers gripped like a vise around his throat. The other hand grabbed the back of his knees and clamped his legs together.

Lane was hoisted up into the air, over the Bellator's head. He was helpless. The beast's strong hands pinned his neck and knees. Lane's arms were free to flail, but no amount of slapping and clawing would dislodge the Bellator's death grip.

Even over the wind and the rain, Lane could hear the gasp of the crowd. He could feel their shock and disappointment pulse through him as the Bellator carried his captured prey over to the platform.

The pain shot through his head. Lane's heart pounded wildly in his chest. The massive fingers dug into his neck.

Is this how it would end? Was he going to die at the hands of his opponent, like a weak and worthless animal? Had the coma finally won?

The Bellator thrust him into the air and presented him to Amo and the high priest. The rain bit hard and cold into his face. The priest stood on the edge of the platform, eyes wide with delight. Behind him, the spectral image of the woman thrashed about, waving her arms, reaching out to Lane, pulling her hair. She was insane with bloodthirst.

As the Bellator lowered him down to chest level, Lane knew this was the end. The fingers tightened. He looked up into the monster's eyes. It was the first time that Lane had been this close to his face. The Bellator's eyes were blue, not fierce and red. His pupils were round, not goatlike. The Bellator was human.

He stared hard into those eyes. The Bellator was caught by Lane's gaze and stopped squeezing for a moment. He stared back.

There was something familiar about those eyes. Lane looked harder. The Bellator's face softened slightly, and the ridge above his eyes, where eyebrows would normally be, lifted in curiosity. This gesture seemed to invite Lane to probe further. Lane looked deeply into the pale blue eyes. Another scene appeared before him. He had seen those eyes before.

It all made sense now. He had been wrong all along. The whole world spun around him.

"I know who you are," Lane screamed over the driving wind and rain. "Look at me. Don't you recognize me?"

PLEROMA

The Bellator looked confused. He cocked his head to the side.

Lane shouted, "Look at me! Dad! I'm your son! It's Lane!"

The Bellator blinked several times. He shook his head. The massive face leaned in, his forehead nearly touching Lane's. At first his brows furrowed and anger began to tighten in his jaws. The grip tightened again around Lane's neck.

"Dad, please. Don't hurt me this time!"

A light switched on in the Bellator's face. His brows shot up and his eyes became round and blue. He loosened his grip and placed Lane on the ground.

The crowd rose to its feet in surprise. The wind whipped through the arena. Thunder clapped, and a burst of lightning lit the scene for an instant.

Yelling as loud as he could, Lane shouted, "I thought you were my coma!"

The Bellator cocked his head again, looking very confused.

Lane shook his hands as if to erase that statement from the record. "I thought I was supposed to come here and defeat you because you were my enemy. Now I see what is really going on. I'm supposed to *free* you."

The Bellator looked surprised.

"Dad, I've seen you here before. I know you don't want to do the things you do. The Altanians own you. They force you to kill. They control you with the nectar."

The massive beast looked up at the priest. He looked at the iron gate that concealed the nectar. He turned and scanned the crowd. The rain beat against his body. Lane's words were starting to penetrate his fuzzy mind.

"Dad! We don't belong here. We can escape this place together."

The Bellator quickly refocused on Lane. He was listening.

"Let's go. We can leave this place and be free!"

A thunderclap accented Lane's words. The beast slapped both bulky hands on either side of his bald head, as if he was trying to keep it from exploding. His eyes flashed back and forth between the iron gate and Lane. The nectar. Freedom. Back and forth. His mouth grimaced as the pain of the decision raced around in his mind. He staggered, then lurched toward Lane.

"No! Please Dad, don't!"

The Bellator grabbed him. This time his grip felt different. It wasn't the painful grip of impending death cinched around his neck. This time the Bellator grabbed Lane around the waist and in one fluid motion hoisted him up to the top of wall on the far left side of the platform. Lane stood at a gap between the tower platform and the stadium seats. He could see ground below him, the tent village that sprawled out to the crest of the summit platform, and the rolling mountain peaks that fell away to freedom.

"Lane!" a small voice fought through the driving wind from the bank of seats beside him. Lane looked to see Jethro jumping over the side of the bleachers. He landed on the platform and ran over to Lane just as the huge form of the Bellator lurched up to the top and stood on his other side.

Jethro cowered in fear next to the beast. With wild and confused eyes, he looked up at Lane, "What are you doing?"

"Jethro, it all makes sense to me now," Lane yelled against the howling wind. "You were right all along. I am not the Pleroma."

Jethro looked even more confused.

"I didn't come here to defeat the Bellator," Lane continued. "I came here to free him."

"Free him? Are you crazy?" Jethro's confusion turned to anger. "What about the children, Lane? What about their freedom? What about the Deltonians? What about me?" Jethro paused as a thought passed through his mind. His expression of anger transformed into one of pain and disappointment. "Lane, you would not betray me, would you?"

Lane got down on his knees in front of Jethro. He grasped the little man's shoulders and looked at him with sincerity. "Jethro, you were right about me from the beginning. I am not the one your people have been waiting for...you are."

Jethro stared in disbelief.

"Jethro, don't you see? The Bellator and I don't belong in this world. We need to find our way home. With the Bellator gone, the playing field will be even again. You can free the children. You can rally your people and overcome the Altanians. Jethro, you are the Pleroma. I'm just a kid who needs to go home."

The rain pelted against Jethro's weathered face. He wrestled with Lane's words. He looked up at Lane, then at the Bellator, then over at the massive crowd of people. The high priest moved wildly on the platform, summoning the guards to gather and pursue the escapees.

Jethro looked at Lane with resolve. He took Lane's face between his hands.

"Yes, Lane. I understand. We can free the children. You must go. Go quickly. The guards are coming."

Lane looked back and saw a group of guards moving toward them along the platform and another group filing out of the main hallway toward the gate. He stood and looked down at Jethro.

"Thank you, Jethro. For everything."

Lane and the Bellator flung themselves over the side of the wall and scaled down to the ground below. They ran toward the tents. A group of soldiers was already coming around the tower in pursuit.

Lane stopped for a moment to look back. Jethro stood on the wall, one arm raised. His voice, barely audible above the wind, called to the people.

"The children! Free the children!" Then he disappeared into the stadium.

Lane spun around and ran through the sea of tents. The Bellator was close behind him. Lane wasn't sure where he was going. All he knew was that he wanted to head east, down the mountain and away from these people.

They came to the edge of the summit cap. It ended in a cliff that fell away into the woods below. A dead end. The soldiers were closing in on them from behind. Lane shot along the edge of the cliff toward the one place he knew would lead down from the summit. They would have to run through the priests' village.

They came to the path that led down to the village. Another group of soldiers moved toward them from the north side of the summit.

Lane and the beast jumped down into the village. They ran down one path, jumped down the wooden ladder in a single leap, then switched back toward the next ladder. Panic and adrenaline pushed them, and soon they were at the base of the cliff, standing in the Altanian village. To the left was the path that he and Jethro had taken on their first trip. He knew that it led back around to the north side of the mountains. Straight ahead was the Main Trade Route. To the right there was another, smaller path that headed south. They took the unknown path.

The two giants ran with abandon. Their long strides put a great distance between them and their halfling pursuers. The soldiers undoubtedly knew this path. They had to get away from it.

There, a small stream. Water finds its way down the mountain, right? Follow the water.

They jumped off of the path and into the stream. It was only ankle deep, so they splashed their way along its path. They ran along the gully for a long time as it wound its way down the mountain side. Sometimes it fell over a small ledge, and they either jumped off of it or fought their way through the trees and underbrush along the bank until the stream leveled off again.

They ran as much as they could. All the time they moved quickly, the hope of freedom and the rush of the chase driving them onward.

After many hours of scraping, splashing, sliding, and tearing over rocks and through the trees, they came to the end of the forest. The trees thinned out, and the ground became rocky. The stream spilled over the edge of a tall cliff. They could no longer follow it.

They were tired. The wind and rain pounded them. It was impossible to hear if their pursuers were close behind them. They had to keep going. But where?

The ridge ran south along the top of the cliff and headed toward another group of rocky peaks. Why not? They took it. It was very narrow. The cliff below them fell straight down into jagged rocks. They leaned hard against a rough stone wall that shot straight up above them. The stone was slick with rain.

Careful steps slowed them down. *Are the guards catching up? It's too hard to hear anything in the storm.*

The ridge wound around a corner and opened up to a wider platform. Two massive rock formations converged, and in the junction a dark crevice formed a cavelike opening. They ducked into the cave to get shelter from the rain.

Soaked to the bone, Lane and the Bellator stood in the cleft of the rock and looked out at the pouring rain. For the first time since that morning, they stopped moving. Lane's feet throbbed from the pounding. Each moment they stood there, out of the rain, he felt a new scrape or gash announce itself. Blood oozed from red stripes that slashed across the Bellator's body as well. Apparently the trees and rocks had protested against their flight. The constant rain had been washing the blood away during the day, and the cold had numbed the pain. Now, in the dark silence of the rocky refuge, Lane's skin began to sting.

Skies that had been dark with storm clouds grew even darker. Streaks of lightning fractured the sky and exposed everything in bright bursts of light. The brilliant snapshots pieced together a picture of where they were. They stood on a rocky precipice at the edge of the Waste. The dry crevices of the desert floor filled with the raging waters of the day's deluge.

A new sensation now accompanied the pain. Hunger. Hunger and exhaustion. Lane's limbs grew heavy, and he felt like he was going to sink right through the rocky floor of the cave. Why had he turned down Jethro's offer of breakfast this morning? He hadn't eaten anything since the day before.

Now, standing in the darkness of a hole in the side of the mountain, alone with a hulking beast that, up to today, had been his enemy, his stomach growling and his heavy feet throbbing, Lane wondered what had come over him. What was he thinking? He left his people behind. He abandoned a man who had truly loved him, who called him "son" in a way that it felt special and real. How could he have abandoned Jethro like that, just so he could run away with this…beast?

He looked over at the Bellator. It was difficult to see him in the darkness, but his hulking frame filled the small cave entrance. He seemed agitated. Restless. Twitching randomly. The beast sat on the ground, his back against the cold stone wall, cradling his head in his hand and rocking back and forth. He moaned.

"Are you all right?" Lane said. "Are you hurt?"

A deep growl bellowed from the beast's throat.

"Does that mean 'yes'? Where are you hurt?"

The Bellator lifted his head from his hands, grimaced, and beat the ground behind him. "Aaaaaarrrrrr!" The roar echoed through the cave.

Lane stumbled backwards.

"Keep it down, man. We don't know if the Altanians are still looking for us. For all we know they could be right around the corner. We've got to keep quiet."

A flash of lightning lit up the cave for a moment. The vision it revealed gripped Lane with fear. The Bellator's eyes glared, seething with rage. Teeth clenched. Muscles rippled. He was standing.

Fear shot through Lane and chased away all the hunger pains and the weight of exhaustion. What was this beast going to do? Why had he released him? This was insane.

The Bellator roared again and lunged toward Lane. He spun out of the way, and the beast's fists pounded against the wall where Lane had been standing.

"What are you doing?" Lane yelled at the top of his lungs. "Why are you trying to hurt me?"

The Bellator roared again. His body twitched, and he seemed to be writhing in pain. He grabbed his head and rocked it back and forth.

"Owen?"

Lane jumped at the sound of the voice. The Bellator heard it and froze.

They stood in silence, trying to see if their ears had played a trick on them.

"Owen, is that you?" A deep and ancient voice came from the back of the cave.

PLEROMA

CHAPTER 28

A small golden glow flickered in the back of the dark cave. A bald and wrinkled forehead poked up over the edge of a rock. It was followed by a pair of eyes that stared out from underneath bushy, white eyebrows arched high in wonder. Gnarled fingers wrapped around the source of the flickering light. The man raised the torch in the air above his head, and the light spilled out onto Lane and the Bellator.

"By all that once was holy!" Now the rest of his face emerged from behind the dark rock. A long, pointy nose hung down over a pure white mustache and beard. "It *is* you!"

The small man was obviously an Altanian. Yet something about him seemed different than any other Altanians Lane had encountered. Perhaps it was his eyes. They seemed kind and inviting ...and wise.

The little man, slightly hunched with age, stepped out from behind the rock and moved cautiously closer to the newcomers.

"Owen, do you remember me?" He looked up at the Bellator's face. The beast stared back at him, blinking fast. After a few seconds the beast's eyes brightened. A look of wonder spread across his face. He obviously did recognize this little man, and the remembrance had a positive effect on him. Lane marveled at how transformational a small smile could be on such a gnarled and hideous face.

"You do remember. I am so glad. I have been waiting for this day for a very long time."

Suddenly a look of concern twisted the man's face. He craned his neck to look past the Bellator and out the entrance of the cave, as if to see if someone else was with them.

"Oh my, they must not be pleased that you are out here all alone." He looked at Lane. "I'm assuming you had something to do with Owen's escape?"

Lane did not respond. He couldn't. Hearing the name "Owen" had paralyzed him. Owen was his father's name. Lane simply grunted "uh-huh."

"Well," the man continued, "I am sure they will be pursuing you. We must not stand here with this torch announcing your presence to the entire world. That would be most counterproductive to our purposes, now would it not? Yes, indeed."

He spun around toward the back of the cave and moved rather quickly for a man of his apparent age.

"Come, come," he beckoned them with a flailing hand raised above his head. "Follow me!"

He disappeared behind the rock.

Lane and the Bellator stood frozen in shock and slight amusement.

After a few seconds of silence, the wrinkled head popped up over the rock again.

"Well, let us not hesitate or procrastinate, shall we. Let us motivate! It only requires moving the feet, one after the other. Come along. We have no time to lose."

He disappeared again. Lane and the Bellator decided it was better to follow a strange little man with a torch into a dark cave than to stand out in the cold rain and be discovered by the Altanian guards. They stepped behind the rock.

The small man led them through a dark crevice, winding back and forth, lit only by the flame of his torch. The rough walls were cold to the touch and felt like fine sandpaper. At one point the crevice became so narrow that the Bellator had to turn sideways and carefully squeeze his body through.

They continued through this dark passage for a while. Eventually a dull orange glow appeared in the distance. As they progressed, the glow intensified. By the time they reached the glow it danced along the rough and jagged surface of the stone wall. A fire was burning around the next corner. As the little man turned the corner, he paused to place his torch in a sconce on the wall. The firelight from the next room lit up his face. He turned and smiled at them.

He disappeared around the corner and they followed. The corridor opened into a large room. In the center of the room a fire popped and cracked, bathing the cluttered room with a warm glow. A loud *pop* sprayed a flurry of sparks from the flame. The fireflies frantically swarmed around each other and flew toward the ceiling. They disappeared into darkness that seemed to rise up into infinite space.

It was obvious from the random contour of the walls that the room was a naturally occurring cavern that had been domesticated by the little man. On one side of the fire sat two cots, a small one that looked like the kind found in this world, and a larger one that looked like it would be comfortable for Lane to sleep on. On the other side of the fire, behind two small, wooden benches that faced the fire pit, nested against the wall and underneath tandem wall sconces, sat a large rectangular table covered with scrolls and papers. Next to the large table were simple shelves upon which sat a few earthenware dishes. At the far end of the cave was something curious. A large iron gate filled what would normally have been a natural archway.

The little man went straight to the fire and attended to a large, black pot suspended above the flames by a spit. He stirred the bubbling brew with a long wooden utensil.

"Ah, our timing could not have been more perfect." A smile widened the white mustache under his nose. His kind, wrinkled eyes twinkled as he looked up at his guests. "The soup is ready. Come in, come in. Sit by the fire and warm yourselves." He motioned for them to enter as he went to the shelves and retrieved three bowls and spoons.

Soon Lane and the Bellator basked in the warmth of the fire, each holding a bowl of savory liquid. The old man eagerly scooped a spoonful to his mouth and slurped its contents with great enjoyment.

"Eat. It will warm your insides while the fire warms your outsides."

As soon as Lane was seated next to the fire, his hunger resurfaced with a vengeance. His logical mind wanted to ask questions and analyze where he was, but a raging, animal hunger overpowered him, and he ate the contents of the bowl in frantic slurps. The Bellator was obviously equally hungry, and he slurped and sloshed several helpings of the meal. The feeding frenzy continued in silence as the old man calmly watched over his bowl, pleased that his simple offering brought such great satisfaction to his dinner guests.

Eventually the hunger pains abated and the frenzy ceased. With a belly full of warm food and his clothes and body toasty and dry, it was time for the fatigue of the day to reassert itself in Lane's consciousness. His limbs felt the weight of exhaustion, and his eyelids battled gravity with every blink.

He looked over and expected to see the beast displaying the same symptoms of fatigue. Instead he saw something that woke him up again. The Bellator rocked back and forth. His knees bounced as his feet nervously tapped up and down. A deep grumble groaned from the depths of his belly, like the early warning signs that a volcano was going to erupt at any moment. His teeth clenched and his mouth contorted into a grimace of pain.

Lane's fatigue was, once again, swept away by another wave of adrenaline. The old man looked concerned and stood up. Gathering his composure, he spoke with a soothing tone.

"Owen. Owen, look at me. I have something to show you that I think you will like."

The Bellator held his bald head and rocked back and forth. At the soothing sound of the old man's voice he lifted one arm so he could see the man, but continued rocking and clenching his face in pain. He was listening.

"I would like you to come over here with me," the old man said as he moved toward the iron gate. "I have been waiting for you for a very long time. I have missed you, Owen. Come in here and let me show you what I have for you."

He reached the gate and pushed it open. It took all of his strength. The opening was huge compared to his small frame, large enough to allow easy entrance for the Bellator. He stood in the doorway and motioned for the Bellator to follow.

"Come Owen. You will want to see this."

Slowly the hulking beast rose to his feet, still holding his head in his hands. He staggered across the room, as if his equilibrium was off-kilter. When he reached the gate he paused, looking nervous and agitated.

"Come inside, Owen. You will like it." The timbre of the man's voice was like a salve that calmed the flames of the Bellator's agitation enough to compel him into the room. The man stood beside him, grasping the handle to the gate, as the beast passed into the room.

At the moment the Bellator cleared the gate, the little man lurched backwards with all his might and pulled the massive barrier toward him. It slammed shut, and the clanging of iron on stone reverberated through the rocky cavern and dissipated into the darkness of the endless ceiling. The Bellator was trapped.

The old man stooped and dropped his head. He still held on to the large handle. He looked at the gate with sadness.

Crash! The gate rattled and clanged. The old man and Lane both flinched. Another loud crash slammed against the gate and sent piercing echoes bouncing through the cavern. The Bellator pounded on the gate in protest.

"What have you done?!" Lane jumped to his feet in outrage, sending his bowl flying across the stone floor. "This was a trap!" Lane looked back at the entrance to the cave, expecting to see the Altanian guards rush in to surround him. He ran toward the gate to free the Bellator.

The old man stood with his back against the gate, hands raised to stop Lane's tirade.

"Did you lure us in here just so you could capture the Bellator?" Lane was upon him now. He stopped just short of throwing the man to the side and ripping the gate open. "Are you working for the Altanians? How did you know we were coming? Who are you?" Lane was in a frenzy at this point. Exhaustion and fear coalesced in his mind and fomented into irrational rage. The pain in his head throbbed again. He grabbed his head and weaved back and forth.

The small man's hands pushed back each of Lane's accusations. His face showed nothing but kindness and patience. He allowed Lane to empty his barrel, and when he saw that Lane was now suffering pain, he spoke with smooth tones.

"Yes, my son. I am sure you have many questions. Rest assured. I have not captured Owen. I am protecting him...and us."

Another crash. This one shook the floor and walls. The Bellator threw his massive body against the gate. The pounding was followed by several minutes of screaming and pacing and the sound of objects being thrown and smashed against the walls. Eventually the chaos subsided and it was silent again.

Wide eyed, Lane backed away from the gate.

The old man continued, "There, now he will sleep. You see, Owen needs some time to heal. It is for his own good to keep him behind this gate.

"Come, let us sit by the fire again." He motioned for Lane to walk with him to the fireside. He placed his gnarled hand on Lane's back and gently led him.

Lane conceded. He sat in front of the fire with a large mug of hot, sweet-smelling liquid in his hands. The steam from the mug filled his head and calmed him immediately. Once again, the fatigue of the day began to drain the last drops of adrenaline from his system, and the weight of a hundred men pulled him onto the bench.

Curiosity battled through the increasing fog in his mind, and he slurred out the question that was begging to be asked.

"Who are you?"

The man sat next to Lane at the fire, also nursing a mug of the sweet brew. "Yes, yes. I suppose proper introductions are in order. Forgive me for my impudence and disregard for protocol. I have lived here in the cavern by myself for so long that I tend to forget the finer points of society."

He cleared his throat and sat up as straight as his ancient back would allow.

"I am Quirinius Maximillian, at your service. Those who

once called me friend found my proper name to be a mouthful and simply referred to me as Quinn. You may do likewise, if you wish."

The name was too complex to fight its way through the thickening fog in Lane's mind. His eyelids were nearly shut and it was everything he could do to mutter the word, "Quinn" in response.

"Come now." Quinn stood and urged Lane to move over toward the large cot that lay next to the wall. "You are exhausted. We are safe here and will have plenty of time to talk after you have slept and regained your strength. Sleep now."

Lane did not resist. He stretched out on the large cot. Soon all was black, and he slept.

CHAPTER 29

"Lane! Lane!" Josh's voice echoed through the darkness. Lane's body was going through the motions of running, but there was no ground under his feet. No walls around him. He floated in a sea of blackness. Josh's voice seemed to be coming from everywhere.

A small light appeared in front of him. Slowly the rim of a window appeared. There was a pane of glass. A small boy stood in the window and peered in, a look of fear and sadness coloring his face. White, translucent curtains hung straight beside the boy, opened just enough to reveal his face looking through the glass at Lane. It was Josh.

More light filled the dark room, just enough to reveal the edge of a white cloth. It was draped over something in front of Lane's face. His feet. The cloth was covering his feet, now he was sure of that. Lane was lying on his back, looking down over his covered feet, at Josh.

This is a hospital room. He tried to reach out to Josh, but his arms would not move. He tried to call out to him, but his voice would not respond. He was paralyzed.

Josh looked back at him, calling to him with his eyes.

The curtain pulled to the side, away from Josh's face, opening up more of the windowpane. A figure stood next to the little boy. A large torso. The curtain pulled back farther to reveal a man's bare chest. Now it was completely pulled back. Icy waves shot down Lane's spine. The face on top of the man's chest was the Bellator. Gnarled brows lowered, and the beast looked out at Lane with a sinister smile. His massive hand slipped onto the back of Josh's neck.

"No!" Lane screamed, sitting up straight in the cot. The darkness was gone. He faced a stone wall, dancing in a warm sea of firelight. He was in Quinn's cave. The dream was over.

"You poor boy," Quinn's voice came from behind. Lane turned on the cot to see the old man stirring a pot over the fire. "That must have been quite a night vision you just had. Would you like to come and tell me about it over a bowl of soup?"

Somehow Lane felt like that was a really good idea. Something about this strange little man set him at ease. It was as if he knew him from somewhere.

Lane received a bowl of savory soup from Quinn. It appeared to be the same meal that they had eaten the night before. Hunger kept him from worrying about repeat meals and he dug in, slurping the rich, gravylike soup. It was delicious.

"Other than a terrible night vision, how has the night's sleep left you today?" Quinn began the conversation.

Lane stopped to assess himself. He looked past the disturbing images he had just experienced and realized that he actually felt pretty good. His mind was clear, his body was warm, and the stinging in the scrapes had calmed down.

"I feel pretty good, actually. My head doesn't hurt anymore. It's the first time since this whole thing started. Thanks."

Lane looked at the gate. Quinn read the question in Lane's eyes and responded. "Ah, yes. I believe our very large friend will be asleep all day today. All we can do at this point is wait."

The two sat in awkward silence for a few moments and ate their soup. Quinn looked at Lane with patient eyes. Lane was not sure what to say or how to begin. His world had been turned completely upside down, and his mind raced trying to keep up with it.

Quinn broke the silence. "Am I correct in assuming that you are the Pleroma?"

"Yeah, right," Lane responded with acid in his voice. "Pleroma. That's a joke."

"You do not believe you are the Pleroma?" Quinn stroked his beard.

"Are you kidding? I don't believe any of this." He shook his head and rubbed his hands through his thick, curly hair. "I can't believe I let myself get sucked into my own delusion like that. What a sucker. My mind got weak."

Quinn's quizzical expression begged him to go on.

"OK, here's the thing," Lane continued, "I'm not really here."

The old man looked confused.

"Well...to you I'm here, but here isn't really *here.*" Lane paused. "What I mean is that I am actually in a hospital room right now. You see, I got in a fight with my Dad, I hid under the bed, he barged in my room, the bed collapsed on my head, and the next thing you know I'm spinning out of control into Oz-land here, full of munchkins and prophecies and craziness." Lane spun his index finger around his temple to emphasize the last point.

"The truth is that I'm in a coma, lying in a hospital bed, fighting for my life. This strange world is actually a construction of my own subconscious trying to communicate to me about what is happening to my body."

Quinn continued to stroke his long, white beard. "So, I am just a figment of your imagination, then?" he asked with a flip of his bony finger.

"Well, yeah," Lane responded boldly. "No offense. But you're not real. I know who you are, now. From the moment I saw you I thought you looked familiar. Now I just realized who it is. You are Mr. Lancaster."

Quinn looked surprised. "Mr. Lan-caster?"

"Yeah, he's my science teacher. Of course you don't look like him, exactly, but you have the same eyes. You see, in this world, everything represents something for me. You must represent science and logic. You must be here to help me figure all this stuff out."

"And how can you be sure that I am this Mr. Lan-caster?" Quinn queried.

"Come on," Lane waved off the obvious question, "look at your name. Quirinius Maximillian. Isn't that what you said?"

"Yes," Quinn nodded.

"Quirinius. Quinn. Q," Lane emphasized each word with a roll of his hand. "Isn't it obvious? Mr. L is a huge *Star Trek* fan. I sure could use an omnipotent know-it-all right about now. I bet you can do whatever you want with the snap of your fingers." Lane looked excited and hopeful.

"I am sorry to disappoint you, but I am afraid that at this age I cannot even snap my fingers," Quinn chuckled.

Lane looked down at the ground. "Figures. That would be too easy wouldn't it?" He dropped his forehead into his hands and rested his elbows on his knees. A long sigh blew through his lips and sounded like the flapping of a horse's mouth.

"I am not sure if I am your 'Q' character, but I would like to help you figure things out. It has been a long time since I have had the chance to talk to someone else about ideas.

"Now, you said that everything in this world represents something. Tell me more about that."

The tone in Quinn's voice was not condescending in the slightest. It was sincere and soothing. It flowed over Lane like a warm blanket and softened the hard edges that had been developing around his heart.

"That's just it. I'm really confused right now. Up until yesterday I thought I had it all figured out. I thought the Bellator represented my coma, and the Deltonians represented my little brother, Josh. I thought that when I defeated the Bellator I would wake up in the hospital and be home again."

"What happened to change that?" Quinn spoke gently.

"When I got into the arena with the Bellator, I realized that I didn't have a chance of defeating him. He's just too strong. He grabbed me like I was a rag doll. For a moment there, I thought I was dead. I figured the coma had gotten the best of me and that was it.

"Then I looked into the Bellator's eyes. It totally freaked me out at first. I had never been close enough to him to notice. But, I'm telling you, those are my dad's eyes. They're his eyes, but not his usual ones. They're the eyes I remember from when I was a kid—before he changed."

Lane paused, haunted by the memories of a life lost.

"So then what happened?" Quinn said, "Please continue."

Lane shook off the memories and returned to the story. "Well, when I saw my dad's eyes, it hit me. Maybe I had been wrong all along. Maybe the Bellator didn't represent my coma after all. Maybe he is my dad, somehow. I mean, when I spied on him, I saw that he was not a military monster, the way everyone thinks he is. He's a prisoner. The Altanians own him. They control him somehow with the nectar."

Lane looked up at Quinn. "I don't know why, and I don't know how, but in that moment, I felt like my real purpose was not to defeat the Bellator, but to rescue him…somehow."

Lane looked over at the iron gate. "Now he's locked up in a cave. Another prison. He's going totally crazy. It's all my fault. I betrayed Jethro, who was like a father to me. I ran away from the Deltonians, who believed in me. I abandoned them when their children were in danger. Who knows if the kids were rescued? Now I'm in a cave with an old hermit and a locked-up killer.

"Aaagh, listen to me. I'm buying into this delusion again." Lane stood up and paced around the cavern. "It's not real. It's not real. Get a hold of yourself man!"

Quinn quietly and patiently observed Lane's pacing. "Come, sit down again. I will fix us some more hot brew. It will help calm you."

Lane acquiesced and received the mug gratefully. He was tired of thinking.

"Now," Quinn said, "you have raised some very interesting points. I believe your intuition regarding Owen was correct. He did, indeed, need to be rescued."

Lane raised his hand to stop Quinn. "Hold on a minute. This has been bugging me since we got here. Why do you call him Owen?"

"Well, that is what I have always called him. I refuse to call him that other, wretched name." Quinn swatted the name away with a wave of his hand. "It was a vile idea from the beginning, and I refuse to validate it by uttering the word."

It was Lane's turn to look confused. His eyes begged Quinn

to explain.

"Yes, well." Quinn settled himself on the bench. "I suppose we should just begin at the beginning, shall we?"

CHAPTER 30

"Many, many years ago," Quinn began, "when I was just a young man, things were very different than they are today. My father was the high priest of the Altanians, which made me heir to that lofty position. Unfortunately, my father died in his prime, and I was thrust into the position before I was wise enough to handle it. Yet I was there, and I did the best I could.

"In those days, the tribes lived in peace and worked together in trade and exchange of ideas."

"Yes," Lane interrupted, "Gustov told me about this. Didn't you used to gather down by the river for the annual Festival?"

"Yes, indeed. Excellent. Excellent." Quinn beamed. "Each tribe had something to contribute to the needs of the others, and we all traded fairly for the goods we desired.

"As the high priest, it was my duty to study the ways of the gods and to seek direction for my people. The Altanians, being mountain dwellers, worshipped the goddess Amo. I was learned in her ways and taught the people how to survive in the difficult mountain region.

"Now, I take it you have been to the skullcap of Amo?" Quinn questioned Lane.

Lane looked puzzled.

"The holy place of Amo at the top of the mountain." Quinn elaborated.

"Oh, you mean the stadium up on the summit? Yes, that's where I met the Bella... Owen, I mean."

"Yes," Quinn continued, "well, that 'stadium,' as you call

it, is a fairly recent aberration. When I was the high priest, life was different in the monks' village. Oh, the village itself has not changed much over the generations, but the high place—the Plain of Meditation, as it was called then—was vastly different. On the high place there was a simple stone altar comprised of a fire ring surrounded by stone benches, much like this fire ring right here. As the priests, we would take turns holding night vigils around the fire.

"It was a simple and elegant ritual. We would throw a small handful of the bitter berries into the fire and then focus on the colorful flames that they released as they burned. As we focused our minds on the flame and cleared our thoughts of all else, if we were blessed that night, we would receive revelations from Amo. Sometimes they would come in a vision, sometimes in a sound, other times in a simple suggestion of thought."

"Hold on a second." Lane raised his hand toward Quinn. "I'm sorry to interrupt, but did you say the bitter berry?"

"Yes."

"Jethro told me that the bitter berry was extremely poisonous and to avoid it at all cost."

"You know of the bitter berry?" Quinn was genuinely delighted. "And of the numa?" he questioned.

"Yes," Lane answered. "When we were crossing the Waste, I saw a numa vanish into thin air."

"Marvelous!" Quinn clapped his hands. "That is marvelous news.

"Now, I am not surprised that your friend told you such things about the bitter berry. The truth is that, back then, I, too, believed them to be poisonous. We never ate them, you see. We were only interested in them for their ability to bridge the gap between our minds and the realm of Amo, nothing more.

"Oh, so much has changed since then, at least in my mind. I am getting ahead of myself though." Quinn seemed a little flustered.

"I'm sorry for disrupting your story," Lane apologized.

"Quite all right. Quite all right, my boy. I will explain about the bitter berry in good order. Now, where was I... Ah, yes.

"When we were not meditating on the flame, we studied the stars and the Three Sisters and observed their migrations through the heavens. It was a simple and tranquil way of life. Through our diligence, Amo guided us through life in the Upper Mountains and allowed us to survive and live in peace with the other tribes and their gods.

"Then, one night, everything changed. I was sleeping in my chambers. My older cousin, Exapator, was holding the vigil that night with three young neophytes. During the third watch of the night, just before the light of day was about to break, I heard a frantic pounding on my door. It was one of the neophytes. He was dumb with terror and could only motion for me to come with him quickly.

"He led me up to the altar. That night my eyes beheld something that would change the course of history. I have spent the rest of my life trying to figure out the true nature of what I saw that night."

"What was it?" Lane was thoroughly engrossed.

"It was her. It was that terrible apparition that they call Amo."

"Wait, wait a second," Lane interrupted again. "Are you telling me that you don't believe that giant woman that appears in the tower is Amo?"

"I am now convinced to the core of my being"—Quinn pounded his fist on his knee—"that whatever that specter is, she is anything but Amo."

"Why?" Lane asked.

Quinn raised a gnarled finger to suppress Lane's question and beg his patience. "I will explain. First, there is more to what I saw that night.

"When I approached the altar, I found the other two neophytes lying down beside the fire, one on either side, with empty goblets lying next to them. The figure of the woman rose out of the fire. She stood as tall as a tree. Her body was pure white, like a flash of lightning, and where her face should be was nothing but pure light. Her black hair was the only contrast to her otherwise radiant appearance. Her body writhed and thrashed, as if she was being burned in a flame.

"Exapator was standing in front of the vision, his arms straight to the side. He was frozen in his fixation. Lying on the ground, in front of Exapator and between him and the fire, was Owen.

"At that point he was nothing more than a massive heap of oozing flesh. I did not know what it was at first, but as I approached the scene, I could tell that in front of Exapator laid a creature that was at least twice the size of any person I had ever seen. He was naked, lying face-down, and his skin looked like it had been badly burned over most of his body. He lay lifelessly. At first I was not sure that he was alive, but then I saw his chest rise and fall. He was alive, but barely.

"The neophyte that had brought me there was frantic. He insisted that he had warned them not to do it. He knew that I would be upset with them, and he begged me to forgive him. I calmed him down, and he proceeded to explain what had happened.

"That night the two neophytes—mischievous young men that I thought should have never been considered for the priesthood, but their families were powerful...another story altogether. That is beside the point, I am sorry." Quinn unfurrowed his brow and continued. "That night, the two neophytes thought it would be interesting to see what would happen if they entered into the meditation after having drunk a goblet or two full of nectar. Their heads were already spinning a little from the liquid when Exapator threw the bitter berries into the flame. As the berries entered the flame, they burst into a huge fireball that sent all four men flying backwards. They heard a large *thud* that shook the ground.

"When he regained his composure, the one neophyte who had not partaken of the nectar looked up to see what I saw when I arrived. The two neophytes were unconscious, lying on either side of the apparition, and Exapator was caught in a trance.

"I rushed up to Exapator. As soon as I spoke, the two neophytes opened their eyes and sat up. The instant their eyes opened, the vision of the woman disappeared, and Exapator was free from his trance.

"'What is happening here?' I asked.

"'Oh, Master, that was the most wonderful experience,' Expator said to me. 'I have seen Amo!'

"I have always wondered if there was sincerity in that statement. I have to admit, it was a sight to behold. Deep in my heart, I would like to believe that, on that first night, Exapator had a pure experience, and that he was truly in awe. All these years later, seeing what has happened because of that night, it is very difficult for me to know."

Just then a terrible sound came from behind the iron gate. It startled both the storyteller and his audience. Lane jumped to his feet in alarm. Something smashed against the gate and sent little puffs of dust clouds shooting out from the seams around the door frame. The Bellator raged. Screams that alternated between terror and anger reverberated throughout the cavern, filling the space with an electrified agitation.

Quinn opened his eyes wide and raised his eyebrows in an expression of mock alarm. "I see someone has not woken well," he said with a hint of good-humored mockery.

"Excuse me for a moment." He filled a bowl with the soup and took it to the gate. At the bottom of the iron gate was a small door, only large enough to fit a bowl. Quinn slid the cover off of this door and pushed the bowl through the small opening.

The bowl quickly disappeared. Only a moment later, the bowl slammed against the small, barred window in the top of the gate, sending its contents splashing back into the main room.

"Well," Quinn said in mock offense, "a simple 'no thank you' would have been more appropriate, I do believe."

Raising his voice loud enough to be heard behind the gate he said, "That was the only bowl for this mealtime. You are going to get pretty hungry if you keep that up!"

The Bellator's face filled the small barred window. He was wild with rage and pounded on the gate for a long time.

Quinn calmly walked away from the door and did not acknowledge the screams. Eventually the face disappeared from the window. A few more objects smashed around the room.

PLEROMA

Then it fell silent again.

Quinn took the opportunity to throw another log on the fire and stoke the embers before he repositioned himself in the storyteller's perch.

"I think he will be out for quite a long time now," Quinn said.

Lane stared at Quinn.

"I suppose, from your perspective, it looks like I am torturing Owen, or at the very least being very unkind to him."

"Yeah, a little," Lane said with thick sarcasm.

"Fair enough," Quinn responded, "fair enough. In order for you to understand, I must tell you what happened to Owen.

"After the vision in the flames had dissipated, the five of us were left standing, encircled around a mass of charred and oozing flesh. A terrible and pitiful sound came from the heap every time his chest rose or fell. It sounded like a long 'oh.' After a while it sounded like he was saying 'Owen,' and the name stuck.

"We were not sure what to do. Of course we were puzzled as to the creature's origins. The way he was laying there, it looked as though he had fallen from a great height. Wherever he had come from, he had obviously passed through a fire. We wondered if somehow he had come out of the fire.

"Then Exapator uttered the words that changed the course of our people's lives. He told me that Amo had sent Owen to us. He said that the vision of the woman was Amo herself and that she had contacted him and told him that this creature was a gift to us.

"Well, at that point we were so flabbergasted by the whole experience that none of us knew what to think. I thought it strange, even in that moment, that Amo would contact Exapator and not me, her high priest. I ignored it, and we focused our attention on the injured creature.

"The five of us were not able to move him, so we woke up several priests from the village to assist us. Eventually we were able to move him down the cliff steps to the buildings below. Owen remained unconscious throughout the entire process. I do believe he weighed three times as much that way."

Quinn shook his head. "It was quite a spectacle to see several priests trying to move a very large, very limp mass of oozing flesh and muscle down a series of wooden ladders. Only a few of the priests were squashed in the process.

"Well, eventually we were able to clear out a storehouse to put him in. It was the only room we had that was big enough for his whole body to fit into. It took all that day to get him settled. Owen remained unconscious and moaned throughout the day. He stayed that way for several days more.

"I will never forget the day he woke up. I was there. I took a special interest in this new oddity and stayed next to him as much as possible. Part of my interest stemmed from a leader's concern to protect his people, but, honestly, the other part flowed from the fact that I was simply enchanted with him and all the possibilities of what he could represent.

"When his eyes opened, I could see that they were filled with panic. At first he was not looking at me. Truthfully, I do not think he was looking at anything in this world. He sat up and stared straight ahead, as if something horrible was coming at him, then he covered his face and curled up like he was shielding himself from a quickly approaching threat. He screamed and scooted his back against the wall, trying to escape whatever terror was pursuing him.

"When he pressed against the wall it must have woken him up or jerked him into the space that his body was presently occupying. He looked around the room, completely disoriented. Finally he saw me sitting there, beside him. When he saw me, and I looked into his eyes, my heart melted. Behind the horrifying mass of charred and oozing skin were the eyes of a truly frightened person. His pale blue eyes, with those strange, round pupils, stared at me. They called out to me, asking me what was happening to him. He opened his mouth to speak, but nothing came out but groans and gibberish. Owen has never spoken a word.

"Over the course of the next few weeks, I took it upon myself to personally oversee Owen's care. He was in great pain. The burns on his flesh were severe. We treated the burns with salve, but I decided that we should give Owen the nectar to ease his pain."

Quinn stopped his recitation and stared into the flames. A veil of sadness fell down over his eyes, and his shoulders drooped. As old as he was, he seemed to age several years right before Lane's eyes.

"Q, what is it?"

After a few more moments of staring vacantly into the flames and fiddling with the embers, Quinn responded in a somber tone.

"It is ironic actually. Living here, all alone for these many years, I have never actually verbalized this story to anyone before. Just now, as I heard myself speak the words, I realized that it was all my fault."

He looked up at Lane, eyes brimmed with tears of regret. "I destroyed our world."

"What are you talking about?" Lane said. "I don't understand."

"I was the one who first gave him the nectar. Do you not see?" Quinn explained. "My motives were pure. I simply wanted to ease his pain. I knew that the nectar had a numbing effect on pain. I had administered it medicinally before, when men from the villages had been badly injured. I had never had any problem with it before. I had no idea what it would do to Owen."

"What happened? Please continue the story," Lane prodded.

"Well, the nectar did a marvelous job of easing Owen's pain. From the first goblet—well, more like a barrel—that boy can drink! Our goblets were far too small for him, so we started serving the nectar to him in the barrel. He could empty one of those in no time flat. It was quite remarkable, really.

"From the first time I gave the nectar to him, it seemed to remove the pain and clear his mind. He growled less and was responsive to my words. I believe it even aided in the healing process.

"Over the next few weeks we fell into a regular routine. Every few hours we would administer the nectar, dress his wounds, and feed him. My duties to the people began pressing upon me again, and I had to tear myself away from this new fascination and delegate his care to some of the other priests. We created a rotation for his care. I wanted someone to be with him at all times.

"As Owen healed, he was able to move about. Over the course of time he began moving freely through the village. As his wounds healed, his scars began to form. He was—how shall I put it—well, you've seen him. He was hideous and a bit frightening upon first glance. Whenever a village priest made his first visit to the monastery after Owen's arrival, it was always the same. The poor priest would shriek in terror like a little girl.

"All of us in the monastery made a little game out of it. It was quite entertaining, actually. When a new priest was approaching the compound, our sentry would signal us and we would all take our places..."

Quinn was smiling again as he tattled on himself, a glint of mischief sparkling in his eye.

"We would place Owen behind a large rock, near the first ladder that led up into the village. Everyone else would conceal themselves in places where they could watch the poor wretch who was about to be made sport. Owen enjoyed the game, and I could see his gnarled flesh form what I believed to be a smile as he waited behind the rock. The poor, unsuspecting priest would climb up off the first ladder and onto the path. The first thing he noticed was that the monastery was deserted. This set him on guard. He would walk cautiously toward the compound, and then it would happen. Owen would step out from behind the rock, right in front of the priest. That was all he had to do. He didn't growl, or roar, he just stepped out from the shadows into the priest's path, and the natural course of events would follow and entertain us all for quite a while.

"I learned that I could use that little game as a way to evaluate the visiting priests, based upon how they reacted." Quinn was laughing now. "There was quite a range of responses, let me tell you. My favorite was old Norfin. He was a chubby little man. Very quiet and analytical. When Owen stepped out in front of him, Norfin took one look up at Owen's face...and dropped flat on his back. I thought he was dead. He just laid there. No screams. No flinching. He just dropped—*plop*—right on his back. It was the strangest thing."

Quinn chuckled to himself. Lane laughed as he visualized the scene.

"The truth is," Quinn continued, "Owen was quite docile and friendly. He became quite helpful around the monastery. Once he was healed, we discovered that he was incredibly strong. His strength, combined with his size, made him a valuable tool for assisting in projects around the village. With Owen's help we were able to accomplish great feats of construction and improvement around the monastery, things that would have otherwise been too monumental for us to attempt.

"Now, Lane, I must tell you about what else was happening during this time. Much of this I did not find out until after the fact, of course. While I was distracted with caring for Owen, Exapator and his two neophytes were becoming enchanted with a newcomer of their own. The three of them went up to the Plains of Meditation without anyone knowing and tried to recreate their encounter with the woman in the flames. The two neophytes drank the nectar, Exapator threw in the bitter berries, and, remarkably, she reappeared.

"Exapator claimed that this vision was a manifestation of Amo and that she was communicating with him—and him only. He began proclaiming this to all the priests in the monastery. You can imagine what a predicament this put me in. Here I was, the High Priest of Amo, and I was apparently out of the loop. During my meditations I would follow the traditional methods and stare into the flame. Many nights I would receive nothing. This was common. Well, as you can imagine, my old-fashioned ways seemed weak and pale in comparison to Exapator's spectacle. It was as if he had Amo at his command. He simply needed to inebriate his neophytes and throw the bitter berries into the fire and—*whoosh!*—she would appear. Of course, she never spoke. We could never see her face, and she always seemed to be thrashing about. I always found her odd, to say the least. Eventually Exapator became so confident in his ability to conjure up this apparition that he began inviting the other priests to join him and watch.

"With a growing audience of spellbound onlookers, Exapator started receiving messages from Amo. He said that Amo was ushering in a new age of prosperity and good fortune for the Altanians. She told him that she demanded that the Altanians build a magnificent temple to her on the Plains of Meditation. She was no longer satisfied with the simple fire pit. She also said this was the reason that she had given Owen to us. He was to help us build the temple.

"And so it began. Things started to shift. Exapator, the self-proclaimed oracle of Amo, would announce her newest revelations to all the priests during the day, filling their heads with these new ideas. Then, when it came time for our official council meetings, he would humbly subject himself to my authority and say something like, 'Of course, Master, all of these instructions fall ultimately to your discretion and wisdom in leadership. I am simply the conduit of Amo's revelation.' Then he would bow to me and look up from under his thick brow with a treacherous smile. I knew what was happening, but I had no power to draw back the tide. I felt I had no choice but to acquiesce to these new revelations. The majority of the priests were already following Exapator's teaching. To resist it would have caused much strife within the monastery.

"Against my better judgment, I agreed to use Owen to build a new temple for Amo. Exapator had received the plans for the monstrosity through his connection with Amo, and soon the building was underway.

"Owen actually enjoyed the project. He grew stronger every day as he felled trees and dug stone out of the ground. The monastery became consumed with the construction project. We fell into a new pattern of living. Some of Owen's wounds persisted, and he required the nectar as a pain reliever. Each morning, a priest would deliver food and a barrel of nectar to Owen's quarters. After a morning of hard work, another priest would deliver his lunch and another barrel of nectar. Then work in the afternoon, dinner and nectar. Some evenings, if the work had gone especially well, I found out that Exapator would bring another barrel to Owen just before bed.

"During the months that followed, two things grew in our monastic life. The first was the temple itself. I was amazed at how quickly we were able to build it with Owen working. It was, and still is, an amazing architectural achievement, unmatched in any of the tribes. The second thing was subtle at the time, but looking back on it, I see how significant it was. Between Owen's huge consumption of the nectar and the neophytes' use of it as an oracular vehicle, our demand for the substance increased dramatically. Many of the priests began drinking it as well. I think they secretly hoped that it would somehow connect them to this new age of Amo's revelations. The Deltonians were extremely pleased with the increased demand. They were becoming very rich in our natural resources as we showered them with furs and precious ore in exchange for more of the nectar.

"After several months, the construction was complete. With a spectacular opening ceremony, Exapator held his first 'visitation' with Amo on the temple platform. The priests were enthralled. Owen was given spacious quarters directly beneath the platform. Next to his chamber there was a storehouse for the nectar. Life seemed wonderful.

"Then it happened. I shudder to think of it..."

Quinn stopped and looked at Lane, as if he were afraid to tell him the rest of the story.

"What?" Lane sat up in protest. "What happened? You can't leave me hanging like that, man!"

Quinn continued. "Owen quickly became settled in his new chamber. It was quite spacious, and I could tell he felt very special. One morning I had appointed a neophyte to tend to Owen. The poor boy was just newly arrived from the village and had no idea about Owen's needs and peculiarities.

"You see, we had kept Owen a secret from the villages. The village priests who visited the monastery were sworn to secrecy.

"So, when this neophyte took Owen his morning ministrations, he made a grave mistake. He forgot to bring the nectar. No one witnessed the event, but I can only imagine what happened.

Screams and roars were heard from Owen's chambers. Several priests ran to see what was happening. When they arrived they found Owen standing in the middle of his chamber, covered in blood, and..."

Quinn stopped again, looking pensive.

Lane was not quite as eager to hear the next part of the story. He feared he already knew. Cautiously, Lane asked Quinn, "So... what happened?"

Quinn spoke quietly, "They found the boy...torn to pieces... lying all around Owen's chambers."

Quinn's chin sunk to his chest. A knot formed in Lane's stomach.

"It does not end there," Quinn somberly continued. "The first two priests to arrive on the scene were greeted by a raging Owen. They, too, were torn to shreds before anyone realized what was happening. By this time several priests had gathered. Exapator was one of them. He ran to the storage room, intuitively knowing the cause of Owen's rage, and grabbed a barrel of the nectar. He threw it into the chamber at Owen's feet. Immediately, upon sight of the barrel, Owen dropped the priest whom he was about to disembowel, ripped open the barrel, and emptied its contents in a few big gulps. For good measure, Exapator threw in another barrel and rushed the remaining priests out of the chambers.

"Owen drank the barrels dry and then collapsed in a heap on the floor.

"The entire monastery was in shock. An emergency meeting of the council was called, and, while Owen was still unconscious, it was agreed that we should shackle him in his chambers before he woke again. As quickly as could be manufactured, an iron gate was placed on Owen's chamber door. Owen was now a prisoner."

Quinn stopped and looked at the iron gate that stood on the side of his home. Golden firelight danced on its metal surface. Only the sound of the sizzling flames and the occasional *pop* of the fire softly punctuated the heavy silence. Each spark that floated into the dark abyss of the ceiling seemed to carry a prayer for the lost priests.

Lane and Quinn sat and stared at the rising sparks for a long time.

"Everything changed from that moment on." Quinn finally continued. "And quickly. Many sessions of the high council were held. The council became divided over Owen. I believed that Owen was genuinely a good soul and needed to be rehabilitated. Obviously he had become dependent upon the nectar in a very unhealthy and dangerous way and needed to be carefully and lovingly weaned from its power.

"Exapator strongly disagreed. He informed the council that he had received new revelations from Amo regarding Owen. The purpose of the gift was being revealed in layers. At first he was intended to build the temple, but now his true identity was emerging. 'Owen is not his real name' Exapator declared to the council. With great theatrics, Exapator stood up and announced to the spellbound council, arms raised, chest puffed, 'His name is Bellator!'

"Exapator explained to the council that Amo desired him to lead the Altanians into preeminence among the tribes. No longer would we be the forgotten tribe, hidden up in the mountains, across the Waste, away from the mainstream of the world. With the Bellator, we would conquer the tribes and bring them into submission to the one true god, Amo. Through our leadership and teaching they would learn the truth and understand that the power of Amo is something to be feared and revered. The Bellator was sent to us as a military force. He would lead us into the tribes and bring them into submission.

"Well," Quinn threw up his hands as if throwing everything he owned into the fire. "If I thought I had been losing power and influence before that point, it was all slipping out of my fingers as I listened to that speech.

"I had had enough. I could no longer stand by and watch everything we believed in be consumed by this madness. I spoke out against Exapator. I challenged his credibility. I ranted against the inconsistencies in the revelations he received. At every turn, he had the same rebuttal. He had the physical manifestation of Amo. End of argument.

"Ultimately, I was overthrown. Exapator was unanimously exalted to high priest, and I was exiled.

"After that, I have only been able to piece together the story. Exapator somehow coerced Owen into leading the Altanians into battle. They invaded the tribes, and, one by one, brought them into submission. The Deltonians felt the worst of it, since they were the producers of the nectar. My heart breaks for that tribe. To be taken from such prosperity to such bitter oppression in the blink of an eye—it is deplorable.

"Well." Quinn slapped his knees with both hands to punctuate the end of his story. "That's it."

He stood up to fetch another log for the fire. "Ever since my exile I have lived here, in this cavern, and have dedicated my life to studying the mysteries of this world and this strange manifestation of Amo."

He threw the log onto the fire and sent another flurry of sparks into the air.

"I spend days wandering the Waste, observing the numa and the bitter bush, meditating on the gods and the stories that were passed down to me by the elders."

He paused again to stoke the fire. He looked at Lane out of the corner of his eye. Lane just sat and stared into the fire. A small and barely perceptible smirk curled on the edge of Quinn's mouth as he observed Lane's deep concentration.

"Most of all…" Quinn said quietly. He paused, then whispered, "I've been waiting for you."

Chapter 31

Lane looked surprised. "For me? What do you mea—" Lane stopped himself short as a wave a realization washed over his face. "Oh, right. The Pleroma. Everybody was waiting for the Pleroma to show up."

Quinn began waving his hands, as if Lane's suggestion was an annoying fly buzzing in front of his face.

"Yes, yes, of course I had heard about the Deltonians' prophecy." Quinn quickly dismissed the idea. "But that is not what I mean. Since the first day I met Owen I had suspicions about his origin. I knew he was not from this world. At first I thought he might have been a special creation of Amo, born from the flames and given to us as a gift. Through the circumstances of my life and the years of study and discovery in the Waste, my theology has been somewhat…hmmm…re-visioned, shall we say? I have some theories about Owen's origin, but no way of verifying them. I have wanted to ask Owen hundreds of questions, but I knew that even if he was free and I had access to him, the information I would gather from him would be extremely limited due to his inability to speak.

"One of my theories suggests that, if Owen did come here from another world, through some sort of passage, then it would only seem logical that someday another creature would pass through as well."

Quinn extended his hand as if he were displaying Lane to a jury as Exhibit A. "And here you are. I have so many questions to ask you…"

Another crash echoed from behind the iron gate. Quinn

and Lane's conversation was abruptly interrupted as they both jumped and stood to their feet. Owen was awake and raging through the small window. His voice seemed tired and forced, but he continued to pound on the gate.

"He is growing weak." Quinn said.

Methodically, Quinn prepared another bowl of steaming soup and walked it over to the window. He stood patiently, holding the bowl in his hand, waiting for the creature's tantrum to subside.

He stood there for quite a while as Owen continued to pound on the gate and roar his mournful groans. Eventually the beast calmed down enough for Quinn to speak.

"Now, Owen, that will be quite enough." Quinn spoke as if to a child. "You are only hurting yourself by acting that way. You need nourishment. I am going to give you another bowl of soup. If you throw this one, you will have to wait to get another."

Quinn bent down to the small slot at the bottom of the door and placed the bowl on the ground, poised to slide through. Just before he pushed it, he said, "Do you think you are ready for this, Owen?"

Owen responded with a throaty whine. Quinn slid the bowl through the slot and stood up. There were a few seconds of quiet, and then the bowl and its contents came hurling at the gate and splattered through the window. The Bellator flew into another fit of wild rage and began thrashing around the chamber. Crashing, pounding, stamping, moaning. He carried on for a long while. Quinn shook his head and returned to the fire pit.

"He keeps hoping I will give him nectar to ease his pain. Right now he is feeling very betrayed and very angry and lonely. He will fall asleep soon and then we can continue."

Over the next few days Quinn and Lane fell into a routine. In the morning they would attempt to feed Owen, who would rage against them and then fall asleep. Quinn and Lane would head out into the Waste and explore. They walked and talked for most of the day, gathering bitter berries in a large pouch along the way. In the evenings they returned and offered another meal to Owen, then settled down next to the fire with a meal of their own and talked some more.

One evening, they walked along the ridge that separated the cliffs from the Waste.

"Q," Lane said, "I have to tell you that these last few days have been great."

"That is nice, Lane,"

"No, really. I mean, I know this sounds corny, but I feel a strange connection to you."

Quinn kept his gaze focused on the path as they walked.

"Please explain."

"First of all, I love talking to you. You actually listen to me. That alone is awesome. And then, even though you're really old…"

Quinn's eyebrows lifted.

"…no offense," Lane stammered.

"None taken. In truth, I am ancient."

"Right, well, most old people get set in their ways, but you seem to be so thirsty for knowledge. I love it."

Quinn smiled.

"I had a really great connection with Jethro," Lane continued. "He was like a father to me. But what I feel with you is different. I could never talk with him like I do with you. I can connect with you on a deep, philosophical level. It's like you can look deep into my soul and pull things out of me that I didn't even know were there. It's pretty cool. I don't know. Is that weird?"

Quinn stopped on the path and faced Lane.

"It is not weird, Lane." He placed his hand on Lane's arm. "I, too, feel that it is… cool." He smirked and then continued along the path toward the mouth of the cave.

One night, after returning from the Waste, Quinn and Lane settled next to the fire.

"Lane, tell me about your life in the other world. I know your father was an angry man who would hurt you when he was intoxicated; that must have been very difficult for you. But, was it always like that for you?"

Lane stared into the fire for a long time. Quinn waited patiently.

Eventually, Lane spoke. "No, it wasn't always like that. The first ten years of my life were wonderful, actually." He looked up and stared at Quinn, eyes brimming with tears. The moisture glistened on the lids of his deep blue eyes as the firelight coaxed a drop down his face.

"Please," Quinn said softly, "tell me more about those times. I think it will do you good." The sincerity and safety of Quinn's face and voice invited Lane into a space that he had not allowed himself to go for a very long time.

He choked back the lump in his throat and continued.

"My mom and dad were awesome. I was an only child, so they were able to shower me with attention. They were both very intelligent—professors, actually. Mom taught literature at the local college, and Dad was a philosophy professor at the U. With parents like that, you can imagine what my childhood was like. I was surrounded with fantastic stories and wild ideas about anything and everything.

"Dad wasn't really into sports or hunting or fishing, or anything like that. He was a thinker. I remember one of my favorite things that he used to do with me. Every Thursday we would have a lunch date. Even after I was in school, he'd pick me up and take me out. We went to this one drive-in place, and he'd let me order whatever I wanted. Of course, I always got the grilled-cheese sandwich and that neon-blue slushy drink. We would play this game. He would start a story and then stop it and point to me. I had to pick up where he left off and add on to the story. I'd take it a little farther and then point to him. We'd go back and forth, creating these fantastic stories until it was time to get back to school."

Lane shook his head and grinned. "Man, we created some pretty crazy stories. It was great.

"Then there was my mom. Every night, before I went to bed, she would come into my room and crawl in bed with me, carrying a storybook in her hand. I would snuggle up next to her, and then Dad would come in and lean over the end of the bed. She would read to us about all kinds of wonderful places and people and adventures. Half the time, Dad would fall asleep as he leaned on the bed. We'd have to kick him when his snoring drowned out Mom's reading. We'd just laugh and roll our eyes at each other, and then Mom would keep on reading.

"Then Mom and Dad told me that I was going to have a little brother. I had just turned nine. I was so excited. It was perfect, really. I had had my parents all to myself as a little kid, and now I was ready to share them with someone else. I couldn't wait to tell him all the stories we had made up and listen to Mom read all those books to him again.

"The day they brought little Josh home from the hospital was a great day. He was so cute. Honestly, I was a little disappointed with him at first. I mean, he just laid there. He wasn't very interesting. He got better though. Soon he was sitting up, and Mom was feeding him really nasty-looking mush out of a little jar. I used to spread a blanket out on the floor before I had to leave for school in the mornings and have baby school with him. I'd show him letters and colors and read to him. As his big brother, I felt it was my responsibility to help him get a head start in life, you know?

"Then one night my parents had to go to a dinner reception at the university, so they hired a babysitter to stay with us. I told Mom that I was big enough to watch Josh by myself, but she insisted that someone sit with us while they were gone.

"They got all dressed up for the dinner party. They looked so good that night that Dad thought it was a good opportunity for a family photo. We all stood in front of the fireplace. Dad put me on his shoulders, and Mom held Josh in her arms. The babysitter was a really funny older lady, and she made us burst out laughing right before she snapped the picture.

"Mom looked so beautiful that night. Her long black hair was so shiny, and her smile was contagious."

Lane looked up at Quinn. The tears had returned to the edge of his eyes. "That was the last time I saw my parents." His head sunk and he stared back at the fire. "The next morning I woke up, and the babysitter was still there. I came down to the kitchen for breakfast and there was, like, this heaviness in the room that I could feel before I even saw her. She had the worst expression on her face that I've ever seen. She looked old and tired, and when she saw me she threw open her arms and started to cry.

"I had no idea what was going on. She told me that, the night before, as my parents were driving home from the dinner party, they were in a car accident. I guess my dad had had too much to drink at the party, so my mom was driving. Dad had his seat back, so when the car flipped it threw him out and sent him flying. Mom was strapped in the car, so when it burst into flames…"

Lane stopped. He couldn't get the words out. It took a few seconds for him to regain composure.

"…well…there was nothing left. The flames were so intense that they consumed her completely.

"Dad was never the same after that. He blamed himself for her death. He became angry and violent after that. It was like a part of him died in the crash with Mom that night. Ever since then he has been mean to us. He used to beat me every night. I would ask him to read to us and he would slap the book out of my hand and yell at me. It was terrible.

"I basically raised Josh by myself. Dad lost his job at the university and had to get some brainless job. I'm not even sure what he does. That didn't help things. He's like an automaton now. He gets up, goes to work, comes home drunk, falls asleep in front of the TV, and then gets up to do it again. I learned that, if I kept Josh out of his way, and I stayed behind closed doors, we were safe.

"I basically lost both of my parents in that crash. I don't even know who the man is that sleeps in my house every night.

"That's why I'm so worried about this coma I'm in."

"Ah yes, the coma," Quinn responded, as if he had just been reminded of a very important piece of an equation that had slipped his mind. "Tell me more about your coma theory."

"First of all"—Lane's head was clearing again—"it's not

a theory. It's a fact. When the bed collapsed on my head, the trauma induced a coma. Right now, as we are having this conversation, I am laying on a hospital bed, fighting for my life. My subconscious has created this world to guide me and show me how to break free of the coma.

"Quinn, you have to help me figure out how to get back home. Josh needs me. He can't be alone with my dad. He's too young. I don't want him to suffer like I have. The poor kid has only known the painful part of my family's story. I'm the only thing he has."

"Indeed," Quinn simply stroked his beard.

Chapter 32

Throughout the days, Quinn continued to offer nourishment to Owen. Gradually, the hulking beast accepted it. The raging and pounding subsided. Quinn spoke softly to him through the barred gate, and he listened without growling.

After about two weeks it was time. Owen was ready to come out from the chamber. Quinn's gnarled fingers laced around the gate handle, and his entire body jerked backwards to swing the door open. It scraped along the stone floor. Lane was afraid the abrasive noise would set the beast off, and he would come raging through the gap. Lane held his breath as the opening widened.

Nothing happened at first. The chamber seemed dead and empty. Quinn poked his head into it and waved his hand to draw out the reluctant inhabitant. A broad smile spread across Quinn's face as he backed away from the door. He looked like a proud father watching his toddler take his very first steps. First a foot appeared from the side of the doorway. Then the entire body followed and filled the empty gap.

Lane was shocked. The figure that stood in that doorway could no longer be described as a beast. His frame was still large, and the skin was still severely scarred, but he was no longer grotesque and hulking. His muscles had reduced in size and mass. He no longer looked like an exaggerated, comic-book character, but had the well-proportioned appearance of a muscular human. The Bellator had truly become Owen once again.

"My friend!" Quinn greeted Owen with outstretched arms. "It is so good to see you!"

Owen looked down at Quinn. A smile twisted around his

scarred face.

"Come, come!" Quinn motioned for Owen to move toward the fire pit. "I would like to introduce you to another good friend of mine."

Lane stood as they approached and moved around the fire pit to meet them. As they came together, Lane did not feel intimidated by Owen's size. The truth is that Owen was only two or three inches taller than Lane. While his shoulders were still much broader and his chest thicker, he did not seem like the mountain of a man that he was before.

"Owen, this is my friend Lane," Quinn said. "He is the one who helped you escape from the Altanians."

At the sound of the name "Lane" Owen's eyes open a little wider and his head cocked to the side. The two giants stood toe to toe. Owen looked intensely at Lane, studying the features of his face. He leaned in closer. A large hand came up on either side of Lane's face and held it. Lane tensed at the touch. Adrenaline was about to shoot through his veins, and fear stood at the door, ready to pounce. But Owen's touch was gentle. Lane looked into his eyes. The blue discs were kind and inviting, and very familiar.

They stared into each other's eyes for a moment, looking deeply, as if probing a hidden storehouse of memories and emotions. A spark arced between them.

"Dad!" Lane threw out his arms. "It *is* you!" Owen's face lit up, and he engulfed his son in a warm embrace.

As they stood there, locked in a long-overdue reunion, Quinn smiled and moved to prepare some bowls of soup for the three of them. He called over his shoulder, "Owen, you will find some proper clothing for you draped over the cot. Perhaps you should put them on while I prepare some food."

Owen complied and the clothing further enhanced his more normal appearance.

"Come, men," Quinn summoned them after he had prepared their places at the fire. "Let us eat together and celebrate."

"This is incredible," Lane said. He was almost too excited to eat. "I mean, that night at the Festival, when I looked in your eyes, I thought it was you, but after we left and you were so out of control, I figured I had just been seeing things.

"How did you get here, Dad? What's going on?"

Owen looked across the flames at Lane with apology in his eyes. He simply shrugged his shoulders. Dumb. No words. He pantomimed shielding his face from something horrible, then he looked over at Quinn and pointed to him, and then simply shrugged again.

"What are you trying to say? I don't understand." Lane was frustrated. "You don't remember how you got here?"

Owen shook his head and conveyed regret through his eyes. He looked over to Quinn for rescue.

"Yes, Lane," Quinn interceded, "this is the difficulty we have always had with Owen. For some reason he cannot speak. Perhaps the best way to communicate would be to ask simple, yes-or-no questions."

"Right," Lane said, "It will be like playing twenty questions and charades at the same time."

Lane searched his mind for a minute.

"Dad, do you remember anything from before you arrived here?"

Owen nodded to the affirmative. Lane was encouraged and continued with enthusiasm.

"Do you remember me?"

Yes.

"Do you remember Josh?"

Yes. Owen cradled his arms like he was holding a baby.

"Are you saying that Josh was a baby?"

Yes.

"How old was I when you last remember me?"

Owen pointed at Lane, then held his hand, palm-down, beside him, like he was showing the height of a young child.

Lane stopped short, shocked by this revelation. He choked down the lump that caught in his throat and squeaked out the next question.

"Dad...was I...ten when you last saw me?"

Yes.

The realization swept through Lane's body like a rush of fireflies swarming under his skin. The questions came faster.

"Is the last thing you remember going to a dinner party with Mom?"

Owen froze at the word. His eyes saddened. Slowly, his head nodded. Yes.

Owen's eyes widened in terror. He threw his hands in front of his face like he was shielding himself from something terrible flying towards him. He fell backwards off the bench and crashed on the floor behind it. Quinn and Lane jumped to their feet to come to his aid.

Owen looked like a frightened child as he lay on the ground. He was scared and confused. Lane helped him to his feet, and the three resumed their spots next to the fire.

They sat in silence, eating their soup, each of them tumbling this new revelation in their minds, trying to make sense out of it.

In an attempt to lighten the mood, Lane refocused the attention of the group.

"Quinn?" Lane held up the bowl of fragrant soup and motioned to the old man. "I've been meaning to say this since I first got here. This is great. What is it?"

Quinn sensed Lane's attempt to shift the focus away from Owen and quickly jumped on board.

"Lovely!" Quinn responded enthusiastically. "I am delighted that you enjoy it."

He paused, placed his hands on his knees, and looked like he was about to tell a big surprise that he'd been holding in for a very long time.

"Well, I suppose since you brought up the subject, this is as good a time as any to tell you."

Lane looked confused and intrigued. "What are talking about?"

"The soup you are eating"—Quinn was very excited, but also a little pensive— "is made from...bitter berries."

Lane spit the contents out of his mouth, threw the bowl across the room, and stood up.

"What!? Are you crazy?" Lane shouted. "Are you trying to kill us? Have you been slowly poisoning us or something?"

He paced back and forth. Owen became visibly agitated by the mounting tension in the room.

"I knew it. I knew this was too good to be true," Lane ranted, more to himself than to the others. "I'm so stupid! Come on, man, when are you going to learn? Every time you let somebody in, they hurt you. This is amazing! Even the people that my mind creates turn on me. I must be totally losing it!"

He grabbed his head with his hands and looked around frantically, like a wild animal that had been cornered and was desperate to escape. He walked to the opening of the cavern, then stopped, turned around, and headed straight toward Owen.

"And you! Why do *you* have to be here? It serves you right that you're all mangled and nasty...and mute. You left me! How could you have left me like that?"

Lane's intense anger instantly morphed into equally intense sadness. He burst into tears, chest heaving up and down. Between sobs, he choked out words. "Why? Dad, why did you have to go? Why did you and Mom leave us? We've been so afraid ever since you left. I loved you so much. Now...now all I feel is anger and...hatred. Dad, I HATE YOU!"

Lane slumped back into his seat by the fire, his body limp. He buried his face in his hands and sobbed uncontrollably.

Quinn and Owen sat silent.

Chapter 33

Lane sat, tear-stained and empty, his body heavy and weak.

Quinn moved over and sat next to him. He spoke softly, his voice like a warm, healing oil.

"That was good, Lane. You needed to let that out. I believe this will help to begin your healing. This highlights a very important truth that I have learned. Oftentimes the very things that eat away at us from the inside are ideas that have been manufactured from our own misperception of reality. Pure fiction. Take this soup for example. It is made from the bitter berry."

Quinn held up his bowl. Lane looked at it, then blinked away some lingering tears and looked at Quinn.

"When you and Jethro crossed the Waste," Quinn continued, "he told you that the bitter berry was poisonous, true?"

Lane nodded.

"And did you have any reason not to believe him?"

Lane shook his head.

"No, of course not. You trusted Jethro, and well you should have. He was your mentor. The truth is that Jethro was being completely honest with you. As far as he knew, the bitter berry was poisonous. His father taught him that, as his father's father taught him. The truth is that everyone, including the Altanians, believed the bitter berries to be poisonous. We only used them for their ability to open up the conduit to Amo's realm in the flames. We would never have ingested them.

"Ever since I first saw Exapator's Amo in the flames, and since I was exiled by my own people and rejected by the goddess I served so faithfully, I have done a great deal of thinking.

I would be lying to say that my faith had not been shaken to its core. I began reexamining everything, trying to look at it from a different perspective. It has been a long and difficult journey, especially in isolation.

"I found my greatest source of insight in the Waste, of all places. For generations we have believed that the Waste was a cursed place that was once a fertile valley and had been destroyed by Amo. Everyone feared it. We believed the numa to be the tortured spirits of those condemned tribesmen, cursed to eat the bitter berry and wander back and forth between the spirit world and our world, never knowing their final rest.

"In my exilic solitude I took to wandering through the Waste...and observing. I put aside my inherited fears and simply watched...and learned. I made some interesting observations."

Lane's scientific curiosity helped dry his remaining tears. He sat up and leaned in.

"First," Quinn continued, "I observed that the only creature that eats the bitter berry is the numa. That much I could explain—it was part of their curse. I also observed that the only time a numa vanished and passed into the otherworld was when it happened to pass through an arch that was formed when the branches of two separate bitter bushes touched and intertwined. Given the sparsity of the Waste, this phenomenon is fairly rare.

"I made it my mission to locate and map every occurrence of these archways that I could find. I observed them carefully for a very long time. This led to my second observation. Of all the arches that I have observed over all these years, I have never seen a numa come out of one. I have seen hundreds of them go in and vanish, but none have returned.

"Our legend claimed that the numa were spirits that wandered back and forth between the worlds. If that were the case, then why did none come back? I started to wonder if, perhaps, there was another force at work here.

"Then one day, I made the big step. Abandoning all fear, I walked up to one of the bitter bushes, plucked a berry, and ate it. I was fully prepared to fall over right there and die. But I did not. Granted, the berry was extremely bitter and tough, but I did not die. That night I expected to die in my sleep. But I woke up. So, the next day I took a pouch into the Waste and filled it with bitter berries. I brought them back and began to experiment.

"After many attempts, I made a wonderful discovery. If you soak the berries in water for several days, they swell up and become plump and soft. Then, if you heat them slowly in a pot, they release a broth that has a sweet, meaty flavor and becomes this soup. It is one of the best meals I have ever had. In fact, it is all I have eaten since I made the discovery many years ago. And it is all you have eaten since you arrived."

Lane was amazed and impressed. "Wow, Q, that was some pretty gutsy scientific exploration. You're the man."

"Thank you." Quinn received the compliment with confidence. "So, you see, my intention was not to poison you."

"I'm sorry about that." Lane said, "It's just that..."

"No need to explain, Lane," Quinn interrupted. "Quite understandable. You have been through a great deal in your young life. Apology accepted."

Owen smiled and looked relieved.

"No, I was not trying to poison you," Quinn continued. "Quite the opposite. I was trying to prepare you. Along with my exploration of the Waste, I have also been developing some new theories. When I walked away from the Plain of Meditation on the day I was exiled, my theological mind opened up to new possibilities. I looked at the stars and wondered what they were and if there was anything above them. I looked at the mountains, the plains, and the sea, the movement of the clouds, sun, and rain, and wondered if there was a force behind them. I looked at the gods and realized that they seem to be just like us. The Sisters with their repeated pregnancies and births, the Great Father and his continual death and rebirth and his never-ending struggle with the underworld. Amo and her temperamental nature and propensity to deception and intrigue. I began to wonder why. Sometimes the gods seem more flawed and twisted than we are.

"Perhaps, I thought, it was possible that the gods were nothing more than metaphors, analogies for elemental forces that are larger than we can explain. Perhaps the universe is bigger than we ever imagined. Perhaps there is something beyond what we know and observe. As my mind began to entertain these thoughts, and knowing that I was safe from those who would stone me as a heretic for such dangerous rantings, I became convinced of something. I know that there has to be a mind beyond all of this. Above it, somehow. Not spatially. Not a mind like ours, but a force, an existence, an intelligence that thought all this up. It made it, it drives it, it knows it—in some way."

Quinn shook his head. "I know this sounds like the ravings of a man who has been alone far too long."

"No," Lane said, "please continue. I'm totally tracking with you."

Quinn looked pleased and somewhat relieved. All pensiveness was now gone, and he became excited as he shared his theories.

"When your mind is open like this, your favorite saying becomes, 'what if?'"

Lane chuckled. He liked it.

"What if there was more to the universe? What if there were actually other universes or realities that coexisted with our own? What if that explains where Owen came from? And where you came from, Lane. And…"

Quinn paused for dramatic effect.

"What if the archways in the bitter bush were passageways to these other realities?"

"Ha!"

Lane clasped his hands over his mouth. His reaction surprised them all.

Quinn looked confused. "Are you laughing at my idea, Lane?"

"No, no," Lane scrambled to find an explanation for his outburst. "It's just that, well… I mean, portals to other realities? Come on. I was totally with you up to that point, but now you're just talking Wood-Between-the-Worlds kind of stuff that comes right out of kids' stories. You've simply exchanged one set of myths for another."

Quinn sat back, looking a little dejected.

Lane walked around the fire pit a few times, processing all that Quinn had said. By the third circle he spoke.

"Here's what I think is going on. Quinn, you are the guide that my mind has created within the context of this world. Your purpose is to show me ways to defeat my coma and wake up. These 'portals,'"—Lane wiggled the first two fingers on each hand in the 'quote marks' gesture—"of yours represent something."

Lane paused and rubbed his chin. His words had caught up with his ideas, and now he needed to regroup and process some more.

He snapped his fingers. "I got it. The portals represent different methods that the doctors are using to bring me out of the coma. In order for me to wake up, I have to buy into this fantasy and explore the portals if I want to break free of this delusion."

"Ha!" Quinn burst out, mimicking Lane's previous interjection.

Lane dropped his shoulders in dejection, half playing along with Quinn's mockery of him and half truly deflated by Quinn's obvious disagreement with his hypothesis.

"You have a problem with my idea?" Lane said in a teasing tone.

"Yes," Quinn answered, "as a matter of fact I do. You just accused me of exchanging one set of myths for another, when my hypothesis is based upon years of observation and an openness to new possibilities.

"Let me ask you a question. On what basis do you believe that this world is not real and merely a figment of your imagination?"

"Well," Lane hemmed, then paused. "My dreams! That's how I know. In my dreams I have seen myself in the hospital room, and I've heard the doctors talking around me. Beside the fact that alternate realities and portals just aren't possible. This is the only logical explanation."

Quinn stroked his beard and stared at Lane for a while. "So, you are basing your hypothesis that Merib, the world in which you have lived for some time now—the world in which you have experienced laughter, fear, anger, love—is pure fantasy, because you have had dreams about the other world? And, further, you deny its observable existence based on the presupposition that it cannot exist? Am I correct in my understanding?"

Lane paused, feeling a little trapped. He finally released a simple and somewhat timid, "Yes."

"Hmm…very interesting," was all Quinn had to say.

The three of them sat in awkward silence for a while as Quinn fiddled with the embers of the fire and chased out flurries of random sparks. They welcomed the distraction and watched the little dancers racing back and forth into the darkness above.

Quinn clapped his hands.

"Regardless of our perception," he offered, "we share a common purpose and desire. We want to explore the archways. I propose that we get a good night's sleep, and tomorrow we embark on a grand adventure."

"Sounds good to me. I'm in!" Lane agreed.

Owen's face lit up, and his crooked smile wrinkled into the distorted position that they had come to recognize as delight.

"Wonderful," Quinn said. "Tomorrow morning it is. Now, we should get some rest."

CHAPTER 34

When Lane's eyes opened, the soft, warm glow of the firelight still danced on the stone wall beside him. It was very difficult to know the time of day inside the cavern. From his prone position on the cot, he craned his neck back in order to look across the room to the cupboard area. Quinn was already moving about, placing objects into a satchel.

"Is it morning already?" Lane groaned.

"Indeed, my young friend," Quinn answered without looking up from his task. "Come, gain some nourishment and prepare yourself."

As Lane shuffled toward the fire, hair disheveled and sticking straight out on one side, Owen appeared in the doorway of his chamber. Soon the three men were eating bowls of soup, and the cobwebs cleared from their heads.

Quinn threw the satchel over his shoulder and beckoned for the others to follow. He led them out of the cavern and into the dark crevice. A torch he retrieved from the wall sconce illuminated the dark, winding crack between the massive sandstone walls.

A pale light appeared in the darkness ahead and grew in size and intensity as they approached. The passage emptied into an antechamber whose far wall opened up to the faint morning sky. Pale, gray light filled the rocky hollow.

They stepped out onto the ledge and looked out across the vast expanse of the Waste. Pale gray gave way to an aura of gold. It filled the air with a song of life and hope and intensity. A small flame ignited on the horizon and burned brightly. The fire spread across the jagged line until it rose up into the sky and revealed the face of the Great Father, poking his nose above the edge of the world to see how his children fared this day. Long shadows bowed before him.

Lane looked up at Owen. His twisted mouth quivered. A single tear ran down his smooth cheek. Lane reached over and touched his arm. Owen looked down and smiled. Thousands of words slammed against the dam of his mute mouth.

"I know," Lane whispered. "It's amazing, isn't it?"

Owen placed his hand on Lane's and nodded.

Quinn had already begun his descent down the rocky apron toward the desert floor. A small, well-worn trail cut a winding path back and forth down the steep slope.

The two giants entered the path. It seemed like a pencil line compared to their larger frames. Yet it was enough to guide them through the rocks and scrub.

Quinn was just pulling a rolled-up piece of parchment out of his bag when Lane and Owen reached him. He spread it out on top of a large stone and smoothed his hand over the surface as if he were caressing the face of a dearly loved child.

"Here is a survey of the Waste that I have compiled over the years. These triangles represent the archways that I have observed. "The question before us right now is where to begin."

He tapped his finger on the parchment and hummed a bright tune as he surveyed the map.

"You seem pretty excited, Quinn," Lane observed.

"Oh, you have no idea, my boy," Quinn beamed. "I have waited more years than you have been alive for this day. From the moment I first stretched and prepared this blank parchment, I have anticipated the day when I would be able to actually experience the wonders and mysteries held within the bitter bush. Oh, yes, I am quite excited, to say the least."

Quinn scanned the map for a few more moments.

"I suppose there really is no logical starting place. The archways seem to be scattered throughout the Waste in an organic pattern. I suppose we should just start with the closest one and work our way across the valley from here"—he placed his finger on the triangle closest to the bottom right of the page, then slid it up—"to here. Then work our way up and down and across until we have reached them all."

"How long do you think this will take?" Lane asked.

"Truth be told, Lane," Quinn said as he looked up at him, "I have no idea if we will make it past the first one. We really do not know what to expect, do we?"

Lane paused. A tickle of excitement pulsed in his stomach.

"I guess not. That's what exploration is all about, right?"

"Indeed it is," Quinn agreed. His mustache widened over a broad smile as his eyes wrinkled into horizontal slits cut into his age-worn face. A sparkle flashed from each eye.

"We will begin here"—he pointed to a triangle that was just above the Upper Mountains. "We are here." He slid his finger a half inch straight down and landed on a green circle on the edge of the mountain range. He lifted the finger and pointed into the desert, straight toward the rising sun. "It is over there, not too far away."

He looked at his two companions, who towered above him.

"Shall we?" he said and then headed into the desert.

He moved quickly over the rugged terrain. The gravelly sand crunched beneath their feet. The hills rose and fell along the surface of the rocky landscape, like petrified waves on a vast sea of stone. Eventually they came to the edge of a dry river bed, and Quinn carefully slid sideways down its steep bank and came to rest on the smooth river rocks that lined its bottom.

The entire channel was lined with short, wispy, brown bushes that swayed in the breeze. A fairly large cluster of stubby, dull-green bushes squatted on the edge of the ravine, directly across from them. Shooting up from the middle of the cluster grew their target—the distinctive shape of the bitter bush.

"I see it!" Lane announced.

"Very good," Quinn said. He headed toward the arch.

Their approach flushed out two numa and sent the gangly rodents scurrying up the opposite bank of the river bed. Their spastic feet scratched along the gravelly rock, sending a spray of pebbles and dust into the air. They disappeared above the rim.

"Sorry to disturb your breakfast, my friends," Quinn said.

Quinn reached the archway first and placed his satchel on the ground, about ten feet directly in front of the opening. As Lane and Owen stepped up next to him, Quinn emptied the contents of the satchel onto the ground. He pulled out a coiled rope, two knives, a smaller pouch with a long cord attached, and two small objects that looked like balls made from cloth. One was brown and the other green.

Quinn picked up the balls and held them in his open hands for Lane to see.

"I have saved a little surprise for you," Quinn said, his voice seasoned with a hint of good-humored mischief. "What I hold in my hands are two ordinary pieces of cloth, stuffed with feathers and lint."

He handed them to Lane.

"Do you see any difference between them?"

Lane turned them over in his hands, weighed them, smelled them, and carefully examined each one.

"No," Lane said, "other than their color, they seem identical."

"Very good." Quinn retrieved them.

He walked over to the archway and looked back over his shoulder to make sure that Lane and Owen were paying close attention. With a quick flick of his hand, Quinn tossed the brown ball into the archway. It flew through and plunked down into the gravel on the other side. Quinn looked to see Lane's expression. He was underwhelmed.

Quinn smiled and turned back toward the bush. This time he tossed the green ball into the archway. It entered the arch two feet above the ground. As it passed through the plane of the branches, it vanished. Without any spectacular flash or sound, it simply was not there anymore. Gone.

Lane's eyes opened wide in wonder.

Quinn turned and beamed.

"I thought you would enjoy that," Quinn said. "You see, there was a fundamental difference between those two balls. I soaked the green one in bitter berry broth for several days and then let it dry.

"I believe that the bitter berry has some kind of transforming effect on matter. Ordinary matter passes through the arch as if it were nothing special. Yet something that has been saturated with the bitter berry will vanish. I believe that is why the numa vanish. They eat the bitter berries regularly.

"Now," Quinn moved closer to the arch, "watch this."

He rolled up the sleeve on his right arm and lifted his hand toward the arch. Slowly he moved it into the opening. As the tips of his fingers reached the plane, they vanished. As if he were submersing his hand in a perfectly still pool of water, Quinn extended his arm until his hand and half of his forearm had disappeared. After a second, Quinn slowly retracted his arm, and the flesh reappeared along the same vertical plane.

He slowly turned, hopeful anticipation in his eyes. He was not disappointed. Lane's jaw slacked wide in pure awe.

"OK, now that's just cool," Lane said.

"I first discovered this by pure accident," Quinn explained. "After I discovered the bitter berry soup, I began eating it regularly, simply because I enjoyed it. One day, after a few weeks of eating it, I was walking next to one of the archways, and I tripped. I sprawled forward and landed on my chest. As I hit the ground, my hand thrust into the archway and disappeared, just as I demonstrated a moment ago.

"Since then I have done the same experiment in many arches, and always found the same results. My hand simply vanishes. As I showed you with the ball, this phenomenon is not limited to organic tissue. Anything that has been saturated with the bitter berry will pass through."

"This is awesome!" Lane exclaimed. "I think I might know what's going on here. We talked about this kind of stuff in Mr. Lancaster's class. Some physicists theorize that there are multiple planes of reality, all coexisting in the same space, but at different quantum phase variations. I wonder if the bitter berry somehow alters the molecular structure at the quantum level and allows matter to pass through the phase shifts. There's got to be some kind of energy in the bush itself that, when focused by the joining of the branches, opens a rift between phases and allows berry-saturated matter to make the jump."

"Hmmm…," Quinn ruminated, "sounds pretty sophisticated, and real to me. Are you sure it is not just a figment of your imagination?"

Lane teasingly scowled back at Quinn. "Of course it's a figment of my imagination. Come on, this stuff comes from a dozen different sci-fi stories and movies. Mr. Lancaster's class got distracted by this kind of nonsense all the time."

Quinn looked disappointed.

"Don't get me wrong," Lane continued, "whether it's real or not, in this world it is real and if I'm going to be able to wake up from this coma, then I have to buy into this reality. So, I guess you could say that I do believe it's real."

Quinn did not appear completely satisfied with Lane's concession, but he said nothing.

"So, what's our next step?" Lane asked.

Quinn raised a finger in the air and walked over to the equipment he had laid out on the ground. He threw the coiled rope to Owen, who had been observing everything with keen awareness and interest.

"Owen," Quinn directed, "since you are the largest of the group, I would like you to tie one end of that rope around your waist. I will tie the middle portion of it around my waist, and Lane will tie himself to the end. That way we will be connected and will not get lost on the other side. I have no idea what we will find when we cross over, so I would like Owen to stay on this side and anchor himself. That way he will be able to pull us back through if need be."

Quinn tied the pouch and one of the knives to his waist and handed the other knife to Lane.

"I have placed some food in this pouch, just to be prepared," Quinn explained.

Lane nodded in agreement as they tied themselves to the rope. Linked together, the three of them looked like they were ready for an expedition up the face of Everest.

Lane and Quinn approached the arch and stood, shoulder to shoulder, squarely in front of it. Owen stood behind, feet spread wide, ready to brace himself. The excess rope lay coiled on the ground.

Lane looked down at the old, wrinkled hermit who stood beside him.

"Quinn, I have no idea what's about to happen. If it goes the way I hope it will, then I won't see you again. I'll jump through, wake up on the hospital bed, and start living my life again. I just want to say how much I appreciate all you've done for me. You've really helped me sort out a lot of things in my head. I know it's kind of weird to be talking to you like this since you are actually me, in a strange sort of way, but...still...thank you."

Quinn simply smiled and nodded. He reached up and gave Lane's arm a gentle squeeze.

Lane looked at Owen. Soft blue eyes stared back at him from the gnarled face.

"It was really good to see you again, Dad." Lane's voice tightened and his throat burned. "I'm going to miss you."

Lane swung around and threw his arms around Owen's chest. The large, muscular arms engulfed Lane's body, and they stood in a tight embrace.

After several moments, Lane pulled back and looked into Owen's eyes. "Dad, I'm sorry for what I said. I don't hate you. I love you. I miss you."

Owen tilted his head and smiled his twisted smile. His bright blue eyes shined back at his son.

Lane turned around and resumed his position next to Quinn.

"I'm ready."

Chapter 35

Quinn went first. In two quick steps he was gone. It was incredibly unspectacular, and Lane was a little disappointed. Quinn simply walked into nothingness. Now it was Lane's turn. He took a deep breath, leaned over to fit his head under the crest of the arch, and stepped through.

The experience itself was much more intense than watching it from the outside. As his foot broke the plane of the entryway, it immediately tingled. A force pulled him into the arch. As his face and head crossed over, an electric pulse shot through his body, and he was completely in.

Darkness. This was unlike any darkness he had ever experienced. Oppressive and heavy, it was like a deep cave painted with thick black tar.

His chest tightened and burned. No air.

He looked around to find Quinn, but could see nothing. He couldn't even see his own hand in front of him.

Panic pressed in around the edges of Lane's mind. He tried to turn, but realized that he was not standing on anything. He felt like he was both floating and incredibly heavy at the same time. The more he tried to move his feet, the more disoriented he became.

All of these observations happened in the moment he arrived in the black sea. In the next moment, just as he was about to tug on the rope to signal for Owen to pull them back, something caught his attention. A small shimmering cloud formed in the distance. It swirled and pulsed like a swarm of shining insects and grew larger. With no visual reference, it was hard to determine whether it was coming toward him from a great distance or was right in front of his face and simply growing in size.

Soon the cloud engulfed his entire field of vision. The sparkling matter now seemed more like a wall of mist. In the center of the wall an image appeared. At first it was a murky smudge against the undulating backdrop. It popped into focus and took the form of a dog, silhouetted against the bright cloud. The dog grew larger and began to move. It was bigger than a dog. A wolf. The wolf's face was now visible. It was not an ordinary wolf. A puppet head. He recognized this face. When he was a kid he was terrified by a puppet wolf that he had seen in a children's movie. That puppet wolf haunted his dreams for years after that. As soon as he recognized the face, it vanished and was replaced by two more images. One was a scene depicting a small-town main street. A large sign stood on the side of the road. The sign was for a family restaurant whose mascot was a large, muscular man with a white T-shirt and a chef's hat. The sign-man stood about thirty feet high. At the base of the sign, a young woman walked along the sidewalk. As she passed the sign, the man came to life and broke free of the sign frame. He looked down at the woman and picked her up. He raised her over his head, held her there for a moment, and then hurled her down against the ground.

While that scene played out, another overlapped it and ran simultaneously. A young woman sat in an icy chamber. She faced to the side, revealing only her profile. Her head drew closer to Lane's face. It turned and revealed the face of a once-beautiful young woman who was now pale-skinned, with large, dark circles marking the contour of her sunken eye sockets. It was the face of death. Lane immediately recognized her as a high-school girl who had been a friend of the family when he was a boy. She took her own life, and he was haunted by this dream for months after her funeral.

More images flooded into the cloud. All of them were nightmares that he had dreamed throughout his life. Each of the images was grainy and partially transparent, revealing the texture of the water vapor onto which it was being projected.

Another image appeared, however, that was crystal-clear. It filled his field of vision and preempted all others. Josh lay in his bed, thrashing back and forth like he was fighting off a monster in his dreams. Suddenly, Josh sat straight up in his bed and looked directly at Lane, as if he actually saw him. Josh reached toward him.

"Lane!" he yelled out.

As soon as the words left Josh's mouth, the image fractured into a million pixels and blew away like grains of sand driven by the wind. In its place the face of the puppet wolf appeared. It morphed into the snarling face of a real wolf and lunged at Lane.

In the few seconds that these images had appeared, Lane had been frantically tugging on the rope attached to his waist. Just as the wolf was about to bear down on him, the rope pressed into his abdomen, and he flew backwards. A pulse of electric shock surged through his body, and bright light blasted all around him. The light seared into his eyes. His lungs filled with air in a huge gasp, like a drowning man who had finally splashed up to the surface of the water.

The momentum of Owen's rescuing rope pull sent Lane skidding across the rocky ground, a spray of pebbles and dust flying everywhere. The jagged stones ripped into his back and brought him to a stop. He lay motionless for a moment. Slowly his eyes adjusted to the desert sun, and his heart rate reduced from a high-paced panic to the level of a normal adrenaline rush.

Quinn! Lane rolled his head to the side to see if Quinn had made it back. The old man's body was just a few feet from him. Owen knelt beside him. Quinn lay motionless.

Lane scrambled to his hands and knees and scooted frantically to Quinn's side.

"Quinn!" Lane grabbed the ancient head in his hands. "Quinn, can you hear me?"

Nothing. Quinn's face looked old and wrinkled. His eyes were closed, and what little color had been in his weathered skin seemed to be fading quickly.

Lane looked up at Owen. "This can't be happening. It can't

end like this."

Lane felt something in his hand. A flutter? A twitch? He looked down at Quinn's face. An eyelid twitched. The other one fluttered. Air rushed into Quinn's nostrils and his chest rose. His eyes opened wide. Immediately his pupils constricted to a flat horizontal line against the flecked golden iris in reaction to the bright sunlight.

Quinn closed his eyes tightly, then blinked several times. Finally, he gathered his senses and was able to look up at Lane, then over at Owen.

A small smile curled up under one side of his mustache. His face relaxed and he looked exhausted.

"Well," he said with a tired and weak voice, "that was an adventure, eh?"

Lane helped him sit up. He carried Quinn over to a rock beneath a group of larger scrub trees and set him in a patch of shade.

Owen and Lane plopped down on either side of Quinn and leaned against the large stone. They sat stunned for a while, not knowing what to say.

"What in the world was that?" Lane finally broke the silence.

"I believe," Quinn responded, "a more accurate question would be, what *out* of the world was that?"

"I think that's a safe assumption," Lane agreed. "What happened to you over there?"

"It was so strange, and it all happened so fast," Quinn answered. "I saw moving images suspended before my eyes. Images that I have only seen in a night vision."

"Yes!" Lane said, "that's exactly what happened to me. Were you able to breathe?"

"Oh no," Quinn looked upset, "it was quite painful, actually. I felt as if Owen himself was stomping down on my chest." Quinn paused and gave a worried look back and forth between Lane and Owen. "I really believed I was going to die."

"I thought you had died," Lane quickly added. "Q, we can't do this again. We have no idea what could be on the other side of those archways. We can't risk losing you."

"But Lane, how else will you get home?" Quinn asked.

Lane ran his fingers through his curly hair and slumped back further against the rock. He started softly banging his head against the rough sandstone, trying to knock loose a solution to their dilemma.

Think, man, think. It can't end like this. There has to be a solution, there's always a solution.

Lane raised his index finger. "There is one thing I know for sure. You, sir"—he wagged his finger at Quinn—"are not jumping through again."

Quinn's eyes softened, and his head sunk deeper into his chest. "As much as I hate to admit it," he said, his voice strained as it was still difficult for him to breathe, "I have to agree with you. This old body could not take another encounter like that."

Lane slapped his knee. "That settles that. Now, Owen, pick up Quinn, I'll grab the gear, and let's head back to the cavern. Maybe something will jump out at me on the way."

They quickly gathered their things and headed back to the cavern. Near the edge of the desert floor, something moved off to the right. The movement caught Lane's attention, and he looked over just in time to see a numa shoot from behind a rock and disappear into a small cluster of brush.

"Well, what do you know?" Lane said, half to himself, but loud enough for the others to hear, "It actually did jump out at me.

"Gentlemen"—Lane put on the airs of a man who was just about to announce the greatest invention the world had ever seen—"I have a plan! Let's get Quinn back up to the cavern, and I'll tell you all about it."

Chapter 36

Back inside the cavern, the three of them gathered around the fire. Quinn was strong enough to prepare some tea and get the flames roused from the smoldering embers. Once they were situated, Lane revealed his plan.

"I'll be honest. That jump into Dreamville really freaked me out. I think we're lucky we got back in one piece. Who knows what other worlds might be like? For all we know, we could walk through the arch and end up embedded in a piece of crystal or something, and," he snapped his fingers, "*poof!* That's it. No more jumping. No more anything.

"So, we can't just go randomly jumping through archways. The problem is, how can we possibly find an archway that leads to my world if we can't look into it?

"We have to have some way of testing what's on the other side without putting ourselves in danger. But what?"

Lane let the question hang in the air.

"While we were coming back to the cavern, something jumped out at me. Answer this: What is the only other living creature that we know of that can pass through the archways?"

Quinn responded, "The numa, of course."

"Of course," Lane extended both hands palms-up toward his two companions, as if he had just presented the whole idea and was waiting for their response.

They both looked blankly at him for a moment. Then the light switch flipped in Quinn's mind.

"Of course!" the old man hooted. "The numa. We could use them as test subjects. If we tied a harness around them and sent them through the arch, then pulled them back through, we could determine whether the other side was hospitable to life as we know it."

"Exactly!" Lane exclaimed. "I couldn't have said it better myself."

"Wonderful, wonderful," Quinn said. This new development was beginning to revitalize him. "The next hurdle to be crossed in the process is to figure out how to capture some numa."

Over the next few days, they worked tirelessly toward that goal. Quinn designed a trap for the large rodents, using his bitter berry soup as the bait. They quickly discovered that the numa preferred the stewed brew to the berry itself. The very aroma would draw the creatures out of hiding. Before long, the room that had been Owen's chamber was a pen full of captive numa. The creatures seemed perfectly content to sit in the room and be pampered with large bowls full of bitter berry mash.

At the end of a long day of trapping, they sat around the fire. "Now," Quinn said, "I believe we have enough of the creatures to begin." He held up a long, thin strap that had two loops attached to the end, "Here is a harness that I believe will allow us to retrieve the numa from the other side." He pointed to a pile of the harnesses next to the wall. "I have been making them while you two have been out catching the creatures."

"It's good to see you've been keeping yourself busy," Lane teased.

"Tomorrow," Quinn continued, ignoring Lane's comment, "we should begin our experiments. Now we should get some sleep."

They retired to their cots for the night. Owen had joined them in the main room. They slept well.

In the morning they prepared themselves for the experiments. Owen grabbed one of the numa and placed it in a large sack. The creature resisted very little and sat still once inside the bag. Quinn consulted his map and determined the location of the next archway. Soon they, along with their unsuspecting rodent, were down on the desert floor and quickly approaching the arch.

"Here it is," Quinn declared.

Owen removed the numa from the bag and quickly offered it some dried berry mash. Quinn had discovered that, once the berries had been cooked and mashed, the thick soup could be dried and cut into small cubes that preserved it for quite a while. These snacks had become a favorite of the numa, and this one was more than willing to receive the treat without any argument. The numa had proven to be very good pets, once they had been won over through treats. Owen, especially, had become very fond of them.

Once the furry creature finished its treat, Owen slipped the harness over its torso and secured it. He nodded to Quinn to indicate that everything was ready.

"All right, Owen," Quinn said, "you know what to do."

Owen nodded and then moved toward the arch with the numa tucked between his left arm and his chest. He reached into his pocket and produced another treat. The numa perked up at the sight of the morsel and strained to reach it. Owen waved the treat in front of the creature and its head tracked the motions. Then, with a quick jerk of his hand, Owen threw the treat into the arch and released the numa. The rodent darted after the treat and vanished in the archway. The rope that was attached to its harness quickly unfurled, drew tight, then snapped back and landed at Owen's feet.

Owen picked it up and they all examined it. A frayed mass of charred strands splayed out from the end of the rope.

"Whoa!" Lane exclaimed. "That's intense. It's like he was instantly consumed in fire."

Owen looked sad and stared at the burned rope for a long time.

"I am terribly sorry," Quinn consoled his large and compassionate friend, "I truly am. But imagine if that had been Lane that jumped through. Your little friend made a great sacrifice today. He should be honored."

"Well." Lane exhaled loudly. "At least we know the plan works. I guess now we just need to load up some more numa and take these bushes one at a time."

They returned to the cavern. This time Owen carried an empty sack and a heavy heart.

Over the next few days they fell into a pattern. Early in the morning they loaded up three or four numa and headed out for the next archway on the map. At the end of the day they returned with an empty sack. None of the archways proved to be hospitable to life. Some of the numa were pulled back through the arch, but they did not survive. Some were frozen. Others were mangled, as if their molecules had been disassembled and reassembled in a haphazard mess. Others seemed to have been turned to stone. Many just disappeared, leaving a frayed rope snapped back at Owen's feet.

Lane and Quinn were discouraged at their lack of results. Owen grew more saddened at the loss of his new pets. All the while they kept reminding themselves that, if they had not come up with this plan, Lane would be dead.

PLEROMA

Chapter 37

A few days later, after they had covered about a third of the archways on Quinn's map, they readied themselves to head out for another day of exploring. The arches were now much further away from the cavern, so they prepared themselves to camp out overnight on this expedition.

Laden with satchels and numa, they set out across the desert. It was midday by the time they reached the first arch. As usual, Owen sent a numa into the arch. A few seconds later he pulled back a dead creature. They were used to the disappointment by now and simply mourned over the loss of the numa, then moved on to the next arch.

Quinn led the small band of explorers over a large rock outcropping and down into the bottom of a wide, dry riverbed. In the monotony of the red-brown dirt and sandy rocks of the riverbed, every place started to look the same. Somehow Quinn was able to distinguish one cluster of scrub from another.

They arrived at another group of desert plants, and the telltale signs of the bitter bush arch were evident. They silently moved into place and prepared themselves for another mission. Owen harnessed the numa, taunted it with the treat, and sent it on its way through the arch. A few seconds later, Owen tugged on the rope, and the numa came hopping back through and immediately went to Owen's hand, looking for another treat.

Lane stared at the rodent and blinked in disbelief.

"Owen," Lane said, "check him out. Does he seem OK?"

Owen lifted up the numa and thoroughly examined its whole body. Everything checked out.

Lane and Quinn exchanged excited glances.

"This is wonderful!" exclaimed Quinn. "Send him back in and let him stay over there for an extended time."

Owen sent the numa back in. The creature willingly followed after the treat and vanished into the arch. Several minutes passed while the rope twitched and moved from one side of the arch to the other. Periodically it pulled tight in Owen's hand and then went slack. Apparently the numa wanted to move past the boundary of the rope that tethered it to Owen.

"Pull him back," Quinn instructed.

Once again, the numa hopped through the arch and greeted its treat vendor with expectation.

Quinn looked at Lane. "Do you know what this means, Lane?"

Lane nodded. "It means that if I jump through that arch I will most likely not die immediately."

"Well, yes." Quinn looked a little set back at Lane's reply. "I suppose that is the truest answer to my inquiry. However, I was focusing more on the fact that this could actually be the one that leads you home."

Lane sat back on the rocky ground and let out a long, slow breath.

"You're right," Lane said. "This could be the one."

He looked at Owen, then over to Quinn. "I'm glad we had these last few days to spend together. The last time I jumped I made big speeches. They still count, right? I'm really going to miss you guys."

He gave Owen a big hug and scratched the numa behind the ear. "Thanks, Furball."

Lane moved over to Quinn.

"Here, Lane." He held out a knife and a pouch full of food. "Since you are going alone, I thought you should take these things."

"Thanks." Lane received the gifts. He looked down at the small, wrinkled man and didn't know what to say. Quinn responded with a squint of his eyes and a knowing smile.

"It is time for you to go, my boy."

Lane positioned himself in front of the archway.

"Well guys," Lane spoke without looking back, "if this is the one, then the next thing I should experience is waking up in the hospital bed. Here goes."

He took a deep breath and stepped into the arch. The same course of electrical shock raced through his body. This time, however, his feet landed on solid ground. He stepped forward and found himself standing in front of a building. It took a moment for his eyes to adjust to the dim sunlight.

He stood on a cement path that led to three small, painted wooden steps. A bike lay on its side. He looked closer. It was his!

He looked at the building in front of him. It was his house. The painted steps led up to his front porch. He quickly surveyed the surroundings. It was definitely his neighborhood. Everything was still. Only the barking of old man Crocker's dog could be heard from a few houses down.

Lane looked through the living-room window to see the shape of his father rising from his chair and moving toward the entryway.

"Dad!" Lane sprang toward the door, jumping all three steps. He fumbled with the knob, then burst through the front door. His momentum sent him stumbling into the small entryway. Josh stood to his left, at the base of the stairs, a look of terror on his face. Josh didn't even notice Lane's entrance. His fright had him focused on something else in the room. Lane looked to the right to see his father approaching. His angry, glazed eyes were riveted on Josh's small frame.

Wait! I've done this before. How can this be? I was supposed to wake up in the hospital room. What's happening?

Lane moved forward into the room and then turned around. The rope was still tied to his waist. It ran out the front door, down the steps, and then disappeared on the sidewalk. He looked down at the belt around his waist. The knife and the pouch were still there. He felt them to make sure they were real. He reached over and touched the banister to see if it had substance and that he wasn't just dreaming. The worn wood was smooth in his hand. Everything seemed real. *How is this possible?*

Lane didn't have time to think about it. His father was going after Josh.

Lane stepped forward and placed himself between his dad and his little brother.

"What do think you're doin', you stupid brat?" He stood about three inches taller than Lane and seemed to tower above him. The drunken and enraged man looked around the room until he locked onto a glass beer bottle sitting on the coffee table.

Lane knew what was coming this time.

The bottle whipped through the air toward his head. He reached up with his left hand and caught his father's wrist in mid-swing.

The sudden jolt startled the man, and he froze in surprise.

"Not this time, Dad!" Lane got right in his father's face and stared at him directly in the eyes.

His bloodshot eyes softened. The pale blue irises stared back at his son. Lane looked closer into those eyes. He recognized them.

In that moment, it felt like the whole world spun around him. Images whirled through Lane's mind. He saw the faces of Gustov and Jethro. Trik and Tora dancing around his feet. The stadium looming over the skullcap of Amo. The stormy morning when he was standing in the pouring rain, staring into the eyes of the raging Bellator.

The hair on Lane's body stood on end as wave after wave of prickling sensation pulsed through him. He knew what was happening now. It was real. All of it.

"Dad!" Lane yelled at his father, as if the rain was pounding around him and he was fighting against sound, time, and space. "Dad, stop! I know who you are. I know where you are. I know what happened to you."

His father looked confused.

"Dad, the night of the accident, I think I know what happened. When you crashed, part of you was lost. It was sent to another place. I know it sounds crazy, but you have to believe me."

PLEROMA

Lane reached down and grabbed the rope that was tied around his waist. He held it up to show his father, and then dragged him to the doorway. By this point his father was so stunned and confused that he complied with Lane's promptings.

"Dad, on the other side of this rope is the answer to our problems. *You* are on the other side of the rope. The Dad I knew when I was a kid, the Dad who loved me and played with me and made up stories with me. Dad, I know it sounds crazy, but somehow, I think your soul is over there."

To Lane's surprise, his father did not protest. His face softened as he watched Lane speak. Then he looked out at the short sidewalk and the rope that vanished into nothing. His eyes filled with sadness and longing.

"Call out to him, Dad. Just call out to him. Call him back!"

Lane's father fell to his knees in the doorway. He sobbed.

"Yes," he said through his tears. "Yes, I know you're right. I've felt it for years. Yes, please come back to me. I need you. Please help me!"

Lane looked out at the sidewalk. On the ground, next to the rope, a toe appeared. It was followed by a foot, then a knee, a leg. Finally, Owen's terribly scarred and disfigured body stepped out of nothing and came into full view on the sidewalk. He looked at Lane with loving eyes and gave him a twisted smile. Then he looked at Lane's father.

Their eyes met. Owen's body changed. It fractured into tiny pieces, like pixels suspended in air. In a quick snap, the pixels were sucked into the center of Dad's chest. The connection sent him hurling backwards into the entryway. He lay motionless.

Lane rushed to his side. Josh knelt next to him on the other side. The two boys hovered over their father's large frame. Josh was frantic with worry. Lane was bristling with anticipation. He shook his father's shoulder.

"Dad, wake up!"

His father's eyes fluttered and opened. He shook his head briefly and looked around, trying to regain his bearings. The bloodshot streaks were gone from the whites of his eyes, and the dark circles around them had disappeared.

"Oh, Lane." He sat up and enveloped his son in a tight bear hug. "Lane, thank you. Thank you for saving me!"

Lane rested in the embrace for a few seconds, then pulled away to get a better look. In that face a set of soft, blue, loving, and very familiar eyes stared back at him.

"Yes, it's me," his father said, "it's Owen."

A flood of emotion rushed into Lane's throat. He threw himself back into the bear hug and squeezed like he would never let go.

Owen's deep voice continued, "You don't know how long I've waited to say these words out loud. I love you, son. I'm so proud of you. I've missed you so much."

"Dad, I can't believe this is happening. I can't believe this is real. I mean, this whole time I thought I was in a delusion created by my own mind while I was in a coma. And now, it's real."

He pulled back and looked at his father with a very serious expression.

"This is real, right?"

Owen laughed and hugged him again. "Lane, this is more real than anything either of us has ever known."

Lane looked over at his little brother. Josh stood with a dumbfounded expression on his face.

"What's going on?" he asked.

Lane laughed. "Don't worry, little J, I'll explain everything, eventually." Then Lane tussled Josh's hair and gave him a wink.

Lane and Owen eventually released their embrace and simply sat and basked in the moment. Lane looked at the rope, which was still attached to his waist. The other end of it lay out on the sidewalk in a loop that had once been around Owen's waist.

"Q!" Lane blurted out. "If you're here," he said to his father, "then Q is standing on the other side, wondering what just happened. I've got to go back and tell him. Quick, Dad, tie the rope around your waist again. I'll just step back really quick and explain everything."

Pleroma

His father agreed and was soon tied off and anchored on the front porch steps. Lane prepared himself and walked back toward the opening. He took several steps forward and ended up at the street. Nothing happened. Lane looked confused and came back to the steps and tried again. Nothing. He ran around the front yard, searching everywhere. The opening was gone.

Disappointed, they returned to the living room and sat down.

"Well," Lane said, "I guess I wasn't supposed to go back."

He leaned back in his chair, letting out a deep sigh, and scanned the room. His dad. For so many years he had lived in fear of that man. He hated him for what he had done. Now, knowing the truth, seeing him reconciled and whole, all he could do was love him.

Josh ran over and clung to Lane. He was still in shock. Lane realized that Josh had never known the dad who existed before the accident. The only father Josh ever knew was the angry shell that had been left behind. It would take a while for Josh to get to know Owen and learn to trust him. But Lane knew it would come in time.

Lane surveyed the living room. It was surreal to be back in his own home after all this time. His mind went back to the Deltonians. Then it struck him. If that world was actually real, then Jethro and Gustov were real too. Lane had left Jethro to be the Pleroma and rescue the children. A twinge of pain shot through Lane's heart. He hoped that they were able to make things right. How he would ever know?

His mind returned to the present, and his eyes continued to follow the perimeter of the room. The familiar furniture brought back many happy memories of being a child in this house. He had not allowed himself to think about those memories for a very long time. He heard his mother's laughter and saw images of him as a young boy running and playing with his mom and dad.

Then his eyes fell on a picture hanging on the wall. Lane stood up and walked over to the image. It was a photograph of his family. They were all smiling—all four of them: Lane, Josh,

Dad, and Mom.

"Dad, what happened that night? I mean, I've never been able to talk to you about the crash."

His father came over and placed his arm around Lane's shoulder. They both stared at the photo for a few seconds.

"It's been so long since I've thought about that night. The whole time I was with the Altanians my mind was in a fog. Honestly, I thought I was dreaming most of the time. It wasn't until you called out to me in the stadium that I started to think again. None of it made sense until I woke up here, just a few minutes ago."

He looked more intensely at the photo. "This picture was taken that night. I remember it now. We had a function for the university. I had too much to drink that night, so Mom had to drive home. She started to swerve, and I looked up to see what was going on. She was screaming about a rabbit that had jumped out in front of the car—she was trying to miss it. The car went out of control, started to roll, I saw a huge ball of flames... and the next thing I remember I was sitting in a room and this strange little man with goat eyes was looking at me."

"So, you don't remember anything about what happened here after the accident?" Lane asked.

"No." His father turned to Lane, and, almost afraid to speak the words, asked, "Where's Mom?"

Lane swallowed hard.

"Dad, she didn't make it. She was lost in the fire, totally consumed. They never found a trace of her."

Owen staggered a bit and steadied himself with his hand against the wall. Tear-brimmed eyes looked at the photograph with a new depth of longing.

"I wondered. I missed her so much, but I guess I always knew," he whispered as he gently stroked the image of her face with his finger.

"Dad, it's been hard for all of us. But there is something wonderful about today. Turn around." Lane gently pulled his father's shoulder and pointed him toward the chair on the other side of the room.

"Dad, I'd like to introduce you to your son, Josh. He's been waiting a long time to meet you."

Josh had been sitting on the arm of the chair. Owen got down on one knee and held out his arms toward the boy. A bright smile lit up his face, and he ran into his father's arms.

Lane looked down at the scene that he had thought would never happen and smiled. He got down on his knees and added his arms to the hug.

"Everything's going to be OK now Josh. Dad's home."

Chapter 38

A few weeks later...

The doorbell rang. Lane set down his fork and looked across the dinner table at Dad and Josh.

"I wonder who that could be?"

"If it's the newspaper boy, tell him I'm not home," Owen said.

Lane waved off the comment and opened the door.

"Heather?!"

"Hi, Lane."

She bit the corner of her lip like she always does when she's embarrassed. Something flipped inside his stomach.

"May I come in?"

"Oh, right." Lane stepped aside and motioned for her to enter.

She sidestepped, facing Lane as she entered. Both hands were tucked behind her back.

"Who is it?" Owen's voice called from the kitchen.

"It's Heather Jyles."

A brief pause. "From across the street?" Owen stepped into the small entryway as he spoke.

"Hi, Mr. Gray." She seemed uncomfortable in Owen's presence. "I brought something for Lane."

"Oh really." Owen looked at Lane with surprised admiration. "Would you two like to be alone?"

"No, no," Heather said, "that's fine. You will want to see this, too."

"Come on in, then." Owen motioned for them all to sit in the

PLEROMA

living room.

Josh joined them from the kitchen.

Heather sat next to Lane on the couch and presented a large envelope. "I hope you're not mad, but I asked Ms. Mitchell if I could be the one to give this to you."

She handed the envelope to Lane. The return address read *Massachusetts Institute of Technology*.

His heart pounded and he sat frozen, staring at the words.

"Open it, Lane!" Josh slapped both hands on his head.

Lane ripped open the envelope and read the letter.

> *We are pleased to inform you that you have been selected to participate in the early enrollment program at MIT. You will spend your senior year of high school on our campus.*
>
> *We look forward to seeing you next fall.*

A stunned and electric silence hung in the air.

"You did it!" Heather wrapped her arms around Lane's body. Owen and Josh shouted and clapped.

Lane felt the warmth of Heather's body against his and couldn't believe this moment was real.

After the celebration calmed down, Lane turned sideways on the couch and faced Heather. "Why did you bring this to the house? Ms. Mitchell could have given it to me at school."

Heather scooted a few inches away as a serious aura took over her countenance.

"Honestly, I needed an excuse to stop by."

"For what?" Lane asked.

Her eyes rested on each of the men in the room, then she spoke to all of them. "I don't know how to say this, so I'll just blurt it out. I saw you!"

Owen's face went white. "Saw what?"

She looked at Lane. "You, Lane. The day you took the test, I was so excited for you. I was watching for you to come home so I could see how it went."

Heat rose in Lane's face.

Heather continued. "I saw you come home and go in the front door, so I started to come over...." She paused, as if the words were trapped in her mouth. "You just appeared, right out of thin air. *Poof!* You stood there with a rope tied around your waist."

Lane's stomach felt sick and a cold sweat beaded on his forehead.

She continued. "Then—I still can't believe I saw this—but the most hideous thing I've ever seen appeared and...." She looked at Owen. "Was sucked into your body."

They all stared at each other. *What do we say now?*

"Well," she said, "are you going to explain? Like it or not, I saw it. You've been different at school and I know you've been hiding something. I want in."

Lane slumped back on the couch and looked at his dad. Owen rubbed both temples with his fingertips, and then raised his hands in surrender. "Tell her. Why not? I still have a hard time believing it myself."

For the next few hours Lane told the story of his time in the other world—Gustov, Jethro, the Bellator, Quinn, and Owen. Heather listened with awe and peppered the tale with questions.

After several cups of coffee and some snacks to keep them alert, the tale was told.

They all sat back and let out a deep sigh.

Heather leaned forward and placed her mug on the coffee table. "So, what about the children?"

"What do you mean?" Lane said.

"I mean, are they OK? Are you going to get them?"

"How? I've tried everything. The place under my bed has nothing. I have no idea what to do."

"We can't do nothing!" Heather clenched her fists and pressed them hard against the top of her knees.

"We?" Lane and Owen said it at the same time.

"I'm sorry to tell you this, boys, but you're stuck with me. We have to find a way to get you back there."

Her eyes fell on the opened envelope sitting on the coffee table. She picked it up and tapped it on her opened palm.

"Maybe you'll find some answers here," she said to Lane.

He looked at her in disbelief. There was that look again. *Is it possible?*

Her eyes sparkled. "So, what do we do next?"

End of Book 1

What about the children?
Can Lane find a way back?

Log on and find out

Sign up for our email list and get the latest
news about the release of Book 2.

www.ingramcontent.com/pod-product-compliance
Ingram Content Group UK Ltd.
Pitfield, Milton Keynes, MK11 3LW, UK
UKHW041952230426
12048UKWH00008B/298